"You're my sister, Jessie."

She shook her head. "No, Cade. I don't think I'd feel this way about a brother."

Bracing his elbows on his knees, he studied his feet. "As much as I wish things were different, the world sees us as siblings."

"Since when do you care what the world thinks?"

"Besides, you're rich and I'm poor," he said, evading her question. "It would never work, Jessie. The other night was an accident—"

"*I* knew what I was doing. Didn't *you?*"

Dear Reader,

At last we can enjoy the flowers of May, and Superromance readers will particularly enjoy our perennials—perennially favorite authors, that is!

We're delighted to welcome prolific author Tracy Hughes back to Superromance. *The Princess and the Pauper* is the tale of a man and woman, brother and sister in name, though not in fact, forced to work together to put their father's ailing cosmetics company on its feet. *He* hasn't the slightest inclination; *she* is determined to succeed. And somehow, along the way, the inevitable happens....

Bobby Hutchinson has created wild and wonderful Sameh Smith, a klutzy, comic, endearing heroine who's somehow not quite from this planet. She meets her match in Adam Hawkins, a cynical P.I. who can't figure her out, but can't help loving her, either.

Lynn Erickson will take you from the glamour of the Big Apple to the haunting grandeur and sandy shores of Israel and Greece, where her wealthy heroine, Alexandra Costidos, travels with hired mercenary John Smith on a mission of love—to kidnap her son from the clutches of his powerful father.

Janice Kaiser always delivers a surprise, and in *The Yanqui Prince*, reporter Michaela Emory, bored with her beat, jumps at the chance to track down and interview the legendary Reed Lakesly, a modern-day Robin Hood whose territory is Central America. Naturally, Lakesly has a few surprises of his own, and suddenly, Michaela has more adventure and passion—and men—than she bargained for!

Happy spring!

Marsha Zinberg,
Senior Editor, Superromance

Harlequin Books

TORONTO • NEW YORK • LONDON
AMSTERDAM • PARIS • SYDNEY • HAMBURG
STOCKHOLM • ATHENS • TOKYO • MILAN
MADRID • WARSAW • BUDAPEST • AUCKLAND

ISBN 0-373-70594-8

THE PRINCESS AND THE PAUPER

This edition published by arrangement with Harlequin Enterprises B. V.

Printed in U.S.A.

ABOUT THE AUTHOR

Prolific author Tracy Hughes has written more than two dozen books in her eleven years as a romance novelist. She is the winner of a Romance Writers of America Golden Medallion, as well as a Lifetime Achievement Award for *Jo*, her well-loved Calloway Corners book. She also writes mainstream fiction as Terri Herrington. When she entered her second marriage, her husband's difficulties in maintaining a relationship with his son inspired an exploration of the ties between divorced parents and their children. The result is *The Princess and the Pauper.* Tracy, who now lives with her husband and children in Mississippi, has already begun work on several new and exciting romance novels, including a Superromance that will appear in December 1994.

CHAPTER ONE

CADE HARTMAN DIDN'T GIVE a damn. Intent on proving that fact to the pretentious acquaintances at the reading of his father's will, he strode through the festive mourners wearing a pair of worn-out jeans with grease stains on the knees, leather boots, and a gray Harley Hog T-shirt bought especially for the occasion. His hair was a little too long, its black ends curling slightly up at the back of his neck, and since he had failed to shave that morning, a shadow of stubble gave him the unkempt look of a mechanic. But that was appropriate, he mused, because that was exactly what he was. A mechanic who didn't give a damn.

Heads turned as he cut through the crowd dressed in their probate-best, and without greeting anyone, he headed for the conference room where the will would be read as soon as everyone was seated. The guests whispered as he passed them, and he imagined what they were saying.

"Who's this low life?"

"Andrew's son."

"Of course. I'd forgotten Jessica had a half brother."

"So did her father."

He pushed into the room and saw Jessica sitting alone in the front corner, her blond hair pulled back in a loose chignon with tiny wisps feathering around her face. Jessica was more beautiful than he would have predicted when she was a child, but that only stood to reason. As namesake of an entire line of cosmetics, and Andrew's only biological child, how could she be anything else?

She glanced up at him, and after a moment of blankness, he saw the beginning of recognition.

Yeah, it's me, he wanted to say. *But don't worry. I don't want anything of yours.*

Sam Morgan, Andrew's attorney, was setting up his front table for the reading, and he looked up and smiled at Cade. "You came," he said, reaching across to shake his hand. "I was worried you wouldn't."

Cade slid his hands into his back pockets. "Yeah, well, you convinced me. Besides, I thought this shindig might need a little cultural diversity."

Sam looked through the door at the people mingling outside, with cocktails in their hands and smiles on their faces, as if they'd come here for a party. "Most of these people either worked for your father or touched his life in some way. He was very generous with them. He would have gotten a kick out of making a party out of the reading."

"I wouldn't know," Cade said.

The attorney didn't quite know how to reply, and he glanced helplessly at Jessica. From the corner of his metallic blue eyes, Cade saw her start to rise. Just in time, he turned his back to her and took a seat across the room. When he caught her in his peripheral vision again, she was back in her chair.

It was quiet in the room for several moments, with Jessica staring at her hands, Cade staring straight ahead, and Sam shuffling papers. Finally Barbara—Andrew's widow and Jessica's mother—breezed in, and the rest of the group followed her. Her perfume, a citrus mixture that had made Cade nauseous since he'd smelled it as a kid, wafted in the air around her, inescapable.

As Sam began reading the will, it occurred to Cade how ludicrous it was that he had come here at all. He shifted uncomfortably and stroked his lip, the sandpaper stubble beneath his nose feeling good against his finger. The truth was, any one of his father's acquaintances who had come here today—from the janitor who cleaned his office to the cook in the diner where he ate breakfast every morning—had known Andrew Hartman better than he had.

Which brought up the bitter question, once again, that Cade had asked of Sam yesterday.

Why do I have to be there?

You were his son.

Adopted son, Cade had reminded him. *From a previous marriage. I barely even knew the man.*

But the attorney had insisted on his attendance, and as he eyed the door now, wishing for an escape from the tedious and cloying lists of items Andrew had left people Cade had never met, Cade wondered if Sam Morgan had read the will himself before today. If he had, wouldn't he realize that Cade was the last person to whom Andrew would have bequeathed anything?

Cade couldn't imagine his father remembering him in his will when he hadn't given him a thought while he was living.

The attorney's dull voice went on in what seemed an eternal monologue, and Cade allowed himself to glance, once more, at the young woman across the room.

She looked up at him, and he saw the red rims of her eyes, the shadows beneath them, and the red tint to her nose, though her makeup was impeccably applied. Her expression seemed haunted, yet she met his eyes with some expectation, as if he, more than anyone else in the room, could understand her grief.

Cade looked away. There was no grief where he was concerned, he told himself firmly. He was the poor relation, the adopted son. The one Andrew had abandoned when he got his mistress, Barbara, pregnant. If Cade had been his real offspring, maybe things would have been different. But Jessica was Andrew's only true heir, and it was her birth that took Andrew away from Cade.

He felt his face reddening with old bitterness, and again he shifted. The chair was growing uncomfortable, and the room was too hot. He wished Sam would hurry up and get this over with. Better yet, he wished he hadn't come at all.

Cade couldn't say he wasn't prepared for being excluded. He wanted nothing of his father's anyway. Andrew's pampered little princess needed an inheritance more than he did, for he doubted she had the wherewithal to make a living. He supposed, if nothing else, his legacy from his father had been a desperate kind of responsibility. There was nothing like poverty to build a strong work ethic.

Still Cade had come out okay, and he'd shown time and time again that he didn't need one dime of the old man's money, or the acquaintance of any of the people in this room.

His eyes drifted back to Jessica, and he watched as her trembling hands dug into her bag for a tissue. Swallowing back a surge of emotion, she blotted her eyes, managing to keep her makeup from smearing, and glanced at him again.

Man, she was beautiful, he thought, making himself look away again. Just the type he was attracted to. Soft hair that looked as if she used an imported shampoo that had to be flown in from Paris. Designer clothes, every stitch of which enhanced her ample shape and gave her the look of aristocracy. And those long legs, which were crossed pristinely at the knee, then accented by the high-heeled pumps that pulled her delicate feet into a point.

Clearing his throat, he leaned forward, set his elbows on his knees and looked down at his feet. Damn it, he wasn't supposed to get turned on looking at his sister. Even if she wasn't really his sister.

It was all too complicated, just as complicated as the taste in women that had baffled him since adolescence. It occurred to him now, as his eyes drifted up to her again, that every woman in his life—including his long-departed ex-wife—had in some way represented Jessica.

"And now, for the final part of the will, the part that his immediate family have, no doubt, been waiting for..."

Cade almost chuckled at the emceelike tone the attorney was using, as if announcing the next Miss America, but nothing about it was really that funny. He should have known that he had come just to have his nose rubbed in it. Skipping to the immediate family—which obviously consisted of Jessica and her mother—made it clear there wasn't anything for him in the will at all. Everyone else in the room had been dealt with first.

He leaned back as the attorney dealt with Barbara, his stepmother, who had been younger and prettier and more ambitious than the woman Cade had called mother. Barbara had been by Andrew's side as he had climbed his way to the top. And she, unlike Cade's mother, had been able to provide Andrew with a flesh-and-blood heir.

She wasn't young anymore, and though she'd had two face-lifts to hold her age at bay, she wasn't as pretty as she had once been. But she was still rich. He listened as Sam Morgan read off the list of things Andrew had bequeathed to her: both of their massive homes, one of which she was to sell immediately. Their Mercedes, though she was to sell the Rolls in his garage.

As Cade listened to the plight of the various material stockpiles Andrew had accumulated over the years, he couldn't shake the memory of the rented apartment his mother had lived in until she'd died two years ago, or the two jobs she'd worked while he was growing up, just to make ends meet.

So lost was Cade in his bitter reverie that he almost didn't hear as Morgan finished with Barbara and reached the final portion of the will.

"...leave half of my shares of Jessica Cosmetics to my daughter, Jessica, and the other half to my son, Cade."

A collective gasp rose over the room, and Cade jerked his eyes up. "What did you say?"

The attorney smiled. "He left you half of his shares of his company, Cade. I told you it was important that you be here. But there's a catch. Let me finish."

Cade shot Jessica a look, half expecting her to be glaring at him for cutting into her inheritance, but instead she was smiling. Tearing his eyes away, he looked back at the attorney. "What do you mean, a catch?"

"Just listen." The attorney began to read on, and Cade sat back, carefully trying to follow. "In order for each of my children to get their half of my estate," Sam read, "they must go to work for Jessica Cosmetics, and together raise half a million dollars in net profit within two quarters."

"Hold it." Cade came to his feet, suddenly feeling as if he'd been caught in a trap. "Wait a minute. There's no way I'm going to work for his cosmetics company. I don't owe him anything, and he didn't owe me anything."

"There's more," the attorney said, gesturing for him to sit back down. But Cade kept standing. "If you don't *both* cooperate, neither of you will get your inheritance, and Hartman's shares will be sold, with first option given to his board of directors."

Jessica's smile faded, and she sat up, rigid, in her chair. "Are you sure about this?"

"It's all right here," Sam said. "Your father was very specific."

The haunted look Cade had seen earlier returned to Jessica's eyes, and she turned back to Cade. "That means that if one of us refuses, we could *both* wind up with nothing."

"I know what it means, Jessica," Cade flung back. "But I've had nothing for a long time. It grows on you. Builds character. And if it's all the same to you, I'd just as soon leave it that way. I don't want a shot at anything of his. In fact, if he'd handed it to me all gift wrapped and ready to go, I still wouldn't want it."

"Just hear me out, Cade," Sam said. "Your father was adamant about your getting exactly what Jessica gets. What he's asking of you isn't unreasonable. At worst, you'll get a good job and some invaluable experience."

"I *have* a good job, and I've had all the experience I can stomach."

Jessica gaped at him, and he saw her nose growing redder as she struggled with her emotions. "Cade..."

Cade shook his head, stemming her plea, and it occurred to him that this might well be her first experience with her father's cruelty. He could see Andrew doing this to him in an attempt to make him stop repairing motorcycles for a living and get a job more fitting of a Hartman—he'd long been an embarrassment to his father—but why would he tie Cade's inheritance in with Jessica's?

It was a game, he thought, and a fresh wave of bitterness crested inside him. He and Jessica were the pawns. He turned to Jessica, whose misty red eyes were still pleading with him, and he shook his head again. "I'm not a game player, folks. And I sure as hell won't be manipulated by a dead man who could hardly remember how to spell my name when he was alive."

Before anyone in the room could stop him, Cade slammed out of the room, bolted through the offices and into the parking lot where his motorcycle was waiting.

JESSICA WATCHED the door slam and turned back to the attorney. "I'm...sorry," she said in a hoarse voice. "This has... it's been difficult for all of us."

She sat back down, her back rigid, and focused on Sam Morgan. "You were saying... that neither of us gets our share unless we both cooperate?"

Sam nodded wanly. "I'm afraid so, Jessica."

"And... if Cade refuses... then that's it? None of Jessica Cosmetics will belong to me? And Daddy didn't leave me anything else?"

"I'm sorry. The company was what he wanted his children to have, but he was very specific about how you were to earn it."

She picked up her bag again, searching for that tissue she'd tried not to need all day. "I see." Finding the Kleenex, she dabbed at her eyes again.

Her mother reached out for her, squeezed her arm. "Darling, I didn't know about any of this. I'm so sorry. But you can convince Cade to join you."

Jessica took a deep breath and tried to smile. "My father always wanted what was best for me. I'm sure he had a good reason for this." She got up again, closed her purse and swallowed. "If you're finished with me, Sam, I'd like to go talk to Cade."

"Yes," he said. "I can finish up without you."

Barbara stopped her again. "Sweetheart, I'll cancel my trip if you need me to stay here in Atlanta."

Jessica turned back to her mother, moved by the fact that she'd even consider canceling her vacation through Europe—something that she hoped would help her through her grief over the man she had loved so devoutly. "No, Mom. You need to get away. I can handle this."

With her head held high and her even stride belying the fact that she thought she might fall apart any moment now, Jessica left the room the same way Cade had left.

But Cade was already gone.

She got to her BMW, slid behind the wheel and leaned her head back on the seat. The tears that had been prodding her all day long broke through her emotional dam and began to flow without hesitation. Weakly she wrapped her arms around the steering wheel and dropped her head into them.

She couldn't believe he was gone. One minute, her father had been a vibrant, happy, aggressive man, and the next minute she was watching them lower his coffin into his grave.

It had happened too fast. He had been planning to teach her the business, but she'd wasted so much time, they'd never gotten started. She shouldn't have taken that last trip to Europe, she thought. She should have gone right to work for Jessica Cosmetics out of college and worked alongside her father like he'd wanted.

But she'd let him down. That was why he didn't trust her with the company now, she thought. That was why he had made it so hard.

She saw the others beginning to come out, most of them beaming about the trinkets Andrew had left them. Her mother, who was standing on the sidewalk looking in her direction with a puzzled expression, started toward her. Not wanting to talk with anyone but Cade until she could sort out the conflicting emotions in her mind, Jessica started her car and pulled out of the parking lot.

She had to find Cade, she thought. Somehow she had to reason with him. Convince him not to throw away everything. In her whole life, it had never occurred to her that there would come a day when she had nothing. Never would she have believed that her father could cease to exist in a matter of moments, and that nothing would ever come easily again.

She drove to her apartment and went inside to wash her face, with hopes that the damage the tears had done could be corrected before she saw Cade. Somehow she didn't want him to see her crying. She wasn't even sure why.

She slipped out of her clothes, pulled on a pair of jeans and tennis shoes, and a bulky sweater, then tried to breathe deeply. Tears flooded her eyes again, and she didn't know whether they were tears of grief or tears of helplessness. Almost by rote, she began taking off her makeup, realizing with a surge of defeat that none of the expensive Jessica Cosmetics could cover the redness in her eyes and nose, or avoid blotching at the onslaught of tears that were likely to come on several more times that day. It was futile to fight them—it was all too fresh. Her father's sudden heart attack, his almost instant death, his funeral only forty-eight hours later. And now this.

Why did Cade hate her so?

It didn't really matter, she told herself. They were in this together. The company could be worth millions to them, if they only met their father's challenge. And she wasn't about to sit back and let it all slip through her fingers just because of Cade's pride.

Pulling herself together, she drove across town to the modest ranch-style house that she'd driven past so many times, though Cade had never known it. She turned into the driveway and gazed at the small, well-groomed yard that she'd caught Cade mowing a time or two, dressed in cutoff shorts and a tank top, his tanned body glistening in the sun. For the life of her, she didn't even know why she drove by. But for years Cade had been like a fantasy figure to her, an untouchable kindred spirit who could share her secrets and protect her from harm, if only he would acknowledge her as more than a piece of fluff that annoyed him each time she was near. Even as a woman, she couldn't shake the need to know this man who was so much a part of her life, yet so absent from it.

Shaking the thought from her mind, she rang the bell, but no one answered. Giving up, she walked around to the side of the house and saw that his Ford pickup truck was parked in the garage. But his motorcycle was still gone.

Feeling suddenly wrung out, she went back to the front steps and sat down to wait for him. He wasn't going to avoid talking to her this time, she told herself. When Cade got home, she would be waiting, and together they would work this out whether they liked it or not.

THE BRISK WIND tearing through Cade's long dark hair didn't make him slow his motorcycle any. At this hour, along this lonely highway, there wasn't likely to be anyone getting in his way.

Besides, he knew of no other way to burn off the rage tearing through his heart.

Why had his father done this? Why hadn't he just continued his policy of forgetting he had a son, and kept him out of the will entirely?

He had been set up, and no matter how fast he flew, he couldn't quell the fury. It was a dirty trick. Dangle something in front of his nose, a game he won't want to play, and then you can look like a good guy while still being a bastard.

But that didn't explain Jessica. He would have expected more from Andrew where she was concerned. No, that wasn't true. His father's loyalties were easily shifted. No one knew what he was actually capable of. The truth was, it was Jessica who was being the most hurt by their father's prank. Cade could get over it. But she...

That wasn't his concern, he told himself as he tore along the edge of the road, gravel crunching under his wheels. Jessica had to grow up sometime. God knew he'd spent enough of his life struggling. He supposed it was her turn now.

But as he pulled off the shoulder and back onto the road, something in Cade's heart felt heavier than it should have. There was no justice in any of what had happened today. But that was nothing new. He'd stopped believing in justice long ago.

Cade saw her car before he saw her, and something in him told him to keep going, that he didn't have to stop right now, that he didn't have to confront this today. She would go away eventually, give up on him and find some way around this fiasco their father had created.

And then he saw her, hunched on his front steps like a child who had no place else to go. Against the twilight leaching the color from the day, she looked pale, tired, and a fresh surge of hate for his father shot through him. For years, he'd considered Jessica and himself as different as night and day. But now, as he pulled his bike onto his driveway, he saw the grief, the misery, the puzzlement in her eyes at suddenly finding herself banished from Camelot, and he realized she wasn't all that different from what he had been all those years ago, before he'd been walloped with life's dirty lessons.

Something about that similarity disturbed him. He didn't want to relate to her pain. He didn't want to feel for her. He didn't want to remember.

Cutting off his bike, he flung his leg over and started slowly toward her.

"I've been waiting for you for hours," Jessica said, her voice hollow, as if she'd cried until she was stopped up. Something tugged at his chest, but he tried to dismiss it.

"Can't say I'm surprised. I would imagine that all of a sudden I have a lot of people interested in me."

He made no move to go into the house. In irritation, she pointed to the door. "Do we have to do this out here, or could we go inside? We really need to talk."

Cade's shoulders stiffened. "I don't see any point. Nothing's going to change. I won't be manipulated by anyone, dead or alive." He started around to the garage, and Jessica followed him.

"Why do you think you're being manipulated? We're both being given a chance!"

"To do what?" Cade asked. "Fail in front of the whole world? No thanks. I'm not stupid enough to take on a business I know less than nothing about."

"Well, *I* know something about it!" she shouted. "And your degree is in marketing. Together we could do it!"

Cade laughed and turned around at the door to his house, his eyes holding no mirth. "You're so full of it, Jessica, you can't even see clearly. Listen carefully. You're being jerked around, too. You should be as mad as I am."

"How I feel about this has nothing to do with it," she said, slapping her hair back from her face and whipping it behind her ear. "The fact is that I've been groomed from birth to take over this company. My face has been on every one of their products since I was sixteen. It isn't fair that I'm being forced to watch it slip through my fingers because of you!"

Again, he gave a dry laugh, and then it faded as sharp anger shot through his eyes. "Don't you get it, Jessica? Nothing having to do with Andrew Hartman has ever been fair! I didn't ask for any of this, you know. If you need to blame somebody, blame him. He's the one who dangled paradise in front of your nose, then snatched it away when you started getting secure! It may have taken him longer with you, but I could have told you how it would end."

"How could you have told me anything?" Jessica shouted back. "You were never around!"

Cade's scathing blue eyes whiplashed across her. "Damn right, I wasn't!"

Trying to rally and recover her calm, she tried again. "Okay, so you didn't want anything from him. Does that mean that I have to swallow whatever you decide? It's *my* future at stake here."

"Whether you want to admit it or not, Jessica, I have a future, too. I'm part owner of a motorcycle shop. I do that because I like it. I don't intend to give that up just so I can start marketing a product that I consider frivolous and wasteful in the first place!"

"That product supported you and me, and gave us a start in life that other people only dream of!" she shouted furiously.

"Wrong!" Cade's face reddened as he glared at her. "My mother worked two jobs to support me, because Andrew's child support was so pathetic. I went to public schools all my life, and got a scholarship to Penn State, which I supplemented by working a full-time job from three to eleven every day." The vein in his neck began to swell as he went on, and his face strained with his ranting. "So don't assume that just because you had a cushy life, I had one, too. We're nothing alike!"

He flung his door open and went inside, reaching to pull it behind him, but Jessica caught it. "Cade, you're my brother," she said, her voice cracking. "Please don't slam the door on me before we work this out."

"I'm not your brother!" he shouted. "I'm not even Hartman's real son. I was adopted when I was three weeks old, so that automatically justifies anything he did or didn't do for me."

"You're *still* my brother," she said as tears pushed to her eyes. "I've always thought of you that way. The truth is—"

"The truth," Cade said, still panting with his rage, "is that we don't even know each other. We've never lived in the same house, we've never spent more than one night in the same place, and we know nothing about each other. And I'd like to keep it that way."

The door slammed in Jessica's face, and she jumped in surprise, stumbled back, then caught her forehead in her hand and tried to blink back the tears, no longer of grief but of rage. Slowly she turned and started to walk away, but something stopped her. That rage, hot and growing, turned her around and propelled her back to the house.

Flying back to the door, she threw it open and bolted inside, surprising him. "Damn you, I won't be treated that way. Not by you or anyone else. And I'm not leaving this house until we have a calm, civilized discussion about what we have to gain and what we have to lose. Have you got that?"

A flicker of something—humor? respect?—passed across Cade's eyes, and he threw up his hands. "What's the matter, Jessica? Is it too hard to not get your own way? Are you going to have trouble with this?"

"Where do you want to do this?" she asked through her teeth. "In here at the table, or in the living room?"

"Why not right here?" he asked, leaning against the counter.

"As menacing and intimidating as you may look standing, Cade, I'm not easily frightened. And I don't generally discuss business with someone who looks as if he's about to pounce. We have to sit down."

Cade pushed away from the counter. "Fine. Sit."

"I'd prefer to go in there," she said, heading for the living room.

Cade gave her a few seconds before he followed, and he watched her pause in the doorway and look around with surprise on her face, probably because he didn't live in some dump with four-day-old food festering on the coffee table.

Slowly she walked into the rustic-looking room, and scanned the unstained wood walls, their blondness casting a brightness on the room that she wouldn't have expected. A huge fireplace filled one corner of the room, with a stone hearth and a mantel made out of a tree branch.

The furnishings were simple but comfortable, in earthy colors that contrasted with the off-white carpet. The look over her shoulder conveyed approval, and Cade breathed a humorless laugh.

Wearily Jessica dropped to the couch. He took the recliner across from her, but leaned forward, his elbows on his knees. "So talk."

"Why do you hate me so much?"

She knew the moment the words were out of her mouth that it was a childish, off-the-subject thing to ask, but for all their other problems, it seemed to be the predominant matter weighing on her mind.

"Come on, Jessica. That little fit in the kitchen wasn't about my feelings, was it? You can do better than that."

Again her lips compressed, and he saw her struggle with the fury pulsing through her. Maybe they did have something else in common, after all, he thought. Today was his landmark day for rage, too.

"Cade, we have to look at this logically, all emotions aside. What do you stand to gain if you cooperate in Dad's plan? You'll get a fortune's worth of his stock in the company, a great job using your degree, a job much better than repairing motorcycles..."

"All right, that's it." He came to his feet and set his hands on his hips. "You can leave now."

"I wasn't insulting what you do!" she said, refusing to budge. "I just mean..."

"That it isn't becoming to a Hartman to work with his hands? Look at me, Jessica. Read my lips. I chose what I do for a living. Nobody told me to do this, and nobody made me. It's my choice, and I happen to like it."

"Then you could go back to it later, if you wanted," she said. "You'd have even more money to put into your shop, or you could buy a whole chain of shops."

"You're forgetting something," he said. "The will said that we have to raise profits by half a million dollars. Give me a break, Jessica. That's a lot of mascara. Dear old Dad knew what he was doing. He had a warped sense of humor, you know."

"He did not," she bit out. "He was a good man." Her voice broke with the last word, and suddenly a rush of tears assaulted her. Cade watched quietly as her face reddened and she pinched the bridge of her nose.

Suddenly something inside him that he didn't even know was there spiraled up, compelling him to reach out for her, offer her comfort, peace.... But he only stayed where he was.

"How could you...really know him...and hate him so much?"

"Hate's too strong a word," Cade said, his voice dropping to a softer pitch. "Call it indifference. I learned it from him."

She breathed in a sob and shook her head. "It's like we're talking about two different people."

"Well, there's only one will, Jessica. If I could sign my part over to you, I would. I didn't expect or want anything from him. I didn't even want to come there today. He fixed it where it couldn't be escaped that easily. But the last laugh is on him."

"And what is that?" Jessica asked. "Watching me lose my chance at everything because of you?"

"No," he said. "The last laugh is that I learned a long time ago that I don't need money to be happy."

"How would you know?" Jessica asked, her voice flat with defeat. "You're a malcontent. You've never been happy a day in your life."

For a moment, Cade only stared at her, his eyes filled with fathomless turmoil and anger so intense that she wasn't sure anything would ever cool it. Not even her father's death.

"Wrong again," he said. "There was a time..." His voice trailed off, and swallowing, he shook his head. "Look, Jessica, there's no point in this. I'm not going to change my mind. I'm sorry for what this has done to you, but not sorry enough to give up six months of my life. It'll be a good lesson for you, you know. Learning to stand on your own feet for the first time."

"You're right, Cade," she said, wiping her face. "You don't know the first thing about me." Slowly, wearily, she got up and started for the door.

"Read the fine print, Jessica. Maybe there's some way I can sign my half over to you."

Her eyes were lifeless when she looked down at him, and the glands under her skin around them were blotched and mottled from overuse. "Wills don't have fine print, Cade."

"Then talk to your lawyer. Maybe there's something you can do."

Jessica only nodded and went to the door. Before she opened it, she gave him one last look. Then, without another word, she walked out into the twilight.

CHAPTER TWO

"I'M SORRY, JESSICA." Sam Morgan leaned his elbows on his desk and steepled his fingers in front of his face. "The will is pretty cut-and-dried. Your father's wishes were very specific."

"But he didn't know Cade would refuse to cooperate!" she said. "If he had, he never would have put me in this position." Wearily she walked to the window across the room and looked out at the traffic milling below. It was funny how the world went on, she thought, when hers seemed to have come to a complete halt. "I mean, think about it," she said, turning back around. "He named the company after me. Would he have done that if he knew I wasn't going to wind up with one cent's worth of interest in it?"

"No, I don't suppose he would have," Sam said.

"Then why can't I contest the will?"

"Because you'd lose. He was of sound mind and body, and he seemed to have reasons for what he was doing. Maybe it was to get his son involved in the company. Maybe he knew that he would never get him to do it unless there was something at stake."

"Something at stake," she repeated under her breath. "Something like my future?"

"Your father was a complicated man, Jessica. I think you know that."

"I know that he was a kind and loving man."

"And he loved his son, too."

"Oh, I know that, and you know that!" she blurted. "But for some reason Cade doesn't know that."

"Then you have to convince him," Sam said. "You have six months, Jessica." Standing up, he patted her shoulder with paternal affection. "I've seen your wiles. You can be pretty darn persuasive when you put your mind to it. Unless I'm mistaken, I think you can convince Cade eventually."

She issued a low moan and shook her head. "He hates me, Sam. *Hates* me. Somehow I represent everything that ever went wrong in his life."

Sam sat back down, clasped his hands over his middle, and settled his astute eyes on Jessica. "Then I suggest you try to get to know him better, find out what those things are. You'll never reach him until you know what makes him tick."

The edges of her eyes began to tingle with that stinging prelude to tears. Except that she wasn't going to cry. Not any more. She was so tired of crying. "Well, thank you, Sam," she said, reaching for her purse. "I know you've done everything you can."

"Keep me informed, Jessica. And the minute you talk him into it, I'll set up a meeting with the board of directors."

"Right," she said without much hope. "I'll bet they're really on my side. If we don't play, they get everything."

"But if you do play, chances are their profits will go up. They're not stupid, Jessica."

Jessica turned that over and over in her mind as she drove home, trying to figure out if, perhaps, *she* was the one who was stupid. Cade's mother had died two years ago, and as far as Jessica knew, he had no other family. She was the only one.

If she wasn't stupid, she could find some way to change his mind. But that was assuming that he had any kind of brotherly feelings toward her at all.

All at once, a bolt of reality struck her and a voice in her mind railed out, *How could he feel like your brother, when he doesn't even know you?*

Sam was right. She had to get to know Cade and figure out what drove him. Moreover, he had to get to know her. Until he had made some emotional investment in their relationship, she couldn't expect to sway him. The problem was, she wasn't sure if Cade ever made emotional investments in anything. But it was time he started.

A slow smile dawned on her face as she checked her rearview mirror, did a U-turn and headed for Cade's shop.

"ARE YOU CRAZY, MAN?" Pete Jenson—Cade's seventy-year-old partner who still traveled on a Harley and wore his hair in a gray ponytail that hung halfway down the back of his leather jacket—dropped his feet from their position on the table and glared at his partner. "You gave up a shot at owning Jessica Cosmetics? Do you know how much that company is probably worth?"

"Not owning it," Cade said, wishing he'd never told Pete or Grady anything about what had happened yesterday. But there really wasn't any way around it. They had been speculating about what was in the old man's will since the day Sam Morgan had contacted him. "Just his shares of it. *If* I go to work for them for six months, *if* I work with Jessica, *if* I manage to pull off a miracle and raise profits, *if* the world doesn't come to an end, *if* there's peace in the Middle East..."

Grady chuckled. "Well, hell, long shot or not, it's better than sitting around in grease up to your elbows. Man, you'd have to be a fool to walk away from that."

"Yeah, well, call me what you want," Cade said, stiffening. "I live my life on my own terms. Not anybody else's."

"But look what all that money could do for our shop," Pete argued. He got up, hobbled a step until the stiffness in his knee subsided, and leaned down to Cade. "We could open another store across town."

"Yeah," Grady agreed. Closer to Cade's age, and with a bleary-eyed charm that young women found fascinating, Grady came to his feet, tossing a can of oil from one hand to the other. "Besides that, you'd get to spend six months with that Jessica chick. Damn, if she's as hot as she looks in her pictures on all those makeup ads, I could think of a lot worse things."

Cade's look was almost lethal, and Pete slapped his arm. "Shut up, man. That's his sister you're talking about."

"She's not my sister." Fed up, Cade got up and started out of the room. "I barely even know her."

"Hey, we're not finished with the meeting!" Pete shouted behind him.

"I've done all the meeting I'm gonna do today," Cade said. "I have work to do. Are you guys gonna keep sitting around planning my life out for me, or are you gonna get the store ready to open?"

They muttered some obscene remarks that bounced right off him as he went to the back of the store. Cade loved working with his hands, rebuilding Harley engines and making things work better than they had when they were new. It was something he had control over, he often thought, something where he could see direct results.

Besides, the thought of Andrew Hartman's son having grease under his nails was something that gave Cade a lot of satisfaction. He could only imagine what the old man had thought when he'd heard that his son had abandoned a career in marketing and now catered to a clientele of bikers. A bitter smile tugged at his lips, then quickly died as he realized that the man was gone. The statement was an empty one. There really wasn't anyone who cared.

No one but Jessica.

He heard footsteps coming into the back, and looked up to see Grady with a lascivious grin on his face. "Speak of the devil."

Cade glanced up. "What do you mean?"

"Guess who just pranced into our shop?"

Irritated, he went back to loosening the bolts to remove an old engine. "Why don't you tell me?"

"Your sister. Miss Jessica, herself."

"Oh, hell." Cade threw his wrench down and gaped up at him. "What does she want?"

"To talk to you, I guess," he said. "You want to come up, or you want me to send her back?"

Cade thought of washing his hands and going up front to meet her, but something about that concession riled him. No, he thought. Let her come back here and see who he really was. "Send her back," he said.

Grady disappeared, and with a new determination, Cade dug into the engine again.

He heard her high heels clicking on the floor before she appeared, and he forced himself not to look up. She came closer, her long legs right in his line of vision.

"Hi," she said in a spritely voice.

Grudgingly he looked up her long, long legs to the short skirt flirting around her thighs, to the blouse that defined the woman she had become. He tore his eyes away. "What are you doing here?"

Despite the fact that she wore a cream-colored outfit that he guessed was made of silk, she pulled up a stool that could very well have been grease-stained, and sat down on it. "I don't know, really," she said. "I guess I just wanted to see where you work."

"And what do you think?" he asked facetiously, as he dropped a bolt into his hand and started unscrewing another one.

"Nice," she said. "Especially the showroom floor. I don't know what I expected when you said you owned a motorcycle shop. Hell's Angels hanging around outside, maybe, or a dark warehouse with a bunch of ominous-looking bikes and the smell of exhaust everywhere. But this is nice."

He hadn't expected the compliment, but he blew it off. Sarcastically he said, "Glad you approve."

"You're lucky."

This time he stopped working and looked up. "How's that?"

"You have a good job. Own a business."

He shrugged. "Yeah, I guess." The small talk made him nervous, and finally he decided to force her to get to the point. "So did you talk to your lawyer?"

She slid off the stool and began to stroll around the shop, examining things on the shelves, looking at the bikes lined up for repair. "Yeah. But he said there was nothing he could do. Daddy apparently knew what he was doing."

"Did he ever," Cade said, going back to his work.

She threw him an eloquent look, but let the comment go. "Well, the point is that there's no way around it. Either we both participate, or we both lose. So... I figure there's only one thing I can do."

"What's that?"

"Look for a job," she said. "Got any ideas?"

He almost laughed, but smirked and shook his head instead. "Well, let's see. You majored in Beautiful in college, didn't you? What do you have? A Bachelorette degree?"

Almost instantly, he wished he hadn't said it. The redness climbing her cheekbones was making him uncomfortable.

"No, actually. I majored in public relations."

"So get a job in public relations."

"I've checked," she said. "There's not much available here in that field right now."

"So go somewhere else."

"I could," she said, "if I had time to wait until just the right thing came along. The problem is how to support myself in the meantime."

"Sell a couple of pairs of your shoes," he suggested. "That ought to raise a grand or two."

Again, he could see he'd hit home. The funny thing was, there was no satisfaction in the fact.

"I spoke to Mr. Thurgood, acting president of the company," she went on, as if the comment hadn't ruffled her, "and he isn't interested in my coming to work for the company alone, even just as an employee. He said that would work at cross-purposes with my father's wishes. He said they were beginning to interview new Jessicas to represent the company."

"New Jessicas?" Cade laughed aloud, but Jessica didn't see the humor. "What are they gonna do? Call up the model agencies and tell them to send over every Jessica they've got?"

"No, Cade," she said quietly. "They're going to find someone to name Jessica. A new face to put on the product."

Cade set his wrench down and got to his feet, grabbing a rag to wipe his hands on. "Well, if you ask me, that would be stupid. You're the only Jessica. They'd be shooting themselves in the foot to change that now. It's not like you've lost your looks. As a matter of fact, you've gotten even prettier since..."

Suddenly he realized what he was saying, and stopped in mid-sentence.

A slow smile tickled across Jessica's lips. "Thank you, Cade."

Angry at himself for giving her that much, he turned away, rifled through his tools and found the one he needed. "I just don't get it. You would think they'd do whatever they could to keep what's worked in the past..."

"Profits are down," she said. "I guess they're panicked. And with Daddy's death, everything's shaky. I can't really blame them. They need new blood. New ideas. New energy. And if you and I aren't going to be their saviors, then I guess they have to look somewhere else. Besides," she said, looking down at her hands, "I get the feeling that they don't have that much faith in us. They'd much rather have Daddy's stock revert back to the company."

"Is that so?" Cade asked, his back tensing visibly through his chambray shirt.

"Yeah. You can't really blame them. I never had a contract with them, and I have practically no experience, and you're not exactly taking the world by the tail back in this shop all day."

Bristling, he leaned back against the counter, crossing his arms. "Not to mention the fact that your reverse psychology skills could use a little polish. It isn't working, Jessica."

"I'm not using psychology," she said. "I'm just stating facts."

His grin was maddening. "The fact is, Jessica, that you need a real job for the first time in your life, and I can't very well sympathize. I've been working since I was fourteen."

"I didn't come here for your sympathy."

"Then what did you come for?"

"Well," she said, looking around. "I wasn't sure until I got here. But now that I've seen this place. . ." A strange determination took over her face, and lifting her chin, she dropped her bomb. "I kind of thought maybe I could work here."

The look on Cade's face almost made her smile. A laugh caught in his throat, and he raked his hand through his hair while narrowing his eyes at her. "You're kidding, right?"

"Nope," she said. "I bet I could sell a lot of bikes. Besides, you seem a little shorthanded out front."

"We're not," he said quickly. "We don't have any openings right now."

"Then hire me on a trial basis. If I don't sell any bikes in, say, a week, then you don't have to pay me."

Cade slammed down his hand. "No, Jessica. We don't need anybody."

"So are you the final word?" she asked.

"Yes," he said. "I mean, no. Pete usually does the hiring for the floor, and I do the hiring for the shop. But don't waste your time. We aren't hiring for either right now."

"You could if you wanted to."

"Well, I *don't* want to, okay? The last thing I need is to have you in my face every day, making my life miserable."

She leaned a hip against the wall and crossed her arms, but the stance looked more suggestive than confrontational. "Why would I make you miserable,

Cade? Most people think I'm a pretty pleasant person."

"I don't need you constantly rubbing my nose in the fact that you lost your inheritance."

"Then you do feel guilty?" she asked.

He grunted. "No, I don't feel guilty! I'm just aware that the only reason you'd take a job here in the first place would be to make my life hell. If it weren't for that, you would never consider working in a motorcycle shop!"

"Well, if it's good enough for you, why isn't it good enough for me?"

"Because you're a jet-setting porcelain doll, for crying out loud! What do you know about bikes?"

"I'm a quick study."

He groaned and realized he'd just unscrewed the wrong bolt. "Look, I don't have time for this! Look in the paper, call an employment agency, bug everybody else you know. But please, let this drop. You're wasting your time."

She sighed and dropped her hands, and nodded her head sullenly. "All right. I see. You don't want me here."

"Damn right I don't want you here!" he shouted. "Finally, you're listening!"

"Okay," she said. "Then I guess I'll have to try something else."

"Good. Do that."

"I will." But she didn't seem defeated, and thrusting her chin up as she started across the room, those high heels looking so sexy that he had to turn away, she left Cade wondering what she might do next.

The answer came half an hour later when Pete came laughing through the door. "This is great, Cade. I think it's going to work out just fine."

"What?" Cade asked.

"Hiring your sister to sell for us."

Cade almost dropped the engine he was moving, and recovering his hold, set it down. "What did you say?"

"It was a great idea, man. Jessica Hartman working on our floor? Do you know how many bikers will decide they need to trade once they see her here?"

"I told her there were no openings! I told her she couldn't work here."

"Well, we created an opening," Grady said.

Cade threw down his rag. "Didn't you think this was important enough to consult me first?"

"Well, hell, she is your sister. Besides, Grady and I agree. That's a two-thirds majority. We outvoted you."

"You're voting for a pair of legs, and not the good of this shop," Cade flung back.

"Maybe so," Pete said with a chuckle. "But I can damn well bet those legs'll sell bikes. And if they don't, well, she'll be a nice diversion for a while."

Before Cade could give voice to his annoyance, Pete walked out of the room.

CHAPTER THREE

THE SUN HAD just disappeared beyond the horizon when Jessica drove her BMW down the winding drive of the cemetery and stopped near her father's fresh grave.

She got out of the car and opened the back door, and retrieved the four pots of flowers she had set on a tray on the floor, along with her hand shovel. Quietly she closed the door, as if any sudden noise would disturb the sleeping residents around her.

But all was not quiet, for up on the hill an old man rode on a lawn mower, trimming the grounds so that those left behind would have comfort in where they'd laid their loved ones. The roar did not bother her, as it gave a peaceful, realistic sound to this place, a sense of home and calm.

She went to her father's grave, freshly covered with black earth, and stood for a moment looking at the headstone that told of her father's date of birth and death. The thought of speaking to him, as though he could hear, offered no comfort. She doubted anything could offer her comfort now.

Wiping a tear from her cheek with the shoulder of her blouse, she set down the tray of flowers and knelt in the black mound of dirt. Taking her shovel, she dug in close to the headstone, making a small trench deep enough to set the potted flowers' roots.

On the hill, the mowing stopped, and she heard the birds chattering in the trees above her head as a soft breeze whispered through her hair. It was a lovely place, she thought. It was too bad her father couldn't see it.

She emptied the pots of the flowers and set the roots in the trench, then scraped the dirt back to fill in around them. Patting the earth to pack the flowers more firmly, she wished she had brought water. She turned her face up to the sky and wondered if it would rain tonight. But there wasn't a cloud above her.

She needed to water them or they'd die, she thought, and her gesture today would be useless. Like her love for her father. That was the hardest thing about death to accept, she thought miserably. The fact that her love didn't die with her father. It just hung there, in a vacuum, unreturned and unfulfilled, with nothing but paperwork to account for what once was.

Suddenly, unexpectedly, her tears seemed to explode in a helpless assault. Sitting back on her feet, she covered her face with her dirt-stained hands and let the grief wash over her. For a moment, nothing existed except the white-hot stab of her pain, and the unreality of sitting on the grave of someone she had loved more than anyone in the world, someone she had joked with only days before.

Daddy, you're getting a little bald spot on the back of your head, so I bought you this can of spray paint to fill in the hole. Be still and let me squirt a little.

Give me that, you! I'm not losing my hair, Princess, I'm just growing more scalp.

Bringing her hands down, Jessica drew in a deep breath and let the cool air fan her tears, as dusk faded into the sky.

"Mighty pretty flowers," someone said behind her.

Jessica started and turned to see the old man who'd been mowing the lawn.

"Thank you. I...I didn't want to bring cut flowers. They'd just die, and..."

"You did the smart thing," the old man said with a kindly, comforting smile that made her feel better. He squatted next to her, checked the buds and nodded in approval. "These'll do well here. I'll water them for you before I leave."

"Oh, thank you," she whispered. "Are you the grounds keeper?"

"That's right. I 'spect I'll be buried here one day, sooner than I think, and I want it to look nice when I am." He held out a hand to her. "They call me Cephus, ma'am. You let me know if there's anything I can do for you."

"And I'm Jessica," she said. "Jessica Hartman."

"And who was this?" the old man asked, referring to the grave beneath them.

"My father," she said. "He died just two weeks ago."

"I remember," he said, nodding. "Big funeral."

"Yes, it was." Her eyes settled again on the headstone, and she recalled her numbness on the day of the funeral. She'd barely noticed anyone at all, though she knew two hundred or more of his friends and acquaintances had turned out. She hadn't seen Cade until the graveside service had ended and she was on her way home in the limousine. He had passed them on his motorcycle, with no helmet and his hair whipping defiantly in the wind. Her heart had jolted like that of a child after catching a glimpse of a favorite star. She remembered a new grief settling over her for his being an outsider at his father's funeral, hanging on the fringes rather than sitting with the family.

Cephus got to his feet, dusted off his pants and patted her shoulder. "You feel free to come here and visit with him any time you like, you hear? These graves are for the living, you know."

"I know," she said. "Then you'll water the flowers for me tonight?"

"You can count on it, young lady."

She smiled as he started away, then, giving the grave one last look, she went back to her car.

A sense of profound melancholy hung over her as she drove home, and she realized suddenly that she couldn't stand that feeling. Nothingness. Emptiness. Loneliness. Aimlessness.

It wasn't like her to feel this way, yet maybe she was expecting too much of herself so soon after her father's death. She needed new goals, she thought. She needed a new purpose. She doubted working in the motorcycle shop would do it.

What had she been thinking, she wondered with a twist in her stomach? It probably wouldn't change Cade's mind. It would only waste time that would be better spent . . . doing what?

She pulled into her driveway and cut off the engine, and for a moment wondered if Cade's indifference could ever be broken. It was a challenge bigger than any she'd faced so far in her life. And she wasn't sure she had the resources to fight it.

Wondering if she should give up on the plan and not show up for work at his shop the next day, she went inside and dropped her purse on the kitchen counter. She noticed a message on her machine and pushed the button to rewind it, then went to the sink to wash her hands and face.

"Jessica, this is Cade," the voice said. She cut off the water and grabbed a hand towel. "I heard about your little stunt today and that you conned my partners into giving you a job. I'm calling to tell you not to bother showing up. The position they created for you has just been uncreated. Give it up, Jessica. You're wasting your time."

Jessica's mouth fell open, and her face turned an obstinate color of red as the machine clicked off. Who did he think he was?

Suddenly her sense of purpose returned to her, and she realized that she had no choice. She still had to go through with this, to do whatever she could to make him change his mind. The worst thing that could happen was that she'd get to know her brother better, and even if he didn't join in her father's plan, at least she'd have that.

Snatching up her purse, she went back to her car and flew to his house to tell him that.

CADE CHANGED THE CD in his player from Yanni to Kenny G, then turned back to the woman sipping wine on his sofa. "We're in no hurry to get to the restaurant, are we?"

Melody smiled in that seductive way she had and shook her head. "Of course not, darling. Come here."

He turned on the stereo, picked up his own wine and sat down next to her. He reached over to stroke her hair—hair that was a little too well coiffed—but he feared messing it up. It was a little stiffer than he imagined Jessica's to be, and he had to admit that the blond in Melody's looked a little too platinum. But she was classy, with her Liz Claiborne sweater and tight stirrup pants that accented the shape of her long legs.

But Jessica's were longer. A memory flashed through his mind of Jessica sitting on that stool in his shop today, with her legs crossed so proudly and pristinely, as if she knew exactly what her weapons were and didn't find one ounce of shame in using them.

"Cade, are you listening to me?"

Cade shook his thoughts free and glanced back at his date. "What?"

"You seem a thousand miles away. I thought we were going to have a romantic evening."

"Well, we are. I was just... thinking about something..."

Melody took his hand and brought the palm to her mouth. "Poor baby. You're thinking about your father, aren't you?"

He gave her a surprised look. "Actually, no."

"The inheritance, then?"

"There is no inheritance," he said, pulling his hand back.

"I asked around," she said, fingering the hair that peeked out above the top button of his white shirt. "I heard about the conditions your father attached. You should really go for it, you know. Even if you aren't able to raise the profits, the experience with Jessica Cosmetics would be good for you. It would look good on your résumé, and maybe it could turn into a permanent job with the company."

Stiffening, he pulled back again. "Who says I want a job with them or anyone else? I happen to like what I'm doing."

"But you're too smart for that," she said. "You have so much more potential."

Her words walloped him between the eyes, and he sat back, gaping at her. "Funny, but you never reminded me of my ex-wife until now."

She looked hurt. "Why, darling?"

"Because she married me for my potential. When she found out I wasn't so easy to change, she bailed out."

"Oh, I'm not trying to change you, Cade. I'm just saying that you should have a more open mind." Sliding her arms around his neck, she pulled him closer, pressing her breasts against him. She was well endowed, and she didn't mind showing it... maybe a little too much. He thought of the way Jessica's ivory blouse today had tapered to her waist, accenting the ample shape of her breasts, while modestly yet sensuously covering them.

He wondered if she was as sensual a woman as she appeared to be, or if she was cold like so many of the other upper-class women who seemed to attract him.

But Melody didn't seem cold right now as she pulled his head down and drew him into a kiss that left no doubt about her intentions.

The doorbell rang, and groaning, Cade broke the kiss. "Damn."

"Don't answer it," Melody whispered.

The bell rang again, and Cade got up. "I can't ignore it," he said. "Let me just answer and I'll get rid of them."

Melody gave a great long-suffering sigh as he went to the door.

Jessica stood on the other side of it, wearing a pair of tight faded Levi's that had dirt on the knees, a T-shirt that cast aside any doubts he may have had about the generous portions she'd been given in the breast department, and her face clean and free of makeup, enhanced only by the silky fall of her hair as it brushed her shoulders.

"I need to talk to you," she said, marching inside without an invitation.

"It's not a good time, Jessica," he said, glancing at Melody, who had gotten up and was ambling closer. "I have someone here."

Jessica pasted a smile on her face and held out her hand. "Hi there. I'm Jessica. I hope you'll excuse me while Cade and I work out a little problem we're having. By the way, Cade," she said, sliding a look over his Hilfigger shirt, khakis and deck shoes, "you clean up nice when you aren't trying to shock people. Better watch out or people will think this is the real you."

His eyes became almost amused as they locked with hers.

"A problem you're having?" Melody whined. "What do you mean?"

"Nothing," he said. "Melody, this is Jessica Hartman. My half-sister."

"Oh. She doesn't look like her pictures." The tension in Melody's face slackened a bit, but Jessica took care of that.

"Beg to differ, Cade," she said with a smile. "The truth is, we aren't related at all except on paper. In fact, we hardly even know each other. But I intend to change that."

"Jessica," he warned, then glanced at Melody, who seemed to be growing more and more irate. Jessica was smiling, quite pleased with herself, when he brought his eyes back to her. "Could we do this some other time?"

"Not really, Cade, since I'm supposed to be at the shop at eight o'clock tomorrow morning. I still intend to be there, you see."

"I told you, there's no point."

"Your partners didn't think so. They liked me a lot."

"My partners like anything in a skirt, and the one you were wearing today was right up their alley. In fact, what you did comes close to coercion."

She smiled. "And there I was, thinking you hadn't even noticed what I was wearing."

Melody bristled. "Why *did* you notice, Cade?"

"Well, it's hard not to," he said, whirling around. "Look, I don't have to explain—"

"And what's she gonna do? Come work at your shop?"

"Darn straight," Jessica said, lifting her chin in defiance.

"The hell she is," he shouted. "Jessica, I'm warning you that if you go through with this, you're going to regret it."

"Why, Cade? Are you afraid I'll convince you to work with me for JC? Or are you afraid that we'll get to know each other, and you might actually like me?"

He gaped at her, unable to answer, then realized that Melody was staring at him, too, waiting for his response.

"Neither. I just don't like having my time or money wasted. And frankly, I don't think we'll get a whole lot of work done if you're there. Pete and Grady will go gaga over you, and I won't be able to keep my mind on—" He stopped, as if realizing he was indicting himself.

"Keep your mind on what?" Melody asked. "What will you be thinking of? Her legs? Her cleavage? Why the hell does she want to work for you anyway?"

"I want to get to know him better," Jessica said without hesitation.

"How *much* better?" Melody asked.

Cade rolled his eyes and threw up his hands. "Look, Melody, this really isn't any of your business. If you'd just leave it to me and my sister—"

"I'm not your sister," Jessica cut in. "I'm just some woman whose skirt you noticed today."

"Damn it, Jessica!"

But before he could finish his thought, Melody was grabbing her purse and heading for the door.

"Where are you going?"

"Home!" she shouted. "Let me know when you work this out with her. I'd be fascinated to know how it ends!"

The door slammed behind her, and Cade kicked at the air, then, setting his hands on his hips, swung around to face her. "You just ruined a perfectly good evening."

"Well, you should thank me." Jessica stretched and dropped down into a chair. "She isn't your type at all."

"How do you know what my type is?" he asked through his teeth.

"One could only hope," she said. "I would think you'd go for a less pretentious type."

"What makes you think she's pretentious?"

"Her car, for one thing. A red roadster just cries out, 'Look at me, look at me.' And then there's her clothes. But I didn't come here to run down your friends."

"No, you just came to chase them off."

"So you'll take a cold shower tonight, Cade. Big deal. You deserve it after the way you've treated me."

Cursing under his breath, Cade flicked off the CD still playing romantically in the background. Somehow the mood was broken. "I don't deserve any of this, Jessica. I never asked to have anything to do with you or my father, and I've made it more than clear that I'm not interested in anything of his. If you could just accept that..."

"Excuse me if I'm having trouble accepting much of anything just now," she said, the timbre in her voice dropping. "One thing at a time, okay? Right now I'm still working on accepting that he isn't at home waiting for me to join him for our Thursday-night dinner together."

Cade's anger seemed to fade at the sudden vulnerability in Jessica's voice, and he sat back down. "Look, I know how you must feel. I lost my mother a couple of years ago. It's a blow, but it gets better. But I can't share your grief for him. If that's what you're looking for, you're not going to get it from me."

Jessica's eyes lost their luster as she stared at him. "You know, Cade, for someone with such soulful blue eyes, you sure are bitter."

He didn't like being called that. Getting up, he walked to the fireplace and stirred the logs. Jessica's eyes followed him, and she noted the picture on the mantel of a little boy posed in baseball uniform, holding a bat as if about to swing it. It was Ben, she thought, and she was instantly ashamed that she had almost forgotten Cade had a son.

"I'm not bitter," he said. "I'm just realistic. I know what I want and what I don't want, and I don't have a lot of patience for anything else."

"That limits your life an awful lot, you know. How can you stretch and grow if you don't try new things?"

"I try all sorts of new things," he said. "I hang glide and skydive, and when I have the chance I bungee jump."

"Yeah, but what do you ever do that really takes a risk?"

"You don't think those things are risky?"

"Physically," she said. "But I would imagine those are real easy for you. Emotionally, though, you're scared to death. Why is that, Cade?"

He hit the log with his poker, then almost knocked the stand over hanging it back up. "Damn it, Jessica, you don't know anything at all about my emotions."

"I know enough. And I can't help wondering why you're so dead set on staying away from me. There must be a reason for it, Cade. I'm waiting to hear it."

"Because you get on my nerves!" he shouted. "You've always gotten on my nerves!"

She was silent for a moment as his condemnation reverberated through the room. "All I've ever done since I was a little girl was adore you," she whispered finally. "I've never hurt you, or taken anything from you."

"You haven't got a clue what you've taken from me!" he shouted. "Not a clue!"

"Then tell me."

For a moment, she saw the anguish in his eyes, as though he would crack and spill out everything he'd spent his lifetime holding in. But after a moment, those eyes hardened again.

"Go home, Jessica," he said in a dull voice.

She sat still for a moment, then finally got to her feet. "All right, Cade, I will," she said softly. "But I'll be at the shop bright and early tomorrow morning, since you haven't convinced me why I shouldn't."

Cade only dropped his head back against his seat as Jessica showed herself out of his house.

TRUE TO HER WORD, Jessica was at the shop when Cade arrived the next morning. Making no effort to hide his belligerence, he ignored her greeting, unlocked the side door and led her in. "Just for the record," he said, "don't expect me to treat you like any other employee. I've made it my mission to run you off as soon as possible."

"Thanks for the warning," she said, bouncing in behind him. "Where's everybody?"

He set down his keys, went to the coffeepot in the kitchen and began making his first pot of the day. "Pete'll be in any minute now, but Grady'll roll in whenever he feels like it. Your guess is as good as mine." He started the coffeepot percolating, then glanced back at her, disgusted. "What are you wearing?"

As if baffled by his question, she looked down at the short white skirt she wore, the high heels and the tasteful jewelry, along with the short-sleeved coral angora sweater that clung too much to her feminine shape. "What's wrong with this?"

"It's a bike shop, Jessica. Not Madison Avenue."

"I like to dress for success. I'm here to sell, aren't I?"

"But you look like an escaped mannequin from Macy's."

Jessica tilted her head and frowned up at him. "Since I can't believe you'd be quite as insulting as you sound, I'm going to take that as a compliment."

The side door opened, and seventy-year-old Pete came in, flung off his sleeveless leather jacket to reveal his sleeveless T-shirt, and pulled off the helmet he'd been wearing. "Hey," he said to Jessica, ignoring Cade completely. "You made it, huh?"

"Yes," she said. She struck a pose. "Tell me, Pete. What do you think of what I'm wearing?"

Pete perused her from top to bottom, an appreciative grin lighting his eyes. "Damn near perfect, I'd say."

Cade bristled and pushed off from the wall he was leaning against. "Why don't you go over the shop rules with her? I'm going to get started in the back."

Pete grinned. "Rules, huh? Don't hit any of the customers, duck if they swing at you, and sell, sell, sell."

"You're hopeless." Cade stopped at the door and threw a look back over his shoulder. "Hey, when Grady comes in, try to keep him off her, okay? I hate it when he makes a fool of himself."

As Pete laughed, Jessica watched Cade disappear from his sight. So, was he worried about Grady and her? Was it a brotherly concern or a professional one? Either way, she told herself, she would play it for all it was worth.

She'd use anything he gave her, she thought, for the clock was ticking and her future was slipping away.

BY NOON, Jessica had sold a fifteen-thousand-dollar bike and had a deal pending for one of the top-of-the-line models. When she took off for lunch and found

Cade in the kitchen, she couldn't get the grin off her face. "I sold a bike," she said with a giggle.

He didn't look up from the newspaper he was engrossed in. "I heard."

"Guess you'll have to pay me now."

"Looks like it."

"And a guy's out trying to get financing for the hog on the floor. I think he'll get it, too."

Cade turned the newspaper's page and didn't answer.

"Aren't you happy for me?" she asked.

"Delirious."

"Pete and Grady are," she said. "Nobody else sold anything this morning. In fact, they're so happy, they're taking me to lunch."

Cade dropped the newspaper and peered up at her. "Is that so?"

"You want to come?"

The newspaper came up again. "No. I'll stay here and man the front. Looks like somebody'd better."

"We have Miss Stevens and Jerry," she said, referring to the sixty-year-old woman who kept their books, and the eighteen-year-old kid who helped where he was needed.

"I'll stay, anyway," he said. "I have work to do."

"Okay," she said, bopping in and pulling out a chair at his table. "Your attitude would probably put a damper on things, anyway." She sat down and leaned up on the table. "So tell me about Melody."

The paper crumpled down again. "What about her?"

"How long have you been seeing her? It couldn't be serious, given her insecurities, but I just wondered—"

"What insecurities?"

"About me. If she could feel threatened by your sister, well, it seems that she needs—"

"You're not my sister," he said. "And she knows it."

She smiled, undaunted. "So what's the relationship? Is it just a casual affair, or are you engaged, or what?"

"I don't know," he said. "We're not engaged, but—"

"Then it *is* a casual affair?"

"No," he said. "I mean, we see each other some."

She leaned back, crossing her long legs, and asked, "What do you like about her?"

He sighed and focused on the ceiling, wishing—the way he'd wished when she was a kid—that she'd just go away. "She's good-looking, okay?"

"Ah, she's good-looking," Jessica repeated, as if that shed a whole new light on things. "Is that all?"

"No, of course not. She's..."

"A good cook?" Jessica provided with a grin.

He shrugged his brows. "Hardly."

"A good listener?"

His paper came back up. "I guess she would be, if I ever talked."

"Oh, so you're the problem," she said.

Irritated, Cade dropped the paper on the table and centered his eyes squarely on Jessica's. "What problem? If I wanted to talk, I'd talk."

"But you don't trust her enough to confide in her, is that it? She hasn't inspired your trust?"

"Yes. No." Cursing, he slid his chair back and got up. "You're getting on my nerves again. I don't want to talk to you about Melody."

"Well, you already did," she said, "and I understand. I wouldn't be able to get serious about someone who cared only about her looks, and couldn't be trusted with my innermost thoughts, either. That explains everything."

Cade didn't remember when he had felt more frustrated, and for a moment he struggled between wanting to throw his hands up and laugh, or throw something across the room. "You shouldn't be working in a bike shop, Jessica," he said as a grin stole across his face. "You should be a politician. An ambassador."

"Or a spokesperson for a cosmetics company," she said softly. "Either way, I've been told I'm a born seller. It's too bad, isn't it?"

Cade only looked at her for a long moment, and for the duration of that moment she felt a connection between them. But the moment shattered when Grady stuck his head in the door. "Let's go, Jessy-baby. We have reservations at Chez Louis."

"Chez Louis?" Cade frowned and gaped at his partner. "You're kidding."

Taking Grady's arm, Jessica tossed him a grin over her shoulder. "See you later."

Cade only set his teeth as she disappeared from his sight, and, muttering "Jessy-baby" disgustedly under his breath, went to the refrigerator to find something to eat.

CHAPTER FOUR

THE FACT THAT JESSICA dined with his partners for over two hours, only to come back and close the sale on the most expensive bike on their floor, added to Cade's chagrin.

Why it bothered him so, he couldn't really say. He was glad she had sold the two bikes. He'd be crazy to complain about that. If she'd been anybody else, he probably would have thrown a party...or, at the very least, taken her to lunch himself.

But she wasn't anybody else. She was Jessica. And he didn't want her there.

Over the next several days, he tried to avoid her as best he could, but even when she wasn't around, someone in the shop was talking about her. Or she would sneak up on him when he wasn't looking, perch herself on that stool that seemed made to display her legs, and pick his brain about things he wasn't ready to reveal.

He shook his head and breathed a low laugh, remembering when Beverly had come in earlier, looking for him. She'd gotten Jessica's attention right away when she'd driven up in her Porsche and floated inside on a cloud of Obsession.

He hadn't seen the sleek brunette in over a month, but when Jessica led her back to where he was, he couldn't help being glad to see her. She had thrown herself at him in front of Jessica, and he had to admit he had eaten it up. He had quickly finished his work for the morning and left with Beverly. It was his turn for a long lunch.

Now, as he came back in the rear entrance, he saw that Jessica was waiting for him. "So," she said with a curious grin, "does Melody know about Beverly?"

He stooped down and resumed his work on the brakes of a bike for the police force. "I don't keep a registry, if that's what you mean."

She slid onto that chair again, crossing her legs, and he deliberately willed himself to keep his eyes on what he was doing.

"Tell me something," she said. "Why is it that you're so dead set on living out this vow of poverty you have, but you only date women who tip more than you make each year?"

Cade shot her a disbelieving look. "I really don't think it's any of your business who I date."

"Oh, come on, Cade. I didn't mean that in any derogatory way. I'm just curious, that's all."

"I don't check their incomes before I ask them out," he said. "For all I know, they could be homeless."

"Homeless and driving Porsches and roadsters? I don't think so, Cade."

"So you think I'm dating them for their cars?"

"Hardly. I'd guess that you're embarrassed to be seen in those cars. You probably take them out in your pickup."

He didn't want to tell her she was right, because she'd probably read some asinine psychological significance into it. Instead he popped his jaw and tried to ignore her.

"And if I'm right, then you're probably a little embarrassed by them, too, with that pauper complex you've got and all."

He stopped working but didn't look up. "Pauper complex?"

"Well, yes," she said. "That desperate need to be as far removed from wealth as possible, like it represents all the bad things in your life." Examining her perfectly groomed nails, she asked, "Didn't your wife have money?"

His jaw tightened even more, and she saw the color rising on his cheekbones. "My wife's family had money, but before your little mind starts working on that, let me tell you that I never took one cent from them for anything."

"Of course you didn't," Jessica said. "I would have bet everything I own on it. Of course, I don't own much now, but..." Her voice trailed off, just long enough for her dig to sink in. "Anyway, I just think it's odd that you would be so attracted to the very type of person you claim to despise."

"Who says I go after them?" he asked. "Maybe they're attracted to me, for just that reason. I'm the challenge. The one from the wrong side of the tracks."

"Sounds exciting," Jessica said, "as long as you don't ever want a serious relationship. Because one built on that kind of foundation would be doomed."

"Tell me about it." His timbre dropped a degree, and she saw that she had hit a nerve. "You don't have to worry. I have no plans for any lasting entanglements. I've had enough of that to last a lifetime."

"Do you ever see Ben?" she asked, out of the blue.

Cade frowned and threw down his wrench. "Damn, I wish I could figure out how you think. One minute you're prying into my love life, then you're analyzing my psyche, then without any segue, you're whopping me with questions about my son."

"I didn't need a segue," she said. "You were talking about your marriage, and I naturally thought of Ben. Do you?"

"Do I what?"

"Ever see him?"

Cade set his hands on his hips and stared down at a grease spot on the floor. Heaving out a deep sigh, he said, "Ben lives in Arlington, Texas, with his mother and her new husband. I see him when I can, but...he's got it made there. They live in a mansion, and he's got all these friends, and a horse... It's hard to figure out when's the best time to see him."

She was quiet for a change, and when he looked up, he saw her watching him with something close to sympathy in her eyes. But that was the last thing he wanted from her.

"I'm sorry," she whispered. "It must be rough for you."

"Forget it." He picked the wrench back up and began working again. It was weird, this power she had to make his emotions go from exasperation to sentimentality. He told himself he didn't want to be close to her, but he found himself wanting to say more. He had a soft spot where Ben was concerned. "You get used to it after a while."

"Do you really?" she asked softly.

He gave a faint smile. "No. I lied. I guess some people can deal with it better than others. The one to lose is probably the one who suffers the most."

"It seems to me like you both lose."

"I hope not," he said, his eyes suddenly growing soft, pensive, and a thousand miles away. "I hope Ben's happy. I hope he feels like he has a family there. I met his stepdad. He was a little arrogant for my taste, but I'd like to think he cares for my son."

Jessica's eyes were understanding, and suddenly Cade felt too close to her, as if she were more than the pseudosibling he'd grown up envying. She was someone who listened. Someone who seemed to care.

"I'll bet you're a terrific father," she whispered, again surprising him.

He gave her a startled look. "He's a terrific kid. He deserves . . . more than he's gotten."

"Can I meet him . . . I mean, next time you get him here?"

"Why?"

"Well, he's my nephew. And he's your son. It's important to me to know my family."

"Family is a relative term, Jessica," he said. "You should know that by now."

Her eyes seemed to mist over as she held his gaze. "I don't have that much family left, Cade. Don't take it away from me. What could it hurt for us to get to know each other a little better?"

He realized that already he'd shared more with her than he'd shared with anyone in years, and he had to ask himself why. It wasn't like him to open up on any level, with anybody. Yet she had sat there on that stool, perched like a little goddess with those silky smooth legs, and drawn out his deepest, most quiet emotions...

"He doesn't come here much, but if he does, I don't guess it could do much harm," he said finally.

Her smile, as it dawned across her face, ignited a slow burning in his heart. No wonder his father had used her face to market his products, he thought. You couldn't buy a smile like that, and you sure couldn't paint it on. It came from deep inside, from a healthy spirit. It was the reason Andrew had named his whole company after her.

But that very warmth he felt toward her collided with the coldness he clung to after years of blaming her for all the ills in his life.

"Did Grady tell you I sold another bike today?" she asked, slipping off the chair.

Cade grinned. "Yeah, he did."

"He's taking me out tonight to celebrate my first-week anniversary."

Cade's smile collapsed. "You're kidding. You're not considering going out with him."

"Well, sure I am," she said. "Why wouldn't I?"

"Because..." He groped for a concrete reason. "He's a womanizer, the worst kind. And Jessica, he's had the hots for you since the first time he laid eyes on you."

Jessica grinned. "Come on, Cade. I'm a big girl. I know how to handle him. Besides, he's been nothing but nice to me."

"Of course he's been nice to you," Cade said. "You're his fantasy. And he'll be even nicer to you tonight, but it won't be for friendship, Jessica."

She laughed. "So he likes me, Cade. What's the big deal?"

"The big deal is that Grady's used to getting more than small talk on a date. I know him."

"If he's so awful, why are you partners with him?"

"Because he knows motorcycles, and we work well together. That doesn't mean I want him going out with my sister!"

Her smile went into full blossom again. "Cade, I think that may be the first time you've actually called me that without flinching."

"Jessica, you're not listening to me."

"You're acting like an overprotective brother," she said. "I like it." Then, turning and prancing back toward the front, she called over her shoulder, "Don't worry, Cade. I'm twenty-five years old. I've been hit on before."

Cade only ground his jaws together and tried to get back to work, but for the life of him, he couldn't remember what he'd been doing.

JESSICA SHIFTED on the bar stool in the sleazy, smoke-filled room to which Grady had dragged her, and told herself that perhaps she should have listened to Cade after all. Heavy-metal music blared from the stage, where a group of greasy, unshaved musicians with dirty fingernails and tattoos screamed out lyrics that she was certain would have been offensive if she could have understood them.

Grady circled his arms around her, pulled her against him, and began trying to tell her something, but she couldn't hear him. "What?" she yelled, her voice cracking from the conversation she had managed until now.

"You wanna dance?"

Jessica frowned and looked at the dance floor, where sweaty bodies had packed to undulate and jerk. Somehow, she didn't think she'd fit in to the leather-and-spike clientele. If she'd known, she mused, she would have cut the sleeves off of her silk blouse, worn red panty hose and no pants, and not washed her hair for two weeks. But who would have ever imagined he would have brought her here?

"No, I don't think so," she said.

"What?"

"No!" she yelled back. "I've got a headache!"

"Want another drink?" he yelled, as if that were the perfect remedy for such a problem.

She didn't think another Sprite was going to do the trick. "No, thanks. I probably just need to lie down. Would you mind taking me home?"

Grady grinned, as if she'd just offered the invitation he'd been hoping for. "Whatever you want, Jessy-baby. We're outta here."

He pulled her between the tightly packed tables, and the moment they were outside, a sudden feeling of liberation took hold of her. Silence. Air. Space.

But Grady was still there, looming over her, smelling of booze and smoke. "You know, you were the most gorgeous woman in there tonight. Gave old Grady's reputation a shot in the arm."

She didn't answer, since she didn't consider it a compliment to be compared to women with black eye shadow and pink spiked hair.

They reached his motorcycle, and something in her stomach rolled. She had forgotten they'd have to ride home on that, and suddenly she felt shaky and a little dizzy.

"Uh..." She hung back, not taking the helmet he offered her. "Could we...could we just stand here for a minute? I'm feeling kind of shaky."

Grady leaned back against the seat of his bike and grinned as if it were his turn to make his move. "Sure thing, honey. Come here."

He took her hand and pulled her close, but she tried to hold back, keeping some distance between them. "You're a little tiny thing, you know that?"

She stiffened and stepped back, fighting the urge to wipe her hand off where he'd touched it. "On second thought, maybe we should go on home. I've had a good time, Grady, but I'm really not feeling well."

"Fine, baby," he said. "I'll take you home, and when we go in, I'll rub your back, and your feet..."

His voice dropped to a seductive level as he pulled her back against him. His breath smelled of Jim Beam, and she grimaced and tried to pull away. But the door to the bar opened, and a few people spilled out. Grady's grip grew tighter, as if he didn't want anyone to see him getting dumped on.

"Grady, I need to go home... alone. It's been fun, but... well, I'm not really a heavy-metal fan, and I'm not used to all that smoke, and I don't drink much..."

"Oh, honey, the night's still young. Loosen up a little. Come here."

He caught her mouth with his dry lips and shoved his tongue between hers. He was strong, and though she struggled to extract herself, she found that her struggle only stimulated him more. She felt his arousal pressing against her, his hand sliding down to her hips.

Turning her head, she broke free of the kiss. "Grady, stop it. I told you—"

"Come on, honey," he said, beginning to breathe hard. "You want me, too, I can tell. I've known it since the first day you came to work for us. Loosen up and let yourself go. We're both consenting adults..."

"*You're* consenting," she said, bracing her hands on his shoulders and trying to break free. "I'm not. Especially not here in the parking lot. Please, Grady."

"Hey, I just wanted to get warmed up here, baby. But when we get home... that's when the fireworks will start. Come here," he said, crushing her between his thighs and kissing her again. When she broke free, he whispered, "Do you know how much I think about you? Do you have any idea how much I've been waiting for this night?"

His grip was tighter, more threatening, and as his mouth sought hers again, she was vaguely aware of the bar door opening again and more people coming out. If she screamed, would any of these people help her, or would they find it an exciting diversion and cheer him on?

She put all her might into fighting him. "Let go of me, Grady. Now!"

"You're a spitfire, aren't you?"

"Get...your...hands...off...me!"

He grabbed her wrists behind her back, held them with a vice grip of his strong hands, and whipped his leg behind her to hold her in place.

Again his mouth crushed hers, but she flung her face to the side. "Let me go!"

Her struggle made her lose her balance, and she started to fall, giving him more power over her. A scream tore from her throat.

Suddenly someone grabbed her from behind and tore Grady's arm off of her.

"She said to let her go, you asshole!"

Jessica stumbled back and saw Cade just before his arm reared back and shot like a cannon into Grady's face.

Grady fell back, bike and all, then scrambled to his feet. "Cade, what the hell do you think—"

Cade jumped over the bike and knocked him down again, then pulled him up by the collar and shoved his face into Grady's. "The lady told you to leave her alone, you sleaze ball. Now, I'm gonna take her home, and if I see you even look at her again, I'll personally see to it that your eyes are no longer of use to you. Got that, pal?"

"Yeah," Grady groaned, covering the bloody place on his lip. "Sure."

Then, before Jessica could add her two cents, Cade grabbed her hand and led her back to his truck.

He opened the door for her, and gratefully she climbed in, sinking back into the soft seats and resting her head against the headrest.

His jaw popped as he got in behind the wheel and pulled out of the parking lot.

Neither of them exchanged a word for what seemed an eternity, and when Cade pulled into the parking lot of her apartment, she looked over at him. "Thank you, Cade. I should have listened to you earlier."

"Damn right you should have." He cut off the engine and jerked his keys out of the ignition. "I'm walking you up, just to make sure the asshole doesn't ambush you before you can get there."

"I think you put him out of commission for a while," she said.

"Don't bet on it. Fighting is his favorite Saturday night pastime. Tomorrow he'll forget it ever happened. But I won't."

"I won't, either," she whispered. He came around to her door, opened it, and she got out.

Again they were quiet while they climbed the steps to her door, and when they reached it, her hands trembled as she tried to get the key into the dead bolt.

"Here, I'll do it," he said quietly.

Surrendering the keys to him, she waited as he opened the door, then, stepping inside, she turned on the light. Turning back to him, she whispered, "Come in for a minute, Cade."

He hesitated, then crossed the threshold and dropped the keys on her table.

Jessica felt tears pushing to her eyes as she went to her cabinet and searched its contents for some Tylenol. Filling a glass with water, she forced the tears back. "Want something to drink?"

"No thanks," he said. "Are you okay?"

She swallowed the pills down and took a deep breath. "Yeah. Just too much smoke and noise, I guess. I can't believe they call that stuff music. No offense."

Cade dropped down onto her couch and glanced up at her with a puzzled look. "Why would I be offended?"

"Well, it is your hangout, isn't it?"

The grin on Cade's face was wry, and he began to chuckle. "Hardly. That's the first time I've ever been there."

Jessica sank down on the couch next to him. "Why did you come tonight?"

His smile faded, and she saw his discomfort in every line of his face. "Because... I was afraid something like this might happen."

"Something like what?" she asked, not following him.

He shifted uncomfortably. "I know Grady, okay? I didn't think you really understood what you were getting into."

Her face softened, and she moved her foot to sit on it and set her elbow on the back of the sofa. Resting her head on her hand, she gave him a puzzled look. "So you followed us?"

"Sort of," he said. "I felt kind of responsible."

"Why?" she asked quietly. "You warned me. I didn't listen. That should have let you off the hook."

"Well, it didn't, okay?" His eyes met hers, and she realized suddenly how close to him she was sitting. She could smell the mint on his breath, see the dark flecks in his eyes, hear his breath coming a little deeper. "I could have killed that bastard. I still might."

She smiled. "Big brother to the rescue."

A strange look passed over his eyes, and as he held her gaze, she became aware that this thing that passed between them was anything but sibling concern. There was something more... something important.

"I... I'm really sorry I've complicated your life," she said quietly.

His smile was infinitesimal. "No, you're not. That's exactly what you set out to do."

She couldn't help matching that smile. "Okay, maybe. But I didn't want to make you miserable."

His smile faded again. "Who said I was miserable?"

"Well, you gave up a Saturday night that you could have spent with Melody or Beverly, and all it got you was a fight."

For a moment, he didn't answer. Finally he said, "I guess that means you owe me."

"All right," she said. "What do you want?"

He sighed and lifted her hand, and she felt a jolt at the contact. She still trembled, and she knew he felt it. "I want you to quit your job at the shop."

Unexpectedly, those tears lying in wait assaulted her again, and she held her eyes wide to keep them from brimming over. "Why?"

"Because," he said, stroking her hand with his thumb, "we both know that you didn't take it because you needed the money. You took it to get at me. And you did. But now there's this thing with Grady, and I don't know how *I'm* going to deal with him, not to mention how things would be with the two of you..."

"You're right," she said. "I never should have gone to work there in the first place, although I really did need a job and I really did need the money. But what I really wanted...was this."

"What?" he asked.

A tear dropped to her cheek, and she closed her eyes. "I don't have any family left, Cade. Just my mother, and she's thousands of miles away right now. I miss Dad so much...and...I just wanted to get to know you better."

He reached up and wiped away the tear, then set his hand on her shoulder and cupped her neck. "I've been living without family for a long time now, Jessica."

"I know."

"And you know that the other reason you came to work there was to drive me so crazy that I'd cry uncle and come to work for JC."

She smiled and focused through her tears. "Did it work?"

"No," he said.

"I didn't think so." She withdrew her hand and pulled her knees up to her chest, hugged them, and set her chin on her knees. "It was a last-ditch effort, I guess. I didn't know what else to do." Swallowing back the emotion in her throat, she sighed. "Well, I guess you can turn in my resignation for me tomorrow. I'm sorry if I've driven a wedge between you and Grady. Is this going to mess up your partnership?"

"If I'm lucky," Cade said. Raking a hand through his hair, he shook his head. "I can't believe he thought he could take a girl like you to a hellhole like that."

"A girl like me?"

"Yeah," he said. "Of course, he's probably never met one like you who'd give him the time of day."

She smiled and started to thank him, but decided it was best left alone.

"And then to practically tear your clothes off right there in the parking lot." His face reddened again, and he shook his head. "Wait till I see that S.O.B. tomorrow."

She touched his shoulder and made him look at her. "Please, Cade. Just let it go. But I do appreciate your looking out for me." Slowly she leaned over and pressed a kiss on his cheek. It was rough with end-of-day stubble, and it made her lips tingle. "Thank you," she whispered.

She didn't pull back as much as she should have, and for a moment, he just looked at her, his eyes stricken, pensive, and she would have given everything she owned to have a glimpse of what was passing through his mind.

"I'd better go," he whispered after a short eternity.

"Yeah, okay," she said.

He stood up, and she followed. "So...what do you think you'll do...about a job, I mean?"

She took in a deep breath. "I don't know. I guess I'll find something." She glanced at her feet, then met his eyes again. "Will you . . . can we . . . keep in touch? I mean, like a brother and sister?"

"We'll keep in touch," he said, though his tone lacked conviction.

"Promise?"

He hesitated. "I'll do the best I can."

Her heart sank. "Yeah, that's what I thought."

He went to the door, and she followed a few steps behind him. Once again, her tears were threatening to escape from their hiding place just behind her eyes, and she held them back as he opened the door and paused before leaving.

"Well . . . see you later."

"Yeah," she whispered. "Later."

He looked as if he had something else to say, but finally he turned and started down the steps.

And Jessica wondered if she'd ever see him again.

CHAPTER FIVE

THE CEILING LOOKED the same as it had every night since her father died, and once again Jessica found herself lying awake staring at it.

Cade.

His name wouldn't leave her lips, and his face wouldn't leave her mind. Tonight, there had been something between them, something that was disturbing . . .

Yet she dreaded the thought of it ending.

Giving up on trying to sleep, she pulled up out of bed, letting her long white cotton gown trail the floor behind her. Going to her window, she sat on the window seat and gazed out into the night.

What was so disturbing about her time with Cade tonight? she asked herself. Was it that he had come to her rescue like a brother, or that he'd looked at her like a lover?

It was crazy, she thought, pulling her foot up and setting her elbow on her knee. Raking her fingers through her roots, she closed her eyes. She had wanted all her life for Cade to think of her as a sister, and now that he had, she couldn't stop her imagination from reaching into some forbidden realm. Was his imagination leading him there, too? Or was it just a one-sided chemistry?

Whatever it was, she doubted seriously that it mattered now. It wasn't likely that she would see him again.

I'll do the best I can. His noncommittal tone had been impossible to miss. He didn't plan to keep in touch at all. It still didn't matter to him whether they had a relationship or not.

Again, those renegade tears erupted in her eyes, and she looked through them to the night below her window. There was a park behind her apartment, where an empty swing rocked slightly in the night wind. A merry-go-round slumbered and a sliding board glistened in the moonlight, reminding her of days when she and her father had gone out into her backyard after supper to play on the toys with which he had indulged her. It had been too much for one child, she knew now, but at the time she'd felt like a princess with the world at her disposal. Now she wondered if that legacy from her father had been a blessing or a curse. Why would he have set her up as a princess, only to dethrone her when he died?

"Oh, Daddy," she whispered, wiping her tears. "I guess you just didn't know how stubborn your son was. But now what am I going to do?"

She leaned her head back against the wall and thought of her options. She could move back in with her mother, who was all atizzy about having to sell one of her homes, even though she never used it more than three weeks out of the year. She could join her in Germany or Norway or wherever she was now until her grief had passed, but somehow that idea didn't appeal to her. She had been on her own too long. It was too late to go back.

She could move away, she supposed, to someplace where there were more opportunities. But the thought of starting over, all alone, with not one friend in town and no relatives to lean on, made her shiver. It was a cold, lonely world out there, and everything she'd ever known—family and business—had been snatched away from her.

Wearily she went back to bed and sank down in it. When she closed her eyes, Cade's face came into view again—the way he'd looked at her, the way he'd held her hand, the sound of his voice as he'd spoken to her. He didn't hate her anymore, she knew that. If her instincts were right, he might even like her.

And as she searched for sleep, she tried to quell the feeling of guilt at her hope that his feelings had nothing to do with brotherly love.

AFTER A SLEEPLESS NIGHT, Cade was ready for a fight when he showed up at the shop the next morning. He waited for Grady to appear, fantasizing about all the ways he planned to break his face and crush his appendages.

Fortunately for Grady, Pete was the first to arrive. "Good," he said. "You're just in time to see me rearrange your partner's face."

"*You're* my partner," Pete said, frowning.

"I'm talking about Grady. He went too far last night."

"Oh, yeah, I heard." Pete tried to suppress a grin. "He called when he got home, ranting about dissolving the partnership. He was pretty hot."

"Tell me about it," Cade said. "Why do you think I tried to mop the dirt with his face?"

"Admirable, Cade, defending your sister's honor and all. I'm sure she appreciated it. She did show her gratitude, didn't she?"

Cade got to his feet and faced his partner eye to eye. "What exactly do you mean?"

Pete chuckled and waved him off. "Never mind."

They heard the side door opening, and Grady appeared with a swollen bruise on his cheekbone, a cut on his lip, and an expression that would have put the fear into anyone in his right mind. But Cade wasn't in his right mind.

Pete's grin faded. "Uh-oh."

Grady pointed at Cade as he came toward him. "Cade, I think you and I have some unfinished business."

"Damn right we do," Cade said. "And the first piece of business is this partnership. I think it's about run its course. I won't work with you anymore. I'll buy you out at market value."

"The hell you will," Grady said. "I'm staying. You can go link up with your sexy little sister and sell lipstick." He ambled toward Cade, daring him to stop him. "Tell me something, man. Did *you* get into her pants last night? She was hot for somebody. I wouldn't blame you if you took advantage of it."

Cade was across the room in an instant, and one shove sent Grady flying back against the wall, crashing into a crate of helmets on a shelf. "What's it gonna be, Grady? Are you leaving willingly or do I have to throw you out?"

Just then, Pete reached the two and pulled Cade off of Grady. "Come on, guys. This is crazy. We're all friends here."

"You did get some, didn't you, Cade?" Grady spit out. "Like you've been wanting all this time, but it made you real uncomfortable lusting after your own sister, didn't it? Kind of like incest, isn't it? But maybe that makes it more exciting!"

Cade shook Pete loose and started back toward Grady, but this time the man backed away. Cade stopped before going after him again, and tried to rally. Taking a deep breath, he turned back to Pete and, in a low voice, said, "It's up to you, man. Either he sells or I do. Your choice, but one of us has to go."

"Aw, man." Pete groaned and looked from one to the other. "Don't do this to me. We can work this out."

"No, we can't," Cade said. "I can't work with someone who'd practically rape an innocent woman in the parking lot of a hellhole. He makes me nauseous."

"Rape?" Grady scoffed. "Man, she wanted it! And she was gonna get it somewhere."

Cade set his hands on his hips, breathing hard as he waited for Pete to decide. "Come on, man. Make a decision. You know I'm the one keeping this shop in business with repairs. Nobody knows how to rebuild a bike like I do. All he does is give the place a bad name."

Pete rubbed his temples. "Come on, man. You're both my friends. I don't want either of you to leave."

"Decide," Grady said. "I'll go with whatever you say."

Pete looked from one friend to the next, then back again. The struggle on his face made him look even older. "All right," he said, his tone already apologetic. "If you're gonna make me decide, I have to go with Grady."

Cade's expression crashed as he gaped at his friend. "What?"

"Come on," Pete said. "You know that you have something to fall back on, Cade. You have Jessica Cosmetics. Everybody thinks you're crazy anyway for passing up this chance. What has Grady got? All he could do is go into competition with us, and that wouldn't do anybody any good."

Astounded, Cade looked around at the bikes lined up for repair, and it occurred to him that they'd be sunk without him. They deserved it.

"Fine," he said through his teeth as he started for the door. "Arrange financing, *pals.* I'll have my lawyer contact you."

THE DOORBELL RANG, cutting into Jessica's shallow sleep, and she opened her eyes, disoriented. The clock said eight o'clock, and while she hadn't meant to sleep this late, she hadn't set her clock since she'd had no place to go.

The bell rang again. Shoving her disheveled hair back, she got out of bed. Quickly she grabbed her silk robe from its hook, a Japanese floral print with deep reds, greens and purples, slipped it on and tied it around her waist as she hurried toward the front door.

The sight of Cade surprised her, and suddenly she wished she'd taken a minute to brush her teeth and hair, and at least apply a touch of makeup to make her look more awake. "Hi."

"Sorry I woke you."

"Oh, no, you didn't. I was just..." The polite lie seemed futile, and finally she offered a self-conscious smile. "I was just sleeping. You know, I meant it when I said keep in touch, but I didn't expect it quite this soon."

Without a trace of amusement, he came in and closed the door behind him.

"Do you want some coffee?"

"No," he said. "Thanks. Look, I should have called. I'm really sorry." His eyes bored into her with mesmerizing intensity. She wished they weren't quite so blue.

At his hard scrutiny, she had the sudden urge to crawl under the table and tell him to go away until she looked better. She tried to finger-brush her hair. "It's okay, really. I'm usually up by this time, but last night I had trouble getting to sleep."

"Yeah, me too," he said. She started making the coffee for herself, adding enough for him, too, in case he changed his mind. "And tonight's probably going to be worse. In fact, the whole next six months will probably be like a nightmare, but..."

She stopped pouring the water in and froze, the pitcher in her hand.

He took a deep breath. "I came to tell you that I'm selling my share of the shop. Pete and Grady are buying me out."

She set the pitcher down with a clash and turned around. "Why?"

"Because I can't work with that jerk anymore, and short of beating him to a pulp—which it occurs to me now would not be a smart thing to do, though it would make me feel a whole hell of a lot better—I can't make him leave. So I'm left without a choice."

She held her breath, waiting. "Cade?"

"Yes, damn it, I'm going to capitulate to Andrew's cruel little scheme. But I'm not going to like it."

Jessica held her relief in check, afraid any show of victory might frighten him away. "I can live with that."

"Maybe, maybe not," he said. "But you should know right up front that I don't do things halfway. If I do this, I'm going to do it right. It won't be easy, it won't be fun, but we'll get the job done. We might wind up hating each other before it's all over..."

"Thank you," she cut in. For a moment, she stood staring at him. Then, giving into her impulse, she cut across the floor and threw her arms around him. "Thank you, Cade."

He felt her loose breasts pressing against him beneath her gown, and something stirred in a part of him where it shouldn't have. Quickly he set her away. "Don't thank me," he said. "By the time this is over, you'll probably be cursing the ground I walk on."

"When do we start?"

He shrugged. "I don't know. I'll go talk to Sam Morgan right now, get the wheels in motion. But the way I see it, we shouldn't waste one day. In fact, I think I'll arrange to meet with the board of directors this afternoon. Plan to be there."

"I will," she said, trying hard to contain her excitement. "Oh, Cade, this is going to be so great! In fact, let me get dressed and I'll go with you to see Sam."

Before Cade could object, she had disappeared into her bedroom, and all he could do was sit and wait.

SAM MORGAN CALLED a board meeting for that afternoon, then made arrangements for Jessica to take Cade on a tour of the plant that morning. She had grown up with free run of every nook and cranny of the four-story building, and as she explained the workings of everything from the laboratory to the robotics in the manufacturing plant on the first-floor and basement levels, she realized what a vital part the company had played in her life.

But Cade didn't have sweet memories of this place, and she couldn't help noting the distaste on his mouth, the stiffness in his posture. Cosmetics were a far cry from carburetors, she thought. He was used to physical work, forging a living with his hands.

"You hate this, don't you?" she asked with a deprecating smile.

He shrugged and slid his hands into the pockets of the suit she would have never guessed he had in his closet. "It's just so silly. All this fuss over powder and blush."

"It's a billion-dollar industry," she said. "Besides, isn't it something of a double standard to scoff at makeup, but only date women who wear it?"

"Who said I only date women who wear it?"

"I didn't notice either Beverly or Melody choosing the natural look. Their makeup was applied to perfection." She glanced at him, and he grinned.

"All right, you win. It makes them look better. But if they didn't wear it, I wouldn't be repulsed. In fact, when you showed up the other day with none on, I thought you looked pretty good."

She smiled. "Gosh, I wouldn't have guessed by the way you kept insulting me and trying to make me leave."

He laughed as they got on the elevator, but when it stopped on the top floor and the doors opened, Jessica's smile faded.

Cade stepped out and held the doors, but Jessica hesitated. "Coming?"

"Yeah." Slowly she stepped out and saw the portrait of her father hanging on the wall. Her eyes caught it and misted instantly.

Cade glanced up at it, and suddenly his demeanor hardened. "So this was where his office was?"

Tearing her eyes from the portrait, she said, "You've never been here?"

He breathed a sardonic laugh. "When would I have been here, Jessica?"

"I don't know. I just assumed . . . he never brought you here?"

"I told you he didn't," he said, refusing to look at the portrait again. Shoving his hands into his pockets, he started up the corridor toward the offices.

Jessica caught up to him, still stricken with the misty memories of her childhood, so different from Cade's. "Well, you're here now," she said, dabbing a fingertip at the corners of her eyes. "I'll show you his office."

"That's okay," he said. "I don't have to see that."

"Yes, you do," she said, her tone brooking no debate. "It was the nerve center of the whole company."

She led him across the plush carpeting, answering greetings from his secretaries and assistants as she made her way to his office. The executive secretary wasn't at her desk, so Jessica stepped around it and led Cade to the double oak doors through which she had bounced so often as a child, running in to see her daddy, to sit on his knee and play with his computers, sample his newest cosmetics coming off the line, or douse herself in perfume and powder until her mother could barely stand to ride home with her.

She almost felt as if she would see him when she opened those doors—that she'd stick her head in, as she had done just over a month ago, catch his smile and say, "Hi, Daddy. Just thought I'd pop up and see what you're doing."

She went to the doors, glancing back at Cade. He hung back, as if apprehensive about treading on sacred ground. Slowly she opened the doors and stepped into the office.

Her breath caught as she saw Jonothan Thurgood, her father's executive vice president for so many years, sitting behind her father's desk.

"Mr. Thurgood," she said, startled.

The man looked up at her. "Haven't you heard of knocking, dear?"

She felt Cade behind her, and her breath caught in her chest. "Uh... I'm sorry. I just assumed Daddy's office was still... vacant."

She glanced around at the new wallpaper with grays and blues, and the burgundy carpeting that her father would have hated. Even the furniture was different. The Chippendale chairs he'd selected for the room had now been replaced with art deco chairs that seemed to have no place here.

"You were told that I'd been selected to replace him as president, weren't you?"

She flushed, and felt her hands trembling as she grasped the door handle again. "Yes. I'm sorry. It was silly of me to think you'd stay in your old office. After all, Daddy has been dead almost a whole month." Her face reddened with the words, and she felt the sting of tears at the corners of her eyes.

She cleared her throat. "Uh, Mr. Thurgood... this is my brother Cade Hartman. He's going to be working here with me..."

Stepping forward, Cade extended a hand. "How are you?"

But Thurgood didn't bother rising. "Ah, yes," he said, limply shaking his hand. "The mechanic." Dismissing Cade, he turned back to Jessica. "As a matter of fact, we have a board meeting this afternoon, if

I'm not mistaken. Is there something I can help you with until then?"

Cade's posture stiffened at the man's easy dismissal of them, and before she could formulate a reply, he slid his hands back into his pockets, glanced around the room without intimidation and said, "No, not a thing. We just thought that, since we're the ones who've been charged with saving this company's ass, maybe we ought to look around."

Thurgood then found it prudent to rise. "I beg your pardon?"

"You got it." Cade grinned. "I've seen all I need to see in here." He ambled back to the door, stopped just as he reached Jessica, and said, "Let's go eat a bite of lunch. I have a feeling we shouldn't have this meeting on an empty stomach."

Jessica glanced back at Thurgood, who looked like a man whose territory was under threat of conquest, then followed Cade out of the room without bothering to close the doors.

In a few steps she caught up to him as he headed for the elevator. "That was great," she said, her spirits rising again. "You sure didn't let him get to you like I did."

"You were going to cry," he said, pressing the elevator button. "You can't do that at the meeting, Jessica. Our job is going to be hard enough without letting them think they can use us for their doormats. We need respect if we're going to get them behind us. It's in their best interests to dissuade us so they can buy his shares."

The elevator bell rang, and the doors opened. Cade waited for Jessica to step on.

"The nerve of him, moving into my father's office, changing all the furniture, the wallpaper..."

"Never mind that," Cade said, following her on. "I'm more concerned with the way he talked to you. Like you were nobody."

Her big eyes flashed up to his.

"You're not nobody, Jessica," Cade said. "You're the person this company was named after. Your father founded it. And it's your face on the boxes of everything manufactured here. You deserve a little respect."

"Not in his mind," Jessica said. "They would have replaced me if you hadn't agreed to cooperate. I'm not indispensable. In fact, you're right. The board members were hoping you wouldn't capitulate, so they could overhaul this company their own way and make a complete departure from Daddy's way of doing things, not to mention get Daddy's shares for themselves. They may even try to make you mad enough to walk at the meeting."

"You may be right," Cade said as the elevator doors opened on the first floor. "They can try. But I think this afternoon is the time to let them know that they're going to have to change gears. And that's the last time they're going to treat you—or me—like we don't make a difference. They don't realize that this mechanic doesn't happen to have anything better to do at the moment. If they push me, they'll only see me dig my heels in deeper."

As Jessica stepped off the elevator, she had a feeling that things were going to be all right now. Cade was on her side, and he was fully armed and ready for battle. All she had to do was ride along beside him.

CHAPTER SIX

JESSICA HAD NEVER SAT in on a board meeting before, and she was surprised at the tension she felt in her shoulders and back as she and Cade sat at one end of the long table, facing the men and women who were now at the helm of Jessica Cosmetics.

But Cade didn't look at all disturbed.

"As I see it," he told them, "my job is going to be cutting out the deadweight in the company. That means starting here, in this building, and then going to every chain store we have in the country and evaluating each one for waste. At the same time, Jessica is going to travel with me and do a big publicity splash in each town."

Awed, Jessica looked from one astonished face to another as Cade spoke, and wondered what they were thinking about Andrew's adopted motorcycle mechanic now.

Sabrina Simpson, the woman who'd stepped up to Thurgood's former position—a woman who used Jessica cosmetics religiously despite the fact that they couldn't do much to camouflage the terminal scowl on her face—wagged her pencil against her thumb and turned to Cade. "I don't think it will be necessary for you to evaluate the offices here, Cade. They're already functioning very efficiently. What we had in mind was for you to get started immediately on the chain stores."

Cade smiled. "Well, I didn't think you'd like the idea. Nobody wants to have someone looking over his—or her—shoulder."

"You only have five months left, Cade," Thurgood interjected, his tone insinuating that he was exercising great patience. "I'm sure you don't want to waste any of that time by digging into things here that are already being monitored."

"Are they?" Cade asked. "Being monitored, I mean?"

"Of course they are," Thurgood said.

"And there's no waste."

Thurgood shrugged. "None to speak of."

Cade sat back in the tall, plush chair at the table, crossed his legs and settled his piercing eyes on Thurgood's. "Then why did you just spend thousands of dollars redecorating my father's office?"

Thurgood bristled as all eyes turned to him. "Young man, I don't have to explain to you one penny I spend."

"Don't you?" Cade asked. "Excuse me, but I thought that the stipulations of my father's will were in the best interest of the stockholders. I think they would be very interested in knowing every instance of waste in this company when the profits keep dropping so steadily."

Thurgood slammed his hand on the table and came to his feet. "You are not an efficiency expert, young man. You are a motorcycle mechanic who's been given a job too big for him. If it weren't for the fact that we have little to lose by letting you go on this wild-goose chase, you wouldn't even be allowed in this building!"

For a moment, Jessica feared that Cade would snap, get up and walk out of there, as he'd done at the reading of the will, claiming that he never asked for any of this and didn't need it now. But he surprised her. He sat very still, stroking his finger across his lip, studying the faces of the board members one by one. "Never mind the legalities of my father's will, or the fact that you're bound by law to abide by them."

He looked around the room, watching as the board members shot eloquent looks to one another. Finally, without disputing Cade's words, Thurgood sat down.

"You will be given use of one of the secretaries already on staff," Thurgood said through his teeth, "full access to our public relations department, and an expense account."

"I'll need to see a list of all expenditures and all profits for the past six months," Cade said.

Thurgood's face reddened again. "You are not an executive in this company, Cade. You are an employee engaged in a contest."

"A contest?" Cade laughed. "You people don't seem to realize that I'm here to save your jobs. If I don't find some way to increase profits, then this company will die a slow death. Now are you going to cooperate with me or not?"

All of the board members were silent, and Jessica looked around the room, stunned at the secrecy, the animosity, the anger. "Daddy wanted us here to help you," she said. "He wouldn't have done this without a reason. If we do what we're setting out to, we'll be the major stockholders in the company in a few months anyway. You might as well accept us right from the beginning."

Sabrina and Thurgood exchanged looks again, and finally Sabrina turned back to Jessica. "It's not your job, Jessica, to get involved in these business disputes. All you have to do is smile, look pretty and say whatever Publicity tells you to say. We'll take care of the rest."

"All right. That's it." Cade's hand slammed down on the table, and he leaned forward, meeting Sabrina's eyes. "That's the last time you're going to talk to her like she's some little tart. She's the namesake of this company. Without her, you people wouldn't have jobs. Got that?"

Sabrina's face reddened all the way to her ears, and she lifted her chin. "I can see right now that we're going to have an excessively long five months."

"Damn right we are," he said. He drew in a deep breath, and steepled his hands in front of his face. "You're not going to make this easy for us, are you?"

No one in the room said a word.

Finally Cade stood up. "All right then. We won't make it easy for you, either."

Jessica rose tentatively, still gaping at the men and women at the table, unable to believe their attitudes. When Cade gathered up his notes and started from the room, she followed him.

No one stopped them.

The moment the doors closed behind him, Cade's step picked up as if he were marching to the greatest purpose ever imposed on him. "We'll show those jackasses," he said.

Jessica fell into step beside him. "I don't understand it. Why are they so hostile? What are they afraid of? They act like we're inconsequential."

"They're banking on us losing," Cade said, "and then we'll have nothing and we *won't* be of any consequence to them. They're also afraid we'll win, and then the stock won't revert back to them. We're threatening to them, but they ain't seen nothing yet."

He stepped on the elevator and punched the garage.

"Where are you going?" she asked.

"Back to Sam Morgan," he said. "I'm going to make him force them to give us the financial records we need. And if he turns out not to be on our side, then by God, I'll find someone who is."

Jessica couldn't keep a smile from spreading across her face as she followed him on.

BY THE END OF THE DAY, Cade had the financial records in his hands, a tour schedule for all the stores in Louisiana and Texas in the next month, airline tickets and hotel reservations.

He also had a headache the size of the company's deficit. "It was so simple, fixing bikes," he said as he left the office building for the final time that day and sank into the driver's seat of his truck. Jessica got in next to him.

"This is a far cry from that," she said, "but I'm proud of you. Daddy knew what he was doing. You have a real business head."

Cade shot her a disgusted look. "Yeah, well, I don't know how he'd know that. Besides, it's mostly bluff."

"Whatever it is, it works. You have those people up there scurrying around like little mice." She looked out the window to the big building that had been such a big part of her life. Her eyes grew misty. "I can't believe they were going to cut me out altogether. Cade, do you really think my face is an asset to the company? Maybe they do need new blood."

He looked over at her, and his tired eyes softened at once. "You're *the* Jessica. No one can take your place."

"Maybe when I was fifteen, made up to look like I was twenty, I was okay. But now...youth is what sells cosmetics."

He grinned and started the truck. "Right. And you're over the hill."

"Well, maybe not in most arenas. But in this one. Don't you think?"

He chuckled. "No, I don't think. If I thought it was time for you to step aside, I'd be the first to tell you. I think you're just the one who's going to make Jessica Cosmetics synonymous with sensuality, excitement and glamour. I may cut the spending, but you're going to increase sales."

"I hope so," she whispered. "We talked awfully big in there."

He pulled out of the parking lot. "You're letting them get to you, you know. You're letting all that negativity beat you down. It's going to take me hours to pump you back up."

"Hours? What do you mean?"

"It means that I'm taking you to my house where I plan to grill some steaks and break open a bottle of wine," he said. "And we're going to relax, and reflect, and think about all the work we have to do, and the fact that we're going to knock their socks off and come back here in five months practically owning the place."

Jessica threw her head back on the seat and laughed for the first time that day.

AFTER THEIR FIRST BOTTLE of wine, Cade slid back into his thoughtful, brooding posture, and Jessica forgot he was her brother altogether. He was an enigma . . . a mechanic who could take on a corporation. A quiet man who had volumes to say when provoked. An angry man who could reconcile when it was his idea.

"What are you thinking about?"

He shrugged and brought those glorious blue eyes back to hers. "Nothing."

He couldn't tell her that he'd been thinking of his father, wishing Andrew could have seen him today, so he'd know that his adopted son wasn't trash at all, that he had brains and guts and that he was as good as anybody who worked in that building. "What are you thinking about?" he returned.

She sipped on her wine, wondering how many glasses she'd had already. Too many, probably. "Daddy."

He felt the muscles in his shoulders tighten.

"He would have been so proud of you today, Cade."

"Oh, I don't know," he said. "Might have destroyed a few illusions about me. I think he liked seeing me as the poor, stupid relation."

Her spine went rigid, and she shifted next to him. "Cade, that's not true."

"Whatever," he said.

She gazed into her wine, as if to find some other subject for discussion, then looked up at him. "I don't know if you realize it, but you really seemed in your element today."

"Wrong," he said. "I loved what I did at the shop. I'm only here because that's over."

"Whatever the reason," she said, "it's going to bring out a whole new side of you. And you know what? I like both sides."

His eyes met hers, and for a moment they held. She looked down at her glass. "You know, when I was little, I had the craziest crush on you," she whispered.

The surprise in his face amused her.

"Oh, I know you're not supposed to feel that way about your brother, and maybe it wasn't a crush, exactly. But I thought you had to be the coolest kid on the planet. And I wanted like crazy to get to know you better."

She laughed and turned her stem glass in a circle on the table. "'Course, you never even noticed me."

"I noticed you, all right."

She saw the sobriety in his eyes, and knew that he didn't mean that in a positive way. "Enough to hate me?"

He shrugged. "If I ever did that, it was because of immaturity. Nothing you did. I'm sorry."

"And what was your excuse a couple of weeks ago?"

He smiled. "A carryover from childhood? You're supposed to be the enemy, so I treat you like it?"

Her smile faded slowly. "I don't want to be your enemy, Cade."

She didn't know if it was the wine or the headiness of the day that put that look in his eye, but when their eyes met this time, her heart tripled its pace, and her mouth went suddenly dry. "What do you want to be to me, Jess?"

It was the first time he'd called her that, and the first time he'd asked her something so pointed. Something so loaded with insinuation.

She struggled for an answer, knowing that she should say "sister" without another thought. But somehow she knew that wasn't what she really wanted. Sister wasn't enough. It didn't even come close.

Choosing the cowardly way out, she turned the question back on him. "What do *you* want to be to me?"

His silence hinted at a thousand things, and her heart sped in terror and hope as she sat there, her eyes locked so meaningfully with his. Had they had too much wine, or would they have come to this anyway?

She could almost feel her heart pounding, pounding in her chest, and her breathing growing harder, though she tried to hold it back. And when he leaned over, narrowing the distance between them, time froze, and the only thing able to move in the world was his head, dipping to hers.

When he kissed her, something seemed to explode inside her, melt into a volcanic eruption that seeped into her veins. She expelled a sigh as his lips found hers. When she leaned into him and slid her hand up his chest, around his neck, and through the soft secrets of his hair, she felt something inside him change. He pulled her tighter, kissed her deeper, and his hands moved sensuously over her back, up through her hair. His hand closed into a fist at her roots, and when she pulled back for a breath, he yanked slightly to pull her back to him.

That small act of masculine control excited her as nothing ever had before, and as they came back together, she savored the taste of wine in his mouth, the feel of his heavy breath against her face, the hammering of his heart against her breast.

She felt him lowering her back, back on the couch, until her head rested on the soft arm of his sofa, and slowly, he came down upon her.

"You're beautiful, Jess," he whispered. "Do you know that?"

Her breath came too hard to answer, and she arched her neck back as he kissed it, licked it, bit it slightly, then made his frenzied way lower, to the opening of her blouse.

"I've always thought you were beautiful."

She shivered as his hand stole over her breast, feeling the turgid nipple even through her clothes. Heaving a deep breath, he stopped himself from touching her there, and rose back to her mouth.

What was he doing? he asked himself as he claimed her in another scalding kiss. She was his sister, and yet...

He felt her hands move between them, struggling to unbutton his shirt as they kissed, and something about that boldness, that stark act of desire, banished all practical thoughts from his mind. She was woman, she was fresh air, she was sustenance, she was beauty, she was sex. And he had never wanted a woman more than he wanted her.

She wrestled the shirt off his shoulders, then pulled his T-shirt over his head and sent it flying across the room. Before he could stop her, she was kissing his neck, the hollow at the base of his throat, the hair on his chest...

He rose up, and as she slipped lower and caught his nipple in her mouth, something snapped inside him.

Her hand slipped down his stomach, hovered at the waistband of his pants, then moved lower until she found what she sought, straining against his clothes.

He moaned and went for her blouse, trembling with the effort of unbuttoning, struggling not to rip it off her and be done with it.

When he opened it, he moaned again at the sight of her breasts filling the lacy bra she wore. He slipped his thumb behind the front clasp, released it, and peeled the cups back.

Her breasts were the most beautiful he'd ever seen, full and round and pointed, and he touched them with reverence, as though he'd been invited onto sacred ground. His mouth went down to one sharp nipple, caught it in his mouth, and encircled it with his tongue. She moaned, a sound that intensified the urgency, and when he scraped his stubble across the nipple, she almost cried out.

Swallowing the sound, she sucked in a breath and pulled him back up to her mouth.

His tumescence settled at the cradle of her thighs, pressing despite the clothing still inhibiting it. It would be so easy, he thought, to discard his pants, watch her slip out of her panty hose and skirt, and take her right here on his couch. It would be so easy to thrust himself inside her, feel her ecstatic contractions against him, spend himself....

It would be so easy, she thought. So easy to revel naked against him, to guide him into her, to feel his sweet, hot burst of completion. It would be so easy to reach her own apex, to cry out against his neck, to feel as free and as validated as she'd ever been in her life.

She slid her hand down his ribs, to the belt buckle pressing into her stomach. Following suit, he reached for her skirt, wadding it as he pulled it up far enough to reach beneath. She felt his hand close over her, felt the burst of excitement shoot through her. Her hands trembled too much to unbuckle his belt, and in frustration she tried harder.

Something about her clumsiness made him rise up to do it himself. Their eyes met, smoky-hot, anxious, hungry.

But there was something about the honesty there that stopped him. In a moment they would be crossing a threshold over which they could never return.

Perhaps they had crossed it already. His hands froze over his belt, and he looked at her, fighting to keep the recriminations from his mind. He could deal with them afterward.

Afterward, when they couldn't look each other in the eye, when people introduced them as brother and sister, when they had a job to do and couldn't stop the guilt raging through them.

He dropped his hands and pulled her skirt back over her legs.

"Cade?" she whispered.

He sat all the way up, put his feet on the ground and pulled the cups of her bra back over her breasts. She watched as he fastened it. Suddenly feeling ashamed, she pulled her blouse back on and buttoned it with shaking hands.

He watched her, still breathing hard, and when she sat up, he slipped his hand behind her neck and pressed his forehead against hers. "My God, I don't think I've ever wanted a woman this much."

Tears sprang to her eyes. "Then why did you stop?"

He got up, rubbing the back of his neck as he took a few steps away. "It was the wine, Jess. You're my sister, for God's sake."

"Not really," she said. "You know that as well as I do."

"It's still wrong," he said. "I should never have touched you. I should never have—"

"Stop it." Swallowing, she got up herself, straightened her clothes, and finger-brushed her hair. "I understand. Just...please don't start that I-shouldn't-have stuff. You couldn't have if I hadn't let you. I was here, too, remember?"

He raked his hand through his hair with both hands. "We can't do that again, Jess. This has got to be just business. Or family. Or whatever. But not...not this."

She took a deep, labored breath. "We'll just write it all off to the wine."

"Yeah," he said, since that was easier to bear than stark, blatant desire. "The wine."

She looked around for her purse, and saw the dishes still sitting on the table. "I should go, but..." She glanced back at him. "The dishes. I'll help you...."

"No," he said. "I'll do it. You can go on."

She hesitated. "I...I don't have my car here."

He caught his breath. "Oh, yeah. I'll take you home." Grabbing his shirt, he looked around for his T-shirt. It was across the room, and as he went to get it, Jessica found herself steeped in shame again.

Quickly he dressed, then grabbed his keys. They walked to the truck in silence.

The air was charged as they drove to her apartment, and when they finally reached it, she didn't get out.

"I'll see you tomorrow, then?"

"Yeah. I'll call you sometime tomorrow. We have a lot to do."

"Okay." She opened the door, gave him one last wistful look over her shoulder and started to slide out.

"Jessica?"

She turned back. "Yeah?"

"It won't happen again. I swear it."

Somehow, that reassurance only deflated her heart further. She closed the door and started walking to her apartment.

Cade watched her receding figure until she was inside.

CHAPTER SEVEN

THE LAUNCH of their "Save the Brass's Asses Tour," as Cade had begun to call it when no one but Jessica could hear, was a black-tie dinner for the press right there in Atlanta. It was to fall on Friday night, which gave them three days to plan it, and the next day, Jessica and Cade were to fly to Dallas where the real work would begin.

But the tensions between the two of them were so thick that Jessica could almost feel the wall looming between them, making it difficult for them to look into each other's eyes. Cade hadn't said another word to her about what had happened the night they'd gotten so carried away, and the way he treated her now was all too reminiscent of the days when she didn't even warrant a glance from him or a comment that wasn't absolutely necessary.

For the most part, they went in separate directions that week, she to find the right dress to be photographed in at the dinner, to work with hairdressers and JC makeup artists on the look that would knock the country's socks off as she went on her tour, and she spent a lot of time writing and polishing the speech that would hopefully be quoted in news stories across the country.

Cade stayed in the JC offices most of that week, evaluating the expenditures in the home office, working with the publicist to prepare for the dinner, setting up appearances for Jessica in Texas for the following week, and planning newsworthy events that would get them as much attention as possible.

Although he was busier than he remembered being in his entire life, he found himself looking up every time someone came into the office, hoping it would be Jessica. Thoughts of her kept him awake nights, and he spent far too much time chastising himself for wanting her so badly. Late at night, when he was too tired to fight the thoughts flitting through his mind, he recalled the fierce desire that had raged through him—through her—the night he could have had her.

What would it have been like, if they hadn't stopped? Would she have stayed with him all night? Would he have awakened to the scent of her perfume, the silky splay of her hair across her pillow? Would she have rolled over to him, and made love to him again?

And then what? he always asked himself. How would he cast aside the guilt of sleeping with his sister? *But she's not your sister,* a voice inside him would always cry out. *She meets none of the definitions of sibling.* She wasn't born of either his biological father or his mother. They hadn't been raised together in the same home. So why did he feel so guilty?

He didn't know why, but he did, and he imagined that she did, too. And he decided that there had to be a way that he could get her out of his mind.

He called Daphne, a woman he'd been out with twice, one of the most beautiful and cultured women he knew, and asked her to accompany him to the dinner. She was delighted to be asked, and told him to pick her up at seven. When he hung up, rather than feeling elated that she'd agreed to go, he'd felt a heavy disappointment that he wouldn't be spending the evening looking at Jessica, laughing with her, gloating over the successes they were sure to pull off in this launch.

On Friday, when they finally came together so that Jessica could rehearse her speech with him, he smiled for the first time since their night together.

"That was terrific, Jess," he said.

She smiled at the use of her shortened name. "Thanks. You don't think it's too arrogant? I wanted to convey a lot of self-confidence. I represent the woman of the nineties, you know. But I don't want to go too far with it..."

"It was perfect," he said. "You're going to be great."

She set her speech down on the table in front of him, and leaned against it. "So...should we arrive together tonight? Sort of a show of solidarity?"

His smile faded. "Uh...no, I don't think so. I'm bringing a date."

Her eyebrows shot up. "A date?"

"Well, yes. I didn't see any reason not to. I—"

"Of course not," she said, rallying and picking up her speech again, only to stack it and lay it back down. "Well, I'm bringing one, too, of course. I just meant—"

"You are?" he asked too abruptly.

"Yes," she said. "The nineties woman always has a handsome man beside her, doesn't she?"

"Not necessarily," he said. "I thought the whole idea of the nineties woman was that she doesn't need a man to complete her."

She forced a smile. "She doesn't *need* one, but she enjoys one. She is a woman who deserves appreciation, and no one can appreciate her better than a man." Her smile grew too strained, and she pressed her lips together. Grabbing her speech up again, she started to the door. "Besides, what makes you think you're the only one who can get a date?"

"I didn't say that."

"I know you didn't," she said. "I'm just a little puzzled at why you're so surprised that I'd have one."

"I'm not surprised, Jessica." The spirit had left his voice, and he was that brooding mechanic again, sitting before her with his guard as high as he could get it.

She threw her chin up. "You didn't think I was hoping that you and I would—"

"Of course not."

"Good, because that's been the farthest thing from my mind," she said. "And you can bet I won't drink wine with you again."

The words slapped him, and he couldn't reply. Was she implying that he'd gotten her drunk and taken advantage of her? Was that what she thought?

"I think that would be a good idea," he said. "Wine seems to act as an aphrodisiac to us. Doesn't matter who we're with."

The barb cut right through her, and he noted the color rising on her cheeks, competing with the already perfect coloring. "Right. They should put a warning on the label. 'The surgeon general advises that drinking alcoholic beverages can sometimes lead to incest.' "

His eyebrows shot up, and his eyes grew dull. "Incest? Don't you think that's a little strong?"

"Not really," she said. "Not when you seem so convinced that wanting me was some sick phenomenon, or some out-of-body experience brought on by the wine. You want to be sister and brother, fine. I just forgot about it for a while, since you've spent your whole life denying it. Funny how you're embracing the concept now."

He watched her grab her purse and the other things she had come here for, and when she left, he stared at the door for a short eternity. He leaned his head back on his chair, closed his eyes, and told himself that it was going to be a long night.

IF JESSICA HAD HAD ANY money, she would have offered a million dollars for the best-looking, best-bred hunk she could find to take her to the dinner. But on such short notice, and without money, she knew she'd have to leave it to luck.

But luck was on her side, and when she called Jerome Holland, the last man she'd dated until she got so bored that she'd told him she "needed some space," he had accepted.

"I'll have a limo pick you up at seven," he told her.

"Oh, that won't be necessary, Jerome," she argued.

"Nonsense," he said. "The face of Jessica Cosmetics needs to arrive in style."

Jessica had realized that the limo was more for him than for her. He never liked having his picture taken unless he looked his absolute best. She supposed he thought he looked his best in a limo. Vaguely she wondered if Cade would be taking his date to the dinner on the back of his bike or in his pickup truck. She would have gladly traded the limo ride for either.

Her arrival at the dinner was celebrated with a plethora of lights, cameras flashing and rolling, and reporters throwing out questions to her, too impatient to wait for the one-on-one interviews she would do later. Stopping at the door, she smiled regally, offering every photographer there the chance to catch her, and hoping that profits would rise with every flash.

For a moment the lights blinded her, but as she pushed through the crowd of photographers, she caught Cade's eye. He was smiling, smiling like a proud lover...or brother. She glanced away from him and turned back to her date, tall and handsome and as polished as anyone she'd ever known. Jerome grinned like a star as he escorted her through the room. Her heart sank as she realized it would be his face in the media with hers, rather than Cade's. The thought lacked appeal.

She reached the front table, where Cade stood with a cluster of guests, talking about the new direction of Jessica Cosmetics. The cluster broke up just as she approached it, and Cade stepped away from it. The beautiful woman who'd been standing beside him followed him, and Jessica's heart tightened like a fist.

For a moment they faced each other, each waiting for the other to speak. Finally they spoke together. "Cade, I'd like you to—"

"Jessica, I'd like you to—"

Both stopped, and said, "Go ahead."

Finally Jessica tried again. "Cade, I'd like you to meet my escort, Jerome Holland."

The two men shook hands, though there was little warmth in Cade's expression. "And this is Daphne Moak. Daphne, my sister, Jessica."

The word "sister" deflated her, but putting on her best smile, Jessica reached for the woman's hand. "So nice to meet you, Daphne," she said. "Any friend of my brother's is a friend of mine."

She saw that the word "brother" hit him as well, and his lips seemed to thin. "You look great," he said stiffly.

She didn't smile. "Thank you. You look very nice, too."

They let their eyes linger on each other a bit too long, but finally a group of reporters intruded.

For the next hour, Jessica mingled with them, giving sound-bite interviews for everyone there, and trying her best to ignore the man watching her from across the room.

HE COULDN'T blatantly look at her. Not without her noticing when she stole a look back. But when he stood up to say a few words and make a toast to the new direction of Jessica Cosmetics, he felt her watching him with an intensity that could have burned a hole through the back of his jacket.

When she stood up to speak, he finally felt he'd been given license to stare openly at her. His heart jolted as her first full sentence was met with a huge round of applause from the pampered press. Man, she was beautiful, he thought, from the perfectly arranged hair French-twisted and wispy around her face to the tight red mini-dress that teased her breasts, hugged her waist and clung to her hips. His eyes fell to the long legs beneath the podium and the delicate feet in three-inch heels. She was gorgeous, and he knew that if she couldn't bring JC back from the dumper, nobody could.

He only hoped he could survive the next few months without going nuts.

His date nudged him, drawing his eyes away from Jessica, and whispered something annoying in his ear. Whatever she'd said didn't register, and shrugging, he looked back at Jessica again. Damn, it had been stupid to bring a date to this when he'd known that he couldn't keep his mind off every move that Jessica made. So much for redirecting his thoughts, or getting her out of his system. If Daphne couldn't excite him and steal a few of his fantasies, then there wasn't much chance that anyone could.

Jessica finished her speech, and as the applause rounded the room, she paused a moment for the flashing cameras before going back to her seat. She knew how to play the press, he thought. Glamour was bred into her. She must have gotten it from her mother.

For the first time all week, memories of his old bitterness arose, and he recalled the pain of being the abandoned one. His mother had been replaced with a glamorous younger wife, and he had been replaced with Jessica. Beautiful, glamorous Jessica.

As the band struck up and the guests began to dance, he watched that Jerome bozo take Jessica onto the dance floor and whirl her around. The evening was turning out to be a huge success, but somehow the victory didn't excite him. Why was he doing all this? For the stock he'd earn if he pulled this off? For the good of the failing company? Or for his father?

Maybe it was for Jessica, he thought honestly for a fleeting moment. Maybe he was subconsciously doing this whole thing to be closer to her.

Ridiculous, he told himself, suddenly angry that he'd had such a notion. She was the spoiled rich girl, the antithesis of everything he was, and she represented all her father had traded him in for. She represented the wealth that mocked his poverty growing up. She represented the beauty that had faded from his mother's face as the stress of years of hard work had caught up with her. She represented the best of everything. Perhaps he had been the worst.

"You can't sweep me off my feet if you don't ask me to dance," Daphne said into his ear, her shoulder pressing against his.

Cade tried to smile. "No, I guess not. Come on." He took her hand and led her onto the dance floor, pulled her against him, and began to dance to the song

"Lady in Red." Ironic that they would play that, he thought, but maybe it wasn't chance. Anyone who saw Jessica tonight, including the band members, had to be awestruck by her. Everyone else in the room looked dull by comparison. Yes, he thought, they'd chosen the song by design.

Someone tapped on his shoulder, and he looked back to see Jerome, standing with Jessica, asking to cut in. Gladly, he handed over his date, then faced the woman who had such possession of his thoughts.

"You don't have to dance with me," she said. "I need a break, anyway."

Reaching for her, he drew her against him. Her hand trembled as she laid it in his hand, and he realized that none of this came as easily to her as it appeared. His heart came alive, sprinting in his chest, and he pulled her closer, unable to stop himself. For a moment, they danced quietly, each straining with the weight of their tension.

It's not the wine tonight, is it Jess? he thought. After a moment, he whispered, "You're doing great, you know. You're a real hit."

"So are you."

"They could do without me just fine," he said. "You're who they came to see."

"They came to see what the Hartman children plan to do with their father's company."

"The Hartman children," he said, the words not pleasant on his tongue.

"So...are you having a good time? Your date seems to be."

He glanced back at Jerome and Daphne, and thought they made a terrific couple. Maybe he should fix them up and they could leave together. "Yeah, it's okay. This black-tie stuff isn't my cup of tea, really."

"Is it anybody's?"

"You seem to be in your element."

She smiled. "It's kind of fun, I guess. Like playing in your mother's clothes and pretending to be somebody."

"You are somebody, Jess."

The words hit right in the place that she'd tried to block off tonight, and she swallowed and became even more keenly aware of his arms around her, the heat of his body against her, the scent of his after-shave...

Her heartbeat accelerated, and she couldn't help replaying the memories of them together on his couch, his hands moving across her breasts...

She jerked her thoughts back to the present and met his eyes.

His eyes dipped to her breasts, and taking a deep breath, he looked away. He couldn't stop the intrusion of the knowledge that her breasts had such a perfect shape, the memory of the way those turgid nipples felt brushing the palm of his hands, the way they'd felt against his tongue. She was passionate, and lovemaking with her would be explosive. But he shouldn't know that. He shouldn't even think of it.

The song came to an end, and they fell apart, as if neither of them could wait for the opportunity. When their dates drifted back to them, they each vowed silently to avoid the other for the rest of the evening.

Tomorrow, when they got on that plane and took off alone together, that would be another story.

CHAPTER EIGHT

CADE WASN'T IN a good mood when he arrived to pick Jessica up at 8:00 a.m. the next morning, a fact that gave Jessica tremendous satisfaction. Had he lain awake last night thinking of Jerome and her, she wondered, as she had struggled with images of Daphne and him? She hoped so. It would mean there was some justice in the world.

"You're early." Abandoning the open door, she turned her back to him and headed back to her bedroom. Cade stepped inside and closed the door behind him a little too loudly.

"No, *you're* late. I told you I'd be here at eight."

He followed her to the bedroom and leaned obstinately against the casing. She glanced up from her open suitcase. "Sorry. I didn't wake up as early as I meant to." *Liar,* she told herself. *You didn't sleep a wink all night.*

"Rough night, huh?"

She smiled and snapped her suitcase shut, a little too forcefully. "Actually, it was very pleasant."

"Good." From the look on his face, she could see that he didn't mean it. "So was mine."

Her smile faded. "Did Daphne have a good time?"

"Yes. Did Jerome?"

"Of course." She lugged her suitcase off the bed and set it next to the other three.

He didn't seem to notice the number of bags. "I should have asked him not to keep you up late. You need to look your best today."

Her lips thinned. "And I don't?"

He shrugged and pushed off from the door. "I wouldn't know. You won't look at me."

She looked at him then, offering him a full view of her hair, worn loose and full around her face, and a teal green suit that accented the green of her eyes. His heart jolted.

"My mistake," he said. "You don't look any worse for the wear."

Her mouth fell open. "Excuse me?"

He picked up one of the suitcases, frowned at its weight, and set it back down. "Well, you said you were out late last night."

"I *said* I overslept. That doesn't mean I was out all night."

"Never thought you were. I figured Jerome brought you right here after the party. And I'm glad it was so pleasant for you."

She couldn't help being suddenly amused at the jealousy apparent in his tone. Crossing her arms and fingering the string of pearls at her throat, she grinned at him. "Tell me something, Cade. Why is it that you assume anything I consider pleasant must have to do with sex? Or that the only pleasure I could get would be from a man?"

He shrugged. "Hey, I'm just going by what I saw."

"And what about what I saw? Daphne draped all over you, practically drooling on you. The woman would have cleared a table and had you right there if she could have."

He grinned. "Yeah, she does lean a little toward exhibitionism, doesn't she? But she waited."

Jessica spun back around and busied herself with her cosmetics bag. "I'll just bet she did."

"Probably as long as Jerome, anyway."

She shot him another look, not willing to tell him that Jerome had indeed had a long wait—was still waiting. She had kissed him goodbye at the door and told him she had to get up early.

Cade checked his watch and told himself to let Jessica think he'd had a long adventurous night of sex with Daphne, when in reality he'd taken her home as soon as the party was over. It was Jessica who'd been on his mind.

He turned his attention to the suitcases again. "Is it really necessary for you to bring everything you own?"

"We're going to be on the road for five months," she said. "I have over a hundred personal appearances scheduled just in the first six weeks. Yes, I need everything and then some." She went through her purse, did a quick check of the contents and glanced up at him. "What time will the limo be here?"

"What limo?"

She didn't like the amusement in his eyes. "The limo to take us to the airport."

"We're going in my truck."

"Your truck? Cade, how's that going to look? We're on this big campaign to glamorize JC, and the two people representing it are going to show up at the airport in a truck?"

His grin was infuriating. "That's right. We didn't give our itinerary to the press. They won't be there waiting for us. And even if they were, they wouldn't be looking for us in the truck. No one will see us. And it'll save money. That's what my job is all about."

"But the company is paying our expenses. Let them pay for a limo!"

"It's the company whose profits we're trying to save. You have to start with the little things, Jessica. Now come on and help me load this stuff into the truck."

Biting her tongue, she grabbed one of the smaller suitcases and watched him pick up the other three without any trouble. When they had gotten everything loaded in, she made one last check of her apartment, locked it and got into the truck.

"I still think this is ridiculous," she griped. "One stupid limo wouldn't have cost that much."

He got into the driver's side and cranked the engine. "Well, you can stop brooding over that. There are more cuts ahead."

"What cuts?" she asked as they pulled out of the parking lot.

"Our seats on the plane. We're flying coach. Have you ever flown coach before, Jessica?"

She dropped her head back on the headrest. "Cade, how are we going to explain flying coach to people who are supposed to see us as successful and glamorous?"

"Anybody who reads next week's *Newsweek* will know that we've been entrusted with boosting profits and cutting waste. You can't do that by spending like maniacs. Everybody but the government knows that."

"But there's an image thing to consider here, too, Cade. What about that?"

"I don't think enough people will be on that plane to ruin our image, Jess. But if they are, they'll be so distracted looking at you that they won't even notice. And it couldn't hurt to have them relate more to you. The glamorous woman who's not too good to fly coach. You aren't, are you, Jessica?"

"Aren't what?" she snapped.

"Too good."

She bit her lip and fixed her eyes straight ahead. "Cade, is this whole tour going to be hand to mouth? I mean, are we going to scrimp on every little thing? Because I don't know if I can stand that."

"You'll get tough, Jess," he said. "But it's not so hard. I've lived hand to mouth most of my life. I know how to make a dollar stretch. And that's exactly what I intend to do. Even if it kills you."

He seemed amused at the warning, but she wasn't. She watched out the window as he entered the airport and navigated his way to the parking area. "You know, you'll pay more for long-term parking than you would have for a limo."

He smiled. "Not really. Daphne's picking the truck up this afternoon for me. We'll only have to pay for a few hours."

She gave him a sharp look. "And how does Daphne feel about dating a tightwad?"

He laughed. "She thinks I'm eccentric, and it amuses her. It doesn't take much."

"I noticed," Jessica said wryly.

He glanced over at her as he pulled into a space. His grin faded when he saw the disgruntled look on her face. "I am what I am, Jess. Andrew knew I was an expert at cutting corners, because I have him to thank for it."

And before Jessica had the chance to reply, Cade was out of the truck and grabbing the suitcases to carry up to the Delta desk himself.

THEY BOARDED THE PLANE and she found their seats, thankful that there were only two on that side of the aisle. Hesitating, she said, "Which is mine?"

"Whichever one you want," he said.

"Which one's cheaper?" she asked.

He laughed. "Pick one, Jess."

"I could let you have the window seat," she said. "Since you've probably never flown. Being so destitute and all."

His eyes sparkled. "I've flown, Jess. Take the window seat."

She slipped into her seat and looked up at him as he shrugged out of his coat and hung it on a hanger in the small closet at the front of the cabin. He was wearing a white shirt that looked as if it had just come from the cleaner's. It accented the bronze hue of his skin and made her wonder when he had time to get out in the sun.

He took the seat next to her, and she pulled a magazine out of the seat pocket and pretended to read.

Undaunted, he set his elbow on the armrest and leaned toward her. "I didn't notice any gasps when we crossed the threshold from first-class to coach, did you?"

She looked up at him. "Is there a point you're trying to make?"

He smiled. "Just an observation."

He waited for a while as she flipped pages, then said, "Gee, it's too bad Jerome didn't show up to say goodbye. I kind of thought he would."

She leered at him. "He's a very busy man. And where was Daphne?"

He grinned again. "Too tired, probably."

Again, she went back to the magazine, feigning interest, though she feared the tips of her ears were reddening as they always did when she was angry.

She turned to a perfume ad and let her eye rest on the half-nude couple writhing in ecstasy, and for a moment she flashed back to the two of them, just days ago, caught in the same intimate pose. Had it weighed on his mind as much as it had on hers?

His eyes also caught on the ad, and where the woman's breasts blurred into shadow he saw Jessica's, when he had peeled back her blouse and confronted the overflowing handfuls of breast, the pink, taut nipples, and her chest heaving in and out with her breath.

Blood rushed to where it shouldn't have, and he looked away. Did she think about that night as much as he did?

The plane's engine came to life, and he felt the jet backing out of the gate.

He wished she hadn't worn that perfume.

She wished he didn't look so sexy in white.

He wished her neckline was a little higher.

She wished he'd stop rolling up his sleeves.

He wished so much of her legs didn't show when she crossed them.

She wished he didn't look so sensual when he was tired.

He wished she'd quit reading that damn magazine.

She wished he'd stop reading over her shoulder.

He wished he could think of her as a sister.

She wished she could think of him as a brother.

He pretended to be asleep, and she pretended to be enthralled by an article on interferon. And neither of them said a word until they were almost to Dallas.

"SO, ARE WE GOING TO WALK to the hotel or take a bus?" Jessica asked as they stood in the baggage claim area waiting to get their luggage.

"We'll take a cab," Cade said. "They have a shuttle from the airport, but now that we're in Dallas, I suppose your image does count for something."

Her eyebrows shot up. "Really?"

"Yeah, but don't get spoiled. Our concessions to your image are only going to go so far."

Deciding to bite her tongue and not argue with him, for fear that the next concession wouldn't come so easily, she smiled as the skycap stacked their luggage and started pulling the baggage cart toward the line of taxis just outside the door.

They were settled in a cab when he named the Doubletree, an extravagant luxury hotel in Dallas.

She gaped at him. "We're staying at the Doubletree? How do you justify that?"

He looked askance at her. "Are you complaining?"

"No," she said. "I just... I'm surprised."

"Well, don't be. You're going to be getting calls from the press about interviews and things, and I didn't think it would look good to be staying at the Day's Inn. Your room, however, will be just a basic-rate room with a double bed."

"No," she said, her voice asserting too firmly. "This is where I have to draw the line. I need a suite."

"A suite?" He laughed and shook his head, as if he'd never heard anything quite so stupid and wasn't sure he'd heard it correctly. "No, darling." He patted her hand. "I realize that a basic room in a luxury hotel is roughing it for you, but this is the way it's going to be."

She jerked her hand back and shifted in her seat to look at him. "Stop condescending to me, will you? I'm not some little idiot who just came of age and started a grown-up job! I've been JC's spokesperson for years, remember? I've done these tours before, and I know a little more about them than you do."

Cade glanced up at the cabdriver, who was watching them through the rearview mirror. Grinning, he shrugged, as if to say, "Women, go figure." The gesture sent her blood pressure rising even higher.

"At least half of my interviews will take place in my suite, Cade. It's better if they do, because it makes them come to me, and they get me in a more relaxed environment. It's very important that I look glamorous when they show up, and I can't do that in a basic room with a double bed in the middle of it and the smell of shower steam wafting around the room."

He laid his head back, and for a moment, she thought he was formulating his next argument—the one that would blow her away. "I hadn't thought of that."

"No, I didn't think you had," she said.

"I guess it would make sense, though. I was using myself as the lowest common denominator. Whatever is good enough for me is good enough for you. But you make a good point."

"Then you'll get me a suite?"

He sighed as the cab pulled into the circular drive of the hotel. "Guess I'll have to."

She breathed a quick sigh of relief as they got out of the cab. Smiling her best Jessica smile—the one that was recognizable because it was all over the Jessica Cosmetics jars—she followed Cade into the hotel lobby. Heads turned as she walked by, and she wished she'd taken a moment to check her lipstick before she'd gotten out of the cab.

They reached the desk, and she waited beside Cade as he asked if it was too late to change their reservations. "I had two rooms booked for Jessica Cosmetics," he said. "I'd like to change that to a suite."

"Two suites?" the woman behind the computer asked.

"No, actually. Just one."

Jessica's head shot around. "What?"

"Do you have one with two bedrooms?" he asked.

The woman typed something into the computer and said, "Yes, we have one available."

Jessica gaped at the woman as she made the reservation, but before he could get the key, she pulled him away from the desk. "Cade, what are you doing? You don't intend for us to share a suite!"

"Actually, Jessica, I do," he said, keeping his voice low. "We can't afford two. But calm down, it has two bedrooms."

"I don't care what it has! How will it look?"

"No one in the world has to know. And besides, even if they do know, they consider us brother and sister. No one would think anything."

Jessica wilted. "You're not going to miss a trick, are you?"

He shook his head. "No, I'm not. I'm supposed to do a job, Jess. And I'm going to do it. I just hope you don't snore. I'm a light sleeper."

He left her gaping at him and went back to the desk to finalize the arrangements.

JESSICA UNPACKED the last of her things and reached for the telephone to call publicity at JC to see if there had been any changes in her schedule. Cade was already on the phone, and she quickly hung up.

She went into the living room and saw him sitting on the couch, his elbows on his knees and his head dropped down as he held the phone to his ear.

"The Doubletree," he was saying, "Suite 624. But I'll come get you. Are you sure?"

She thought of going back into her room to give him privacy, but the thought that they were in such close quarters, that she wasn't free to go into her living area, riled her. Besides, who was he talking to? One of his bimbos? No, she thought defiantly. She wasn't going to give him the satisfaction of privacy.

She opened the pay bar, searched the contents for a snack. On the phone, she heard him saying in a quiet voice, "Sounds fine. Look forward to seeing you."

She heard him hang up and turned back around. "Got a date?"

He was staring at the floor, his face as sullen as she had seen it since their father's funeral. "You might say that."

She shrugged and reached for a pack of crackers from the pay bar.

"Don't get that," he said. "It's too expensive."

She dropped it and rolled her eyes. "Well, do I get to eat on this trip, or am I supposed to fast for five months?"

"Of course you can eat," he said. "Reasonably priced food in reasonably priced restaurants. But not a pack of crackers that costs three dollars."

Sighing, she closed the door. "Well, since you're going out, and I don't look forward to eating alone, do I have your *permission* to order room service?"

His face resumed that long look she had caught earlier. "I don't know if I'm going out or not."

"Well, isn't she meeting you here?" Her tone seethed.

"She?" He looked up, nonplussed.

"Whomever you were talking to."

He smiled. "Not she. Ben. My son."

Jessica felt like kicking herself. She was turning into a raving idiot, she thought, and she didn't like it. "I'm sorry, Cade. Ben lives in Dallas? I thought you said Arlington."

"Arlington's a suburb. He's going to come by for a while."

"So why the long face?"

He shrugged. "I don't know. I feel like I'm taking him from something he'd rather be doing."

"Cade, you're his father."

"Yeah, I guess. 'Course that's a relative term."

"Father? No, it's not."

"Sure, it is," he said. "To me, a father is someone who raises you. I'm not raising him any more than my father raised me."

Sitting down next to him, she asked, "So how long has it been since you've seen him?"

He shrugged, trying to look neutral. "About a year, I guess."

"A year! Cade, how can you stand it?"

"What do you do when your ex-wife marries a millionaire and decides to take your son halfway across the country?"

"Still..." She let her thought drop, unwilling to heap further blame on him. "How old is he now?"

"Twelve," he said. "His voice sounded like it was starting to change. He's probably grown a foot."

She smiled. "How's he getting here?"

He shrugged. "I offered to rent a car, since I was going to do that tomorrow anyway, and go get him. But he said he'd have his mother's driver bring him."

She stared at him for a moment, noted the dejection on his face, and asked, "So what's the problem?"

He sat quietly for a moment, pondering her question, then finally got up. "No problem. None at all."

He started to the bedroom to get ready for his son, but that look of apprehension and loss remained draped over him, stemming any further discussion.

CHAPTER NINE

THE BOY THAT CAME to their suite an hour later was anything but a kid. He was a five-foot-five-inch man-child with hair cropped short around the sides and top of his head, and long waves in the back that tickled his collar. Except for his hairstyle, he was the spitting image of his father.

For a moment, Ben stood at the open door, hands stuffed in the pockets of faded jeans that looked as if he wore them every day. He stared at his father with dull, brooding eyes, an expression that was all too familiar to Jessica. Cade had worn it for years.

Cade's smile was strained as he awkwardly reached out and drew his son into a clumsy hug. Ben stiffened. "Look at you. You're a giant, for Pete's sake." There was a strange, poignant wistfulness in the offhand greeting, and when Cade pulled Ben into the suite and turned back to Jessica, her heart jolted.

Were those tears in his eyes, or was the light just pooling there to create an illusion?

"Buddy, I'd like for you to meet my... I'd like you to meet Jessica Hartman."

She saw the look of surprise Ben threw his father. "Hi, Ben. It's so nice to meet you. I've always wanted to, but Cade and I were never very close. I'm glad to have the chance now." She stopped, wondering if she was rambling, and glanced back at Cade, waiting for him to say something. Father and son only looked awkwardly at her. She doubted either of them would have admitted it, but their eyes silently pleaded with her to intervene and help them out of the strain of their awkwardness. "Oh, Lord, Cade, the poor kid looks just like you. And you didn't tell me he was so tall."

Cade's smile was sad as he messed up his son's hair. "I didn't know. What did you do? Shoot up overnight?"

"No." Ben tilted his head away and finger-combed his hair back into place. "It's just been a long time since I've seen you." The tone was accusatory, and Cade received it as it was intended.

"Yeah, well. You know how it is."

"Right." Hands still in his pockets, Ben focused on his shoes.

"So...does your mother want you back soon, or do we have a little time to knock around?"

Ben shrugged. "Mom's in Seattle with Richard."

"Seattle? Who's taking care of you?"

Again, he shrugged. "I can take care of myself. But our housekeeper is at the house, and Pete, the driver, stays there, too."

"Oh."

Jessica saw the consternation pass over Cade's eyes, but he didn't pursue it.

"Well, then, we could go out to eat or something. You have any favorite places?"

Ben came farther into the room and plopped down onto the sofa. "Not really."

"You know the area better than I do. Any suggestions?"

"Nope."

Cade raised his eyebrows helplessly. "Well, do you want to go to Chuck E. Cheese, maybe play some of the arcade games?"

Ben shot his father a disbelieving look. "I'm twelve," he said. "A little old for Chuck E. Cheese, wouldn't you think?"

Effectively shot down, Cade tried to smile. "Yeah, I guess so. Bear with me, buddy. Ever since I last saw you, I've had this picture of a kid. It's a tough adjustment to make, seeing you practically grown up."

"Is that my fault?" The belligerent question was like a bullet fired unexpectedly, momentarily stunning Cade.

"Well, no. No, it's not."

Unable to watch any more of this, Jessica jumped in. "You know, you could probably get the concierge to tell you where a good pizza place is. You like pizza, don't you, Ben?"

"It's all right."

"Good," Cade said. "Then pizza it is. We can go right now if you're ready."

The boy sat still for a moment, then finally got slowly up from the couch, as if forcing himself to make the effort.

Jessica's heart sank, and she wondered what on earth the two men would talk about over pizza. Would Ben's belligerence pass and at some point give way to a little boy's charm? Would Cade suddenly be inspired to say whatever Ben needed to hear? Somehow, she doubted it. The two men would struggle over small talk, feinting and parrying until they were both sorry they'd made the effort at all.

Taking a chance, she feigned a pout and said, "You guys go ahead. Don't mind me, really. I'll just stay here and eat crackers or something."

Cade smiled, and she knew he was grateful for the offhand offer to rescue them. "You want to come, Jess?"

She lifted a shoulder. "Well, I do love pizza. But I don't want to intrude."

Cade gave his son a sidelong glance. "What do you think? Should we take her along?"

Ben shrugged, but she could see the relief passing over his eyes. "Sure. She's got to eat."

Grabbing her purse, Jessica pranced out the door behind them. "All right, I'll come," she said. "But be prepared. I expect you to spend a fortune on the jukebox, and head-banging is a requirement on each appropriate song. Is everybody clear on that?"

For the first time since he'd shown up at the door, Ben smiled.

DESPITE JESSICA'S SUCCESS in keeping the conversation going all night, neither she nor Cade could escape the fact that Ben didn't want to have a good time with his father. It seemed more important to keep that fort built up around him. She wondered if he was trying to keep Cade out or keep his own feelings in.

Whatever his intention, one thing was certain. He was just like Cade had been as a child.

When they got back to their suite, Ben phoned his driver to pick him up. Jessica decided it was time to leave the two of them alone. Despite the tension between them, they had to have a few minutes to sink or swim if they ever expected to forge a relationship. Bidding good-night to Ben, she went into her bedroom and took a shower.

IN THE SITTING AREA, as they waited for Ben's driver, Cade tried again to find some way to reach his son. "So what do you think of Jess?"

Ben looked down at his feet. "She's nice. I thought you hated her."

"Whoever said I hated her?"

"You."

"I never said that."

Ben drew in a deep breath. "You said that she was pampered and spoiled. One time we saw her on a commercial for that makeup stuff, and you turned the TV off."

Cade tried to smile. "Oh, yeah." He looked at his son, wishing he only remembered good and noble things about him, since there were so few memories. "Damn, you have a good memory. I hate that."

Ben smiled in spite of himself. "So what happened? Why are you friends now?"

"Well, my father...her father...he died. And he left this—"

"My grandfather died?"

Cade paused. "Yeah. A few weeks ago."

"Why didn't you tell me?"

It was the first time Cade had even considered that his son might be interested. "I'm sorry, Ben. I didn't think it would mean anything to you. You'd never met him."

"Is that my fault?" the boy asked for the second time that night.

Cade let out a tightly held breath. "Well, no. It's mine. I wasn't close to him."

"You hated him, too," Ben accused.

"No, Ben, I didn't hate my father." Cade sank onto the couch. Clasping his hands between his knees, he tried to go on. "Look, it's real complicated. A lot of stuff happened when I was growing up. It's hard for me to explain in a way you'd understand."

"What's to understand? Your parents divorced, like mine."

Cade looked at Ben, searching for remnants of the little boy he used to wake up by rubbing his whiskers across his feet. The little boy who could wrestle him to the floor when he was five years old. The little boy who followed him around the house like a shadow.

Can I come with you, Daddy?

Sure. Go get your shoes on and brush your teeth. And no tricks this time. I'm gonna smell your breath and check your toothbrush.

That was a long time ago—another lifetime.

"Well, I guess it is similar, in some ways," he said quietly. "I shouldn't have hated Jessica. I didn't even know her." He struggled for the right words, and finally chose to take the most direct approach he could find. "But my father devised this stupid game in his will, where we have to work together and try to raise profits for JC."

"What about the bike shop?" Ben asked.

As it always did, any mention of his motorcycle shop from Ben immediately put Cade on the defensive. A mechanic didn't quite measure up to the world traveler and money man that Ben's stepfather was. Bridgit had left him as soon as she'd realized he was nothing more than a mechanic camouflaged in a white collar. "I sold out," he said. "And I came to work for JC."

If it was possible for Ben's face to fall further, it did. "So...you're not riding anymore or anything?"

"Of course I am," he said. "I still have my Harley at home."

Ben's face relaxed a shade. "Oh. Good."

Noting the surprising reaction, Cade said, "Maybe this summer you can come over and stay a couple of weeks with me, and we can ride."

Ben lifted then dropped his shoulders. "Yeah. Maybe."

But he wasn't counting on it, Cade knew, for nothing with Ben ever worked out like he planned. The first summer after Bridgit had moved Ben to Texas, Cade had tried to get him for the whole summer. But the boy had been involved in softball, and then they took a trip to Italy, and by the time they got back, it was time for school again. Cade had been so disappointed—and felt so discarded—that he'd never tried again. It was just too reminiscent of the years after his own father had left, when he'd hoped each summer for a long visit, for time to spend alone with his father. It hadn't happened. There had been the new wife, the new baby, the new company, and his father had been so busy... And when he'd been there, it hadn't been the same. He was like an outsider, a guest in strangers' homes, and as a guest, he was treated politely. But not like Andrew's child anymore. Jessica was the only one who had that privilege now.

The phone rang, and Cade picked it up. The concierge told him Ben's driver was waiting, so he told him they'd be right down.

Cade rode the elevator down with him, and when they reached the lobby, he touched the back of Ben's neck. "I'm gonna be here for at least a week. Why don't we get together again?"

Ben's face looked strained, and his lips quivered slightly as he said, "Whatever."

"Will you be home tomorrow?"

"Depends," Ben said.

"On what?"

"On what comes up," Ben said. "You know. Baseball practice, the guys..."

Cade smiled, but his heart wasn't in it. "Well, why don't I give you a call, and if you're in, maybe we can go see a movie or something? Or I could come to one of your games, if you have one this week."

Ben gave a noncommittal shrug and didn't say whether he had one or not.

He started to walk away, and Cade fought the urge to reach out and pull him into a big bear hug, like the kind they used to wind up in when they'd wrestled on the floor. He wanted to hold him, rock him to sleep, wash his face...

But his son had grown out of that little child who had loved and trusted him, and now he didn't even know how to talk to him.

"See you later," Ben said as he started away.

Cade didn't stop him. "Sure, buddy. See you later."

CADE WAS SITTING alone in the dark living room when Jessica came out of her room.

"Where's Ben?"

"Went home." He looked up at her, and she felt his melancholy eyes sweep over her wet hair, along her white robe to the bare feet peeking out beneath it. But even as he looked at her, she felt he didn't really see her.

Turning on the lamp, she sat down across from him. "You okay?"

"Yeah," he said, rubbing his eyes roughly. "It's just tough. He's not mine anymore. Hasn't been for a long time."

"Of course he's yours," she said. "He'll always be yours."

Cade didn't answer.

"So when are you seeing him again? Tomorrow?"

He shook his head. "I don't think so. I think I'll just leave the kid alone."

"What?"

He brought his eyes to hers and for a moment she could see all the fathomless pain he usually kept so well hidden. "He made it pretty clear that he's got better things to do than hang around with his old man. Probably has box seats for a Cowboys game, or plans to flit away with his mom on their Learjet to Paris. Tough life."

Jessica frowned. "You sound jealous," she said. "Is that it? Are you jealous of him?"

His face tightened even further, and she saw from the sharp look there that she'd made a wrong call. "Jealous?" he repeated, as if the word tasted sour on his tongue. "Well, yeah, maybe. Jealous that another man is raising my child. Jealous that he was taken away from me, and not because of anything I did wrong. In fact, I had no say in the matter at all. You want to call that jealousy? Fine."

She sat back, looking at Cade with eyes too insightful. "I'm sorry, Cade." She was quiet for a moment, then said, "He's so much like you. Sometimes tonight, I felt like I was looking at you as a kid. You were just like him when you used to come visit. You'd sit there with your arms crossed, acting bored and bothered, answering questions in polite monosyllables. And Dad would try and try to find something you could do together, but you didn't want to do anything. And I would turn flips and cartwheels around you, practically begging you for a smile, and you'd look right past me."

"You're exaggerating."

"No, I'm not."

He settled his eyes on her, but she knew he was seeing those years in his mind. "It wasn't the same thing, Jessica. I didn't leave Ben's mother and go marry someone else, and have some perfect little kid to replace him."

"That's not what happened! I didn't replace you!"

"Of course you did. Just like your mother replaced my mother. We were dispensable."

Indignation rose inside her, along with an irrational need to defend her father. "Cade, you're so wrong. You have no idea how much he hurt over you. Just like you're sitting here hurting for Ben."

"Oh, really?" Cade asked. "Well, a lot of good that did me. It didn't make life any easier." He got to his feet, went to the window and stared out on the lights of Dallas.

"What do you mean, easier?"

He turned back to her. "I mean, I was the one at home alone nights while my mother worked two jobs. I was the one who didn't get to play baseball because we couldn't afford the uniform. If your father loved me so much, why did I have to work three part-time jobs in college to supplement my scholarships?"

Jessica started toward him across the plush expanse of carpet. "He paid child support. I know he did."

He breathed a laugh. "Oh, yeah, he paid child support, all right. Enough to almost cover the rent. As long as we lived in a run-down house in a high-crime neighborhood. Ever wonder why he never brought you with him to pick me up, Jess? It was because he didn't want you to see where I lived."

Her face reddened, and she struggled to quell the rage rising in her heart. "He told my mother that your mother blew everything he sent her. That he didn't think any of it was getting to you."

"That's bullshit!" he shouted. "She provided my home, my clothes, my food... Do you think she would have chosen to work days and nights if she was out blowing my father's money?"

Stunned by the revelation that made no sense to her, Jessica shook her head. "But that can't be. He had plenty of money. I know he didn't want you to suffer. There must have been something you didn't know about."

"What, Jessica?" he asked. "Why would my mother hide it? The plain simple truth is that my father forgot about me. He had you. I wasn't even his biological son. What difference did it make?"

"My father was not that kind of man," she bit out. "He talked about you all the time. He always thought you had such a lousy time each visit that you didn't want to come back."

"And he was right."

"But why? Couldn't you have at least pretended to enjoy the visits?"

Cade rubbed his hand through his hair, leaving it tousled, and shaking his head, he finally looked at her again. "It wasn't my job to make the visits fun, or to maintain any kind of relationship with my father. It was his job, Jess. I was just a kid!"

"Ben's just a kid, too," she threw back. "But it's all different when it's someone else! Fine, Cade. Think of me as the little girl who disrupted your life and stole your father. And think of Ben as the little boy who found a father he liked better. Then go wallow in it all, if that's what you want to do!"

Something snapped inside him. Striding across the floor, he put his face close to hers. "My relationship with my son is no more your business than my relationship with my father. When I want your opinion, I'll ask for it!"

Then he bolted out of the room, slammed the door and left Jessica to deal with the feelings ricocheting inside her.

IT WAS AFTER MIDNIGHT when Jessica realized she wasn't going to be able to sleep. No matter how she tried to push Cade's pain from her mind and forget the things he'd said, it wouldn't go away.

Cade wasn't making up the things he'd said about her father, yet it didn't make sense. Why would Andrew seem to love Cade, only to ignore him and turn a blind eye to his poverty? Why would he dote on her and practically forget his other child existed? Was Cade right? Was it because he was adopted?

She got up, went to the window, saw the lights of the Dallas skyline. Ben was somewhere out there, probably as sad and lonely as Cade. It was a cycle spinning out of control. Andrew's neglect, spawning Cade's pain, spawning Ben's loneliness.

She racked her brain for memories that coincided with Cade's. It was true that, even though they'd lived in the same town, she had never known where he lived. Was it really because her father was ashamed?

She thought of one Christmas, when Cade was Ben's age and she was only five. They'd had a glorious ten-foot tree that year, that reached almost to the ceiling, and beneath it had been what seemed like hundreds of wrapped gifts. She'd dug through them alone, checking for the names on the packages. None of them had been for Cade.

"Daddy, when are you putting Cade's presents under the tree?" she'd asked.

"They're under there." Andrew had shot a questioning look to his wife. "You did buy Cade something, didn't you, honey?"

"Of course I did."

It only now occurred to her that her father had shown little interest in *what* she had bought him, and only when Jessica had dug through the mountain of gifts had she finally come across one for Cade.

That night, she'd spent hours in her room, coloring cards for her brother, decorating them with massive amounts of glitter and glue, cutting out Christmas trees and sprinkling glitter stars all over them. She had carefully wrapped them in tissue, tied a clumsy bow around them and written Cade's name on the package—the only name she'd yet learned to write besides her own.

Before she went to bed that night, she'd taken it to her father. "I'm putting this under the tree for Cade," she said. "When is he coming?"

"We're not sure, yet," Andrew had said.

Cade hadn't shown up at all, and Christmas morning, after all the presents had been opened, only two remained under the tree. One small box for Cade, and the cards she had made him.

Now, so many years later, she wondered if he'd ever gotten them.

Oh, she had questioned her father over the years, and always, Andrew would get a saddened look on his face and tell her that Cade was growing older and didn't really have much fun when he was visiting.

She'd ask if they could take him on vacations with them, but something always came up. Whenever Cade's birthday came around, she'd ask if she could buy him something nice. Always, her mother or father claimed they'd get him something, and now she didn't know whether they ever had or not. When Cade had finally reached college age, she had wondered why he chose an inexpensive state college and lived at home. It never occurred to her that her father wasn't paying his way.

Feeling as if she were an accessory in a great crime against a child—a crime that she was certain had an explanation, if only her father were here to give it—she pulled on her robe and padded across the carpet into the living area of the suite. Cade's door was open a few inches, and for a moment she stood staring at it.

There was nothing but silence within, but something she couldn't name compelled her to go through that door and try to find some answers to the questions keeping her awake. She saw Cade lying on his back, hands behind his head. Moonlight cast horizontal shadows on his face as it was broken by the vertical blinds, and she saw that his eyes were open.

"Cade?"

He started slightly, then saw her standing at the door.

"I couldn't sleep," she said. "Can I come in for a minute?"

He hesitated, then sat up. His sheet fell around his bare waist, and something stirred inside her. Was he naked under the blankets? "Yeah, what's wrong?"

She didn't quite know where to go—whether to stand or sit—so she leaned against the wall facing him. "I've been thinking a lot about what you said tonight..."

He rubbed his face. "Yeah, so have I. Look, I'm sorry for coming down so hard on you. I shouldn't..."

"No." Her protest cut him off, and when she stepped into the broken moonlight her eyes were brimming with tears. "It's okay. But I was remembering back. Times when you weren't around..." Her shaky voice fell off, and she studied him for a moment. "Cade...when I was five and you were eleven, did Daddy give you the present I made you for Christmas?"

He frowned. "No."

Somehow, this was much more important to her than she could explain. "Are you sure?"

"Positive. I usually got something like a pair of pajamas that didn't fit me. And it almost always came in the mail. What was it?"

"It was...just some cards and things I had made for you. I worked really hard... 'Course, I was only five. I couldn't write anything but your name and mine." Her voice trailed off, and tears came to her eyes. "Why wouldn't he have given it to you?"

"I don't know."

For a moment her eyes locked with his in the darkness, and a tear dropped to her cheek. "Cade, I don't know why things worked out the way they did, but I'm so sorry."

"Hey." He set his elbows on his knees under the covers. "It wasn't your fault."

She tried to laugh. "You probably would have thrown it away, anyway, if you'd gotten it. You really never liked me."

He looked at her for a moment, struggling with the truth that had been so obvious. After a moment, he sighed and reached out for her hand. Pulling her to sit on the bed facing him, he whispered, "It wasn't you. I was angry, and I felt abandoned. If you'd been anybody but my sister, I would have liked you fine."

"But I really liked you, Cade," she whispered. Another tear plopped onto her cheek and rolled down. "I used to dream about you coming to live with us, protecting me, playing with me, teasing me..."

"But you had a different perspective than I had. I guess the reality is that I shouldn't even blame him for it. He wasn't even my real father, after all."

"When you adopt someone, they're yours," she whispered. "Biology doesn't matter." She looked down at the comforter over him, traced a finger over the paisley print. "Did you ever look for your real parents?"

"Hell, no," he said, watching her finger move across the spread. "That seemed pretty futile."

"Why?"

"Well, what do you think would have happened if I'd found them? Do you think I would have found some nice stable couple who would have embraced me with open arms? They gave me up for a reason, and it wasn't so I could come back to haunt them years later." He sighed, and looked wistfully into the shadows across the room. "When I was really little, Mom and Dad made adoption seem like something really special. My mother never could conceive, and they said they had chosen me out of hundreds of babies. I thought I had to be the luckiest kid in the world."

His dry laugh had no heart, and it died a painful death. "Then, when Dad left, I found out differently. My being adopted probably eased his conscience. Made it easier to walk away."

"Cade, I know he loved you."

"As much as he was able, I guess," he said, but she knew he didn't believe it. "I shouldn't have expected things to stay the same. Expectations can be deadly sometimes."

She grew very still as she watched him. "So now you just keep your expectations low, don't you?"

He smiled wanly. "I guess I do. It keeps me from being disappointed."

She took a deep breath and pulled her feet up onto the bed, hugging her knees. "I guess I've always expected the world, and to be perfectly honest, I've usually gotten it."

"There's nothing wrong with that," he said. "If I'd kept being raised the way I started out, I might be that way, too. I had to be the most spoiled kid alive until I was five. I was the center of my parents' world. Dad used to..." His voice caught, and he stopped, unwilling to finish the sentence.

"He used to what?"

"Nothing. It doesn't matter now."

"Please, Cade. What were you going to say?"

He sighed. "Just that he used to put shaving cream on my face when he was shaving, and let me use a razor without a blade in it. Sometimes I'd go to work with him, and he'd give me some kind of job to do. Then he'd pay me and we'd go get ice cream afterward. And we used to go to the beach...."

"Gulf Shores," she whispered. "So did we."

"I know," he said. "I didn't get invited after you came along. Your mother didn't care much for me."

Her heart burst with regret and sorrow, and she covered her face as new tears rushed forward. "Oh, Cade. I'm so sorry."

"You were just a little kid," he said. "You couldn't have changed a thing."

"No wonder you hate me."

He reached out to her then, pulled her hands away from her face and whispered, "Hey. I don't hate you. I wouldn't be here if I did."

But his words didn't stop her tears, and as she surrendered more fully to her sobs, he realized helplessly that her grief was not only for his past, but for hers as well. Without meaning to, he had tainted her sweet memories of her father. For the first time since he could remember, Jessica's grief became more important to him than the bitterness he had clung to like a shield.

Reaching out, he pulled her into his arms. She came willingly and buried her face in the crook of his neck. He threaded his fingers through her hair, stroking gently as he felt her sobs subside. "If I hated you," he went on softly, "I wouldn't have wanted you to come with Ben and me tonight. I wouldn't have shared a suite with you. I wouldn't have..."

She pulled her head off his shoulder and looked up. "What, Cade?"

"'I wouldn't have gotten so carried away the other night."

She was too close, and her lips shimmered from her tears, and he found that letting her go would take too much effort. He liked holding her, not as a big brother comforting his sister, but as a man, struck with a sudden tenderness that had been foreign to him all his life. There was a chemical buzz that blurred his mind, made it hard for him to think. There was a desire so powerful that he wanted to pull her down on the pillows with him, to touch her breasts beneath that gown. There was a need so strong that he knew all hope for sleep tonight was gone, and that, if he sent her away, he'd just go after her again.

He looked down at her and tipped her chin up to his face. Their eyes locked in a moment of terror, a moment of hope, a moment of capture and surrender.

He wet his lips, and she wet hers. His breath came more heavily. Hers was ragged. For a moment—a thrilling, electric, terrifying moment—they looked at each other, and some voice in his head told him it could be the most important moment in either of their lives. What happened now could change them forever. There would be no turning back.

Slowly he pulled back, let her go, and gently stroked her hair back from her face.

She felt it the instant he made the decision not to kiss her, and while her heart sank, she didn't feel the chill she had felt the last time.

"Well, I guess I'll try to go to sleep," she whispered. "Tomorrow's going to be a long day."

"Yeah."

She made no effort to leave, and finally she reached for his hand. "Cade, I don't know why Daddy treated you the way he did. But don't repeat the cycle with Ben. Call him tomorrow. If he turns you down, fine. But don't be the one to do it."

He dropped his gaze to the spread draped over him. "I'll think about it."

"Good." Quietly she got up from the bed, smiled softly and disappeared into the darkness beyond his door.

CHAPTER TEN

CADE WAS SURPRISED when Ben said he'd see him that night. It made him feel as if there was still time to straighten out his life. Jessica was right. He was crazy to let the cycle repeat itself. From Andrew to Cade to Ben. Somewhere, it had to stop.

He spent his day at the first Jessica Cosmetics store on his list, a store that should have been raking in the dollars but whose management had gotten lazy. There were too many employees in the store, and when he examined their inventory, he found that they were out of most of their most popular items. In the first hour that he was there, he watched fifteen people come and go. Only two bought anything. Eight asked for something that was out of stock. And five browsed, then ambled out without a salesperson ever greeting them.

He studied their budgets closely, their advertising allowance, their telephone and utility bills, their payroll. And he decided that, by the time he was finished here tomorrow, he'd have the store on its way to making more than it spent.

The first thing he did was fire the young redhead who'd had two dozen personal calls that day, and the lazy brunette who had lost three customers because she'd made them feel she was losing patience with their indecision. He'd ordered the manager to cut the number of employees on the floor each day, and not to replace the salespeople he'd fired. By the time he left there, he wasn't popular, but he felt he'd accomplished what he'd set out to.

While Cade was cutting expenditures, Jessica hooked the customers as she made the interview circuit in the Dallas-Fort Worth area. He caught two of her interviews on local news shows, one at noon and another at six, and a long call-in radio show where she'd answered listeners' makeup questions. Poised, graceful and gorgeous, she represented the company better than any top model could have done. Her quick laugh and self-deprecating humor gave her an aura of accessibility that made teenage girls think her product could make them beautiful in spite of pimples and freckles, and made disillusioned housewives feel it might bring some sensuality into their lives.

He left a message for her at the hotel, telling her that she had been wonderful today, and that he was warning all the managers in the Dallas area to batten down the hatches, because there was going to be a mob scene tomorrow when she made personal appearances at the first of their stores. Then he told her he was going to pick up Ben.

Donning the T-shirt and jeans that had been his uniform before he'd had to start wearing suits, he rented a motorcycle and rode it to the mansion where his son lived, hoping he wasn't miscalculating Ben's interest in bikes. If he had read him right, he'd been disappointed that his father had given up his pastime before Ben had ever gotten to enjoy it. Now he'd have the chance.

Ben heard him drive up and came to the door with a smile on his face. His eyes were childlike as he swept them appreciatively over the bike. "Where'd you get the bike?"

"Rented it," Cade said. "Come on. We'll go for a ride."

Still grinning, Ben followed him out. Cade tossed him a helmet. "Put it on."

Ben's smile collapsed. "Do I have to?"

"Yep."

"Aw, man. That takes all the fun out of it."

"So does crushing your skull on concrete. Wear the helmet."

Grimacing, Ben pulled it on, and together they got on the bike. They rode for over an hour without saying a word, then finally, as they came to a red light, Cade looked back over his shoulder. "You eaten?"

"No."

"What are you hungry for?"

"I don't care."

He pulled into a Sonic, and they ate at one of the tables outside, the sound of idling engines and the smell of exhaust around them. It was the best time he had had with his son in years.

"I saw Jessica on TV today," Ben said.

Cade grinned. "Yeah. She's great, isn't she?"

Ben nodded and studied his burger. "What made you change your mind about her?"

Cade glanced at him. "I guess I wasn't giving her a fair shot. Once I got to know her, I found out she's a pretty neat lady."

"So... are you two an item?"

Cade frowned. "Ben, she's my sister."

"Not really," Ben said. "Don't you think she's pretty?"

Cade's mind drifted back to last night, when she had come into his room and he had held her and almost...

He tore those thoughts away and remembered the last time he'd held her, when he'd gotten her shirt unbuttoned, felt her breasts against his chest, and almost...

Leaving those thoughts suspended somewhere in the back of his mind, Cade said, "Yeah. She's pretty."

"I mean, really pretty."

Cade grinned. "Yeah, so? You've seen beautiful women before."

"Yeah, I guess," Ben said. "Mom's pretty."

Cade nodded.

"But Jessica's different," Ben went on. "She's fun."

Cade wondered if that meant his mother wasn't, but he suspected he knew the answer. Bridgit was a woman who thought only of herself. He supposed he'd been so attracted to her because she was such a challenge. He didn't like admitting that he'd married her to prove—to his father, among others—that he was good enough for her. He had loved her in his way, but when she left him, the feeling had turned to bitterness. "So when is your mother due back?"

"Probably this weekend."

"Does she travel often?"

"Sure, all the time."

Cade's stomach tightened. "And she just leaves you there?"

"I told you," Ben said defensively. "I can take care of myself. I do even when she's there."

"But it couldn't be much fun, being there alone all the time."

"I told you the staff is there. I'm not alone."

"Okay, whatever you say." He checked his watch. "It's still early. You want to go find some empty parking lot somewhere, and I'll teach you how to drive a Harley?"

Ben's eyes lighted up. "You mean it?"

"Yeah, if you'll follow my instructions to a *T*."

"Cool."

Feeling as if he'd hit pay dirt, Cade handed Ben his helmet and they took off to find a safe place to learn how to be father and son.

JESSICA'S FIRST appearance at the store in the Galleria the next day brought out teenage girls in droves, along with their mothers looking for the chance to get tips and free samples of products that they hoped would change their lives. Makeovers were given as door prizes, and everyone who was willing to wait in line received a free sample bottle of Jessica Perfume with a tag signed by Jessica herself.

Cade finished working at one of the stores across town, picked up Ben for the third day in a row and made it to the Galleria just as Jessica's appearance time was coming to an end. Still, hundreds of women were lined up, along with dozens of men who claimed to want her autographed perfume for their wives. But he suspected they really just wanted an up-close look at the woman whose face graced almost all the products in the Jessica cosmetics line.

Just outside, a television crew was setting up to push its way through and focus on the anxious crowd and the poised celebrity.

Ben grinned and looked at his father. "Wow. Is it like this everywhere she goes?"

Cade laughed. "This is her first public appearance on this tour. Looks like it's a success."

Ben raised his brows, slid his hands into his pockets and followed his father into the store.

"I have to check the samples," Cade said quietly, trying to be inconspicuous. "Just find a place to sit while I go through them. We might need to go restock." He started away from Ben, then turned back. "Hey, don't worry. This has to die down soon. Then we'll go get something to eat."

"Don't worry about it," Ben said, his eyes still lingering on the crowd. "I can help, if you need something carried."

Cade grinned. "Okay. I'll be right back."

He checked the boxes beside Jessica, trying not to interrupt her animated conversation with each member in line. He saw that the supply was dwindling, and turned back to the manager of the store. "Do you have any more of these in the back somewhere?"

"No, sir," she said, "we're almost out. But it doesn't matter. She was supposed to quit half an hour ago."

Cade gave her a disgusted look. "She'll stay as long as there's a lineup out there. We can get more supplies."

"But the people will keep coming. I was supposed to take off at six."

Cade stood up and gaped at her. "Don't you realize how much this is going to boost sales?"

"Yes, but I—"

One of the young women behind the counter, a plain girl who'd done a lot with her features by applying the techniques on which JC prided itself, spoke up. "I'll stay, Mr. Hartman. I wouldn't miss this for the world. I was supposed to get off at four, but I couldn't make myself leave. Look how much we've sold today already. This has to be a record."

Cade checked the figures, and a feeling of pride shot through him. He wondered if the manager had even checked the figures, or if she'd been too busy trying to avoid the extra work. "Fine," he said. "You stay. Truth is, we're only interested in having enthusiastic employees here during our peak days, anyway. If your mind is somewhere else, by all means, take off."

The manager hesitated. "I *am* enthusiastic, Mr. Hartman. I just don't see any point in overdoing it. She's making appearances at each of our stores for the rest of the week. If anyone's turned away, they can catch her again later."

"So it doesn't matter to you if you send that business elsewhere?"

"I'm not on commission, Mr. Hartman."

"I see." He nodded, as if her statement had just made all the sense in the world, and gestured to the door. "Well, in that case, you're welcome to go."

The woman paused a moment, as if not certain whether he was making this a permanent offer. Not willing to give it much thought, she got her purse and started out. "All right. Sarah, I'll see you at eleven tomorrow."

Cade waited until she was gone, and turned back to the young woman with so much excitement in her eyes. "Sarah, you can come in at eight-thirty tomorrow. I can see that I'm not finished with the changes to this store yet. I think maybe I need to rethink the dedication involved here. Maybe a promotion is in order. And maybe others need to be let go."

Realizing that he could, quite possibly, be meaning to promote her to manager, the girl's eyes lighted up. "In answer to your question about the samples, Mr. Hartman, we do need at least one more box of the perfumes, and the sample cosmetics are low, too. Do you have any more?"

Cade had rented a van that morning to transport the supplies from store to store, and now he started to the door. "I'll get them right now."

"I can get them, Dad," Ben said.

Cade nodded. "It'll take both of us. Come on."

Together they hurried out to the van, and each grabbed two boxes. The Dallas heat bore down on Cade, and he wished he'd taken his coat off before he came out. By the time they'd made it back to the Galleria, he was damp with perspiration.

Jessica had just run out of supplies when they made their way back into the store, and she looked up at them with gratitude. "Thanks, guys."

It was funny, that way she had of looking into someone, making them feel they were the only one on the face of the earth, no matter how many people stood around. But that was her talent, Cade thought. She made every one of them feel that way. Not just him.

Ben was opening the boxes with a pocketknife from his back pocket, even before Cade had the time to take off his coat. And rolling up his sleeves, Cade set about helping his son.

By the time the last of Jessica's admirers had left the store, it was near closing time for the mall. Their sales for the day had rocketed to three times higher than ever before, and with the samples and coupons that had been given out, Cade suspected that the high sales figures would continue until most of the coupons had been redeemed. After that, he hoped, they would have the repeat business of those who had never tried Jessica Cosmetics before, but were hooked now that they'd been given the chance.

Since both of the saleswomen in the store were busy with sales while Jessica autographed, conversed, laughed and made herself a good friend to everyone who had come there, Cade and Ben had pitched in, too. Cade talked at length with anyone interested in the quality that went into their products, while Ben took appointments for makeovers.

When the doors were finally locked and everyone had time to breathe a sigh of relief, Cade shot Jessica a thumbs-up. "Great going, kiddo."

She smiled and kicked off her shoes. "Do you think we'll have this kind of response at every store?"

"I'd bet on it," Cade said. He turned to Sarah, the young woman who'd worked with a vengeance when they needed her most. "Sarah, how long have you worked here?"

"Two years," Sarah said. "I started during my third year in college."

He extended his hand. "Then it's about time you got promoted. Congratulations. I'm making you the manager of this store."

Sarah took his hand as her eyebrows lifted in excitement. "Do you mean it?"

"Yes. I'll be here when Cecile gets here in the morning and let her go. It was pretty obvious today who had the right stuff. I think your promotion is well deserved."

The other salesclerk let out a tiny squeal and threw her arms around Sarah, and Cade realized that no love was going to be lost between the former manager and her employees.

Jessica congratulated the young woman, too, then looked at Cade and said, "I'm starving, but I'm too tired to go out. I think I'll go back to the suite and order room service."

Cade looked at Ben. "I'll bet you're starving, too, aren't you?"

"I'll live," Ben said, bending over to package up what was left of their samples. "You want me to take these back to the van?"

"Yeah," Cade said. "I'll help you. Then we'll go get something to eat."

Ben shrugged. "We could do room service, too. I'm pretty well beat, myself."

Cade grinned. "Okay. You don't mind if we join you, do you, Jess?"

Jessica's smile revealed no fatigue. "I'd be honored."

She watched, still smiling, as Cade and his son hoisted the boxes and went out the back door.

CADE KNEW he was making real progress with his son when Ben invited him to watch him play baseball. He rushed through his last hour of work that day, then flew to the baseball field, searching for Ben's team on the six different fields there. He found the red-and-gray team with the words "Juniper Hardware" stamped on the back of their jerseys.

He sat down in the bleachers among the fathers and mothers there, and wondered if Bridgit and Richard came to Ben's games when they were in town. Somehow, he couldn't conjure a picture of his pristine ex-wife risking getting her bottom dirty on these wooden bleachers, or lugging a lawn chair from her Rolls. And the whole business of baseball was probably a bore to her.

The thought saddened him, and he realized what a lonely life his son must be living.

He found Ben among the players clustered by the dugout, and smiled at the fact that he was a head taller than any of the others. As the cluster broke up and Ben went to the pitcher's mound, Cade swelled with pride.

As he practiced pitching to the catcher, Ben saw his father, and a grin crept across his face. As if his presence had raised the stakes, Ben adjusted his cap, and his face grew more serious. He caught the ball, then focused on the batter stepping up to the plate.

Ben struck the first batter out in three easy pitches, which brought Cade to his feet. And as he sat back down, waiting for him to do it again, he whispered, "That's my boy."

It only seemed to take moments for Ben to pitch the third out, and as Cade came out of the bleachers, whooping and yelling with the other parents, someone tapped on his shoulder. He swung around and saw Jessica, dressed in a pair of cutoff jeans and a yellow sun shirt, laughing at the exuberance she had never before seen in Cade. "What are you doing here?" he asked her.

"The interview I had for tonight was postponed until tomorrow, so I got a cab. Who's winning?"

"Ben's team, of course," he said, even though no one had scored yet. "You should see this kid. He's a born pitcher."

"Look, he's up at bat."

Cade felt as involved as if he were holding the bat himself. He held his breath as Ben swung and missed. The second time he swung, the bat made a loud crack against the ball.

Cade rose to his feet as the ball flew into the outfield, bounced out of someone's mitt and rolled several feet before it was recovered. Jessica grabbed Cade's arm, jumping up and down as Ben made it past first, then to second, then tried for third.

By the time the ball was back under control, Jessica and Cade were exhausted. They sank back to their seats, only to leap up when the next batter hit the ball. They screamed as Ben slid into home plate, as if it were the winning point of the game rather than the first point scored.

"He's going to the pros," Jessica said. "I can see it now."

"He's amazing, isn't he?" Cade echoed.

"A regular prodigy," Jessica said.

Cade looked at her, and they both crumbled in laughter. "Is this the best entertainment around, or what?"

"It's the most fun I've had in ages," Jessica agreed. "Will we get to see any more games this week?"

"No, this is the only one while we're here." His face sobered a shade, until he caught Ben's eye and flashed him a thumbs-up. Ben returned it.

Jessica's smile was poignant as she caught Cade's eye. "You know, I think you look happier right this minute than I've ever seen you."

Cade reflected on that for a moment and realized that it was true. Sitting here, sharing such excitement with his son, had already set a record on his personal happiness scale. But having Jessica beside him, and seeing the delight she took in Ben, made it even better.

"Thanks for coming, Jess," he whispered. "I know how hard it must have been to get away."

Her eyes sparkled as the next batter got to the plate. "I wouldn't have missed it for all the fame in the free world."

And as the batter hit a grounder, and she got on her feet again, he knew that she meant every word.

DRIVING BACK to the suite after taking Ben home from the game, Cade thought back over the last few days. They'd taken Ben out for pizza after their 20-14 victory, and Cade had found Ben more talkative than he remembered since he was a little boy and they still lived together.

They were making progress as father and son, he thought, and now he felt as if there was hope for them. But in the back of his mind, he couldn't help wondering if they could maintain their new relationship after he and Jessica left Dallas. He told himself he'd have to cross that bridge when he came to it.

A deep melancholy fell over him as he realized that no matter how hard he tried, he wouldn't ever be a common fixture at Ben's games, or give him frequent pitching tips or take him for warm-ups at the batting cage. When Ben needed encouragement and looked out into the bleachers, Cade would not be there for him.

Life sucks, he thought. It dangles the promise of happiness in your face, then snatches it away every time. Feeling beaten and miserable, he got to the suite and found Jessica sitting on the couch in her robe with her feet tucked under her. She smiled up at him, and he realized that there was very little in life that her smile couldn't brighten. "Did you get Ben home all right?"

He tossed the keys to the rental van on the table, and sat down on a chair across from her. "Yeah. I thought you'd be asleep by now."

"Too wound up, I guess." She laid aside the magazine she'd been reading. "Some day, huh?"

He leaned his head back on the sofa and looked up at the ceiling. "Yeah. But I wouldn't have missed that game for the world."

"Neither would I," she said. "If I lived here I'd be at every game. That was such a blast. And it didn't hurt having the star of the team in our family."

Our family. The words felt good to Cade, and he realized they seemed right. But were they really a family, when he couldn't decide whether to think of her as sister or lover, and when Ben lived hundreds of miles from them?

"Are you okay?" she asked, noticing his melancholy and dropping her bare feet to the floor.

"Yeah, I'm fine. I just . . . keep thinking that I only have another couple of days with him." He forced a smile. "You know, I really appreciate all you've done with us this week. It took some of the pressure off, and helped a lot. But there must have been places you'd rather be."

"There's no place in the world I'd rather be," she said.

He met her eyes, almost startled, then said, "You know, you don't owe me that. I mean, I know you're carrying around some kind of guilt about the past, but...you're really not to blame. You don't have anything to make up to me."

Instantly he saw the pain in her eyes. "Is that what you think I'm doing?"

He shook his head, honestly unable to figure out what he believed. "If not, you're one of the sweetest women I've ever met. And I don't know how to deal with that."

Her eyes softened. "Maybe I'm really just the stupidest woman you've ever met."

He knew he shouldn't ask, but he couldn't stop himself. "Why?"

She dropped her gaze to her hands. "For getting the lines so blurred. For not being able to tell the difference between fraternal and romantic love."

Cade's heart jolted, and as her face colored slightly, he saw that the admission hadn't been easy for her. "You're my sister, Jess."

She shook her head. "No, Cade. I don't think I'd feel this way about a brother."

Dropping his head and bracing his elbows on his knees, he studied his feet. "There's something inherently wrong with that, Jess," he whispered. "And as much as I wish things were different, the world sees us as siblings. I can't let myself think of you as anything else."

THAT NIGHT, Jessica cried herself to sleep, wishing from her soul that she'd never said a word. She had ruined everything. Now it would be hard to relax around him, and looking him in the eye would cause instant discomfort.

As the hours turned into morning, she told herself that she would have to force herself to embark on the most difficult undertaking of her life. Raising the profits for JC would be a snap by comparison.

For the life of her, she'd have to convince herself, and Cade, that her feelings were only rooted in sisterly affection, and that the thought of anything else between them had absolutely been put to rest.

While Jessica struggled with her thoughts, Cade also lay awake, wondering why her confession of her feelings had shaken him so badly. What was he so afraid of?

He was afraid of getting that close to anyone, he thought. He was afraid of being that honest. He was afraid of waking up one day, only to find that she, too, had abandoned him to move on to better things.

He was afraid of knowing that foreign, unadulterated feeling of love, only to be left alone again.

It was his fault, he told himself, that she felt the way she did. He had given her confusingly mixed signals. And that was because he was confused himself.

There was nothing he could do, he thought, except change his feelings. He would start acting more like a brother, and maybe she'd *seem* more like a sister.

No more tender moments. No more close calls. No more honesty.

And somehow, he'd be able to let her go when the time came to move on.

THE OPPORTUNITY to act like a brother came the next day when Cade got back to the suite before Jessica did, and found a note asking him to take the company credit card and buy her the three dresses they were holding at an extravagant little boutique at the Galleria. The bill was a thousand dollars.

He was pacing and furious when she came in, looking like a million bucks, and asked if he'd gotten them.

"No, I haven't gotten them!" he said. "Are you nuts? Have you gone insane?"

"What's wrong?"

Cade stared at her for a moment. "You've got to be kidding. Jessica, we're not on this tour to spend money, but to save it. And if we have to offset everything we save by spending more on your clothes, we're not ever going to accomplish what we set out to do."

"But you've said yourself that we were doing great, that we would reach the goal! What difference would another thousand dollars make?"

"A thousand dollars for *three* dresses?" he shouted. "No, Jessica. You can't have them."

"Then what am I going to wear to all these interviews?" she returned.

He got up and stormed into her bedroom, and started pulling dresses out of her closet and throwing them on her bed. "How about this, and this, and this? How about any one of the two dozen dresses you brought?"

"But I'll be wearing the same things over and over, Cade! Besides, these are old. I haven't bought anything new since Daddy died."

"Good lord, Jessica," he said, feigning a gasp. "You don't mean to tell me that it's been a whole month since one of your shopping sprees!"

"Stop treating me like that, Cade. I have a high-profile job where I'm supposed to look my best, and you know it."

"You can look your best with what you've got."

She dropped down onto her bed, fighting the urge to fling herself at him to strangle him. "Cade, we can't skimp *all* the time! We've got to splurge every now and then, otherwise none of this is worthwhile!"

"It'll be worthwhile only if we reach our goal. And I'm going to see to it that we do."

"A thousand dollars is a drop in the bucket!"

He shook his head and glared at her. "Only a woman who's never had to look at price tags could make a stupid statement like that. In my book, a thousand dollars is a fortune. And twenty bucks can go a hell of a long way, too."

"Twenty bucks? Give me a break, Cade. Are you going to pinch twenties, too?"

"Jessica, what do you think twenty bucks can buy, besides imported fingernail polish and silk panty hose?"

She huffed out a breath. "Well, it doesn't look like I can stop you from telling me, Cade, so go ahead."

"Twenty bucks can buy several days' worth of groceries, a basic phone bill, four days' worth of electricity. It can buy a cheap pair of jeans that a kid could wear every day of the week if he had to."

It was the last straw, and she snapped. "When are you going to stop feeling so sorry for yourself? I am getting sick to death of hearing how slighted you were, and how poverty-stricken. Forget I ever asked. Just forget the whole thing!"

"Fine!" He stormed out of her room, and she threw the door shut behind him. Then she fell back onto her bed, hating him for getting to her from so many angles, but most of all, hating herself for letting him.

CHAPTER ELEVEN

"OUR VIEWERS WANT secrets. They want the low-down, Jessica. How do you really manage to look so beautiful all the time?"

Jessica settled her knowing eyes on Dave Forsythe, the Channel Five anchor whose interview in her suite had run on an hour too long already. The lights had long ago gotten uncomfortably hot, but Dave's crew didn't let him sweat. Every time they cut, someone rushed forward to powder him.

"Well, frankly, Dave, my secrets are all in our product line. Everything I use comes from Jessica Cosmetics. But if I don't get out from under those lights, you're going to see a meltdown, and I don't think it would be pretty. Besides, I have to be at our Fort Worth store in half an hour. You have enough footage, don't you?"

Dave smiled, flashing those perfect white teeth. "Is it that late? Time flies, doesn't it?"

"Yes, it does," she said.

When he didn't conclude the interview on camera, she assumed he planned to edit it later. Getting up, she stepped out of the lights. Finally he allowed the weary crew to turn off the cameras and start packing up.

"How about a glass of wine?" Dave asked, going to her mini-bar and withdrawing two small bottles.

She took them back before he could open them. "Can't... Cade would have a fit."

He chuckled. "Cade? Why?"

She wished she had just said no and not reacted so quickly. It wouldn't do to tell him Cade was such a cheapskate that he'd rather dehydrate than drink any of the high-priced items in the bar. "Well, it's best if I don't have alcohol on my breath when I make an appearance."

"Then how about tonight?"

She glanced up at him as he leaned an arm on the table and looked down at her. He was too handsome, too pretty—the kind of man her mother might have picked out for her. All morning, he'd flirted unabashedly with her, as if she had nothing better to do than make herself his prey. Instead she'd found him tedious and a little irritating. "What *about* tonight?" she asked demurely.

His cheeks dimpled when he grinned, and his teeth were either the first perfect teeth in the history of the universe, or they had all been perfectly capped. "Me, you, the moonlight, and a bottle of Dom Pérignon from the best restaurant in town?"

His grin became more seductive, and she noticed the looks passing among his crew members. They were used to this, she thought. He probably came on to every woman he interviewed.

"Well, I don't know. I'll be at the store until after five."

"No problem. I have to anchor the five-o'clock news, anyway. And if we're late, they'll hold our reservations. The maître d' knows me."

She sighed and thought of Cade's reaction to seeing Dave come to the door. It would serve him right after the things he'd said to her.

You're my sister, Jess... I can't let myself think of you as anything else.

And then he'd thrown that fit about the dresses, as if she needed his permission to stock her own closet. She'd allowed him too much control over her, but this was one area she would control herself.

"All right, Dave," she said. "I'd love to have dinner with you."

Dave wasn't surprised, and she realized with some consternation that he was rarely turned down for anything. "You'll have the night of your life," he told her suggestively.

But Jessica couldn't help wishing the night was already behind her.

IF CADE HAD EVER DOUBTED that his father had outlined the terms of the will to cast him in a living hell, he was to confirm it as fact over the next few days. Angry at the way he had spoken to her, Jessica had ignored him completely the next morning. That evening, as he and Ben had ordered a pizza and started to watch a ball game on television, she had fluttered in, changed clothes, freshened her makeup and hair, all without uttering a word to Cade.

When that guy from the news had come to the door to pick her up for the date she was obviously going on, the reality of it walloped Cade right between the eyes. Damn, he hated women, he thought.

But when he had taken Ben home, and midnight came and went, he wasn't so sure hate was what was keeping him awake. What it was, he refused to think about.

She came in at one o'clock, and when he heard the front door close, he lunged out of bed and dashed into the living room. "What the hell are you doing?"

She smiled a victorious smile that made him want to kill her. "Whatever do you mean?"

"Staying out so late! For all I knew, you could have been kidnapped, or raped, or..."

"Dave is not the kind of man who rapes women," she said. "He doesn't have to."

Nothing she said could have sent Cade further over the edge. "You have a reputation to keep up, Jessica! It matters what you do with your time!"

"My *free* time is none of your business, Cade! You may be able to tell me what and when I can buy, where I have to be during the day, and how I'm supposed to act when I'm in the public eye, but you will not ever tell me what I can do when I'm off work! I will date whomever I please, whenever I please, and if you can't handle it, then I guess you have a problem."

Cade's face mottled red as she took refuge in her room. He paused for a moment, staring at the door, then bursting forward, threw it open. "That's it, isn't it?" he shouted. "It's a control thing. You feel you've lost control, so you're flexing your muscles."

"Flexing my muscles?" she repeated, whirling around. "That's ludicrous. You're the one ambushing me when I come in from a date, and lambasting me with these ridiculous accusations about control!" She put her face close to Cade's, and through her teeth, said, "Get a grip, Hartman! You're losing it!"

Before she knew what was happening, he had taken her by the shoulders and his mouth was ravaging hers with brutal force, frightening but exciting her at the same time. She started to fight him, but suddenly she realized that she didn't want it to end... didn't want him to go back to his own room...didn't want to stop touching him. Daring to want more, she slid her hands up his bare chest and threw herself into his kiss.

Her compliance heightened his desire, and suddenly they were pulling at each other's clothes, touching in places they'd never touched before. It was hard to know who was pulling whom toward the bed, for the whirlwind of passion sweeping them in that direction was too blurred, too fast, too hot for fine distinctions.

With one tug, he had her skirt off, and he flung it on the floor beside her blouse. She was wearing thigh-high stockings rather than panty hose, and the effect sent him over the edge. Savagely he pulled off her panties, took her mouth again, and with one thrust, united with her.

Their union was the culmination of years of anger, days of restraint, hours of agony. It was the most intense hour of his life, the most satisfying, the most terrifying. And it was her most ecstatic experience as well, her most explosive, her most devastating.

The moment it was over, they lay still entangled, their breathing still hard, and Jessica felt a surge of emotion so deep that she didn't think she could ever reach the bottom of it.

There wasn't a thing to say, for the being was enough. She rolled into his embrace, lay her head on his chest, closed her eyes, and fell into the deepest sleep she'd had since they'd left home. Cade held her, stroking her hair, studying the peace on her face, and wondering why she didn't look tormented, ashamed, angry.

She should hate his guts. *He* should hate his guts.

He had just made love—the best he'd ever known—with his sister.

No, his mind cried out. She wasn't his sister. They had never lived together as children. There was no blood relation between them. Just a matter of an adoption paper. Introduced by a man they both knew, who Cade didn't even know well. They were man and woman...beautiful, gorgeous, classy woman...a woman who would be sought after by the wealthiest, most affluent men in any city they would travel to. Was it the forbidden aspect that had made her throw herself so completely into making love with him? Was that why he had wanted it so badly?

Or was there more? Something more, that he didn't dare admit?

And how could he ever think that she would have the strength to buck the social stigma of what they had done, and choose him over the dozens of other men she had to choose from?

He felt the emotion stinging his eyes, the massive weight of indecision on his chest, and the comfortable way she fit into his arms, so small, so soft, so trusting...

Ah, what would his father have said if he had seen them here, like this? That he had violated his precious little princess? That he had taken advantage of her vulnerability?

Funny, though, she hadn't seemed that vulnerable when she'd screamed for him to get a grip. And she had been right. He was losing it.

Carefully he turned her over, slipped out from under her, and went back to his own bed, wishing from the bottom of his soul that he knew how to confront this new aspect of their relationship in the morning. But it was too much.

And the man who was fearless, the man who thumbed his nose at the world, was scared to death to look into her eyes again.

CADE WAS GONE when Jessica's alarm clock went off. She sat up, groggy and confused, and looked around for him. "Cade?"

There was no answer, so she got up, pulled on her robe and walked through the suite. No one was there.

The euphoria and sense of well-being she had felt upon waking vanished, and she sank to the sofa, trying to put herself in his head. Why would he have left after making love so intensely? Was it going to be a subject they had to avoid, a moment they would pretend had never happened? Did he think he could disappear before she woke, and forget how perfectly they had melded the night before?

Why would he want to forget?

She closed her eyes as tears seeped through her lashes, and told herself that she didn't want to forget, for it was the most right she'd felt since meeting him again after her father died. She didn't want to pretend that it wasn't the best night of her life, or that she wasn't falling in love with him.

She wiped her tears and told herself that, if it was in her power, she would not let him off the hook for this. He was going to confront his feelings for her, just as she had confronted hers for him.

And somehow, together, they would work out this...whatever it was...that had ignited between them.

THOUGH CADE'S and Jessica's paths did not cross that day—due to careful calculation on Cade's part—Cade wasn't able to banish thoughts of the night before from his mind. The smell of Jessica's hair seemed to have penetrated his skin so that he sensed it at each turn, and it made him close his eyes and experience again the sensation of his fingertips on her skin, the soft, firm muscles of her thighs against his hips, the feel of her nails scratching gently through the hair on his chest...

It was driving him crazy, yet it was wrong. Dead wrong. The guilt gnawed at him almost as much as the desire did, and he didn't know which would win out. But he knew which should.

By the time he'd finished with his changes to the final store in the Dallas area, it was almost dark, and Cade was exhausted. He wondered how Jessica's appearance across town had gone that day. He hadn't gone to see, as he'd done on each of her others. He wondered what she was thinking about him.

When he picked Ben up for their final night together—he and Jessica were moving on to Houston the next day—he noticed a change in Ben's attitude. It seemed that all the headway he'd made with his son in the past few days had been lost, and once again they were strangers.

"So how was your day?"

"Fine."

"Did you hear from your mother?"

"Yeah."

"When's she coming home?"

"Sunday."

"Are you looking forward to seeing her?"

"Not especially."

Again, there was silence as Cade drove his van through town, aimlessly searching for a place to eat that might bring the smile back to his son's eyes.

"You know, you can come and join me anytime you want to this summer. I'll be at a different place every couple of weeks, and I'll have to work like a bandit every day, but I want you to know the invitation is always open."

Ben didn't answer, so finally Cade gave up trying to make conversation and pulled into a hamburger place. They ate in relative silence, broken by Cade's efforts to talk about baseball, school, the company and Ben's mother. When they had almost finished eating, Cade realized they had no place else to go but back to the hotel where they'd been spending all their time. But tonight was different. Tonight, he wasn't ready to face Jessica. Not in front of Ben.

"How about a movie?" he asked Ben finally. "That Schwarzenegger movie sounds pretty good."

"I've seen it."

"Oh." He shrugged. "Well, what haven't you seen?"

Ben thought for a moment. "I've seen just about everything. I go to a lot of movies."

"By yourself?"

"Usually."

The loneliness in that fact struck him, and for a moment, he was sorry that Bridgit hadn't been in town this week. He would have liked to take her out for coffee and lambaste her about ignoring their child. But he didn't suppose he could boast of much better parenting efforts than hers.

"Did you like the Schwarzenegger movie?"

"Yeah, it was good."

"Want to see it again?"

Ben shrugged. "Sure, I guess."

The movie killed two hours, and when it was over, Cade looked at his watch. "I hate to say this, buddy, but I probably ought to go ahead and take you home. Jessica and I have to catch a plane pretty early in the morning. Okay?"

"Fine."

They were quiet for a while as they drove through town to the mansion where his son lived, and suddenly Cade was struck with the same old reality, the same old twang of pain he felt each time he had to say goodbye to his son, with no guarantee of when he might see him again. It was too debilitating—the knowledge that he had no part in his life, that he was nothing more than a visitor who came and went. He didn't want to think that Ben was once again indifferent to him. It had helped, the past few days, to think that they were becoming friends. If he had to leave him, he at least wanted to take that hope with him.

"Ben?" he asked as they reached his street. "Are we okay? I mean, I'm sensing something here tonight. I don't know what it is, but—"

"Everything's fine."

He pulled into the gates of the estate and let his engine idle as he regarded his son. "Hey, Ben?" he asked, stopping his son from making a quick exit from the van. "Thanks for hanging out with your old man this week. It did me a lot of good."

"Yeah," Ben said without looking at him. "Same here."

"I'll call you every few days, okay?"

Ben made a face that indicated he'd heard that before and didn't put much stock in it.

"And you have my itinerary. You can reach me anytime. You know that."

"Yeah." Ben sat there for an awkward moment, then finally put his hand on the door and opened it. "Well, I gotta go."

Cade stopped him and pulled him close, embracing him in a clumsy hug. The boy seemed uncomfortable with the whole idea, and finally Cade let him go. "Take care, okay, kid?"

"Yeah," Ben said. "You, too."

He was out of the van and running up the front steps to his house before Cade could tell him he loved him. Cade sat still for a moment, watched him get safely inside, and blotted at the mist in the corner of his eye. It was probably just as well, he thought, shifting his car into drive and heading back to the gates. Ben didn't seem in the mood to hear that tonight. And Cade was quite sure his son wouldn't have been comfortable saying it back.

Depressed and feeling more lonely than he'd felt since his father died, Cade headed for the hotel bar and stayed there until he was sure that Jessica had gone to bed.

JESSICA DIDN'T GET AWAY from the store where she'd signed autographs until the mall closed that night, and wearily she went back to the hotel, anxious to confront Cade about avoiding her all day. But Cade wasn't there.

She packed for their departure tomorrow, ordered room service and waited for him to come home. But when midnight came and went, she realized that she couldn't wait up any longer and went to bed.

She was sound asleep by the time he came in.

When she woke up the next morning, she showered and dressed, then came out of her room to see if he was stirring. He was drinking a cup of coffee and talking on the phone to JC's public relations department. A knock on the door startled her, and Jessica answered it. It was the bell captain, come to take their luggage down. She pointed to the ones in her room, then to Cade's, all the while waiting for the moment he would hang up.

The bell captain was gone when Cade set the phone back down. "Good morning," he said, hopping up from the couch and stuffing papers into his briefcase. "We ought to get on down. The plane leaves in a little over an hour."

"No," she said, blocking him. "We have to talk first."

He rolled his eyes, something that set her off more than anything else he'd ever done. "Can't it wait? We'll have plenty of time on the plane."

"You avoided me all day yesterday, Cade. I woke up and you were gone, and now we can't even talk about what happened?"

She could see the struggle on Cade's face as he finally looked into her eyes. "It was wrong, Jess. You're my sister."

"Not by blood."

"It doesn't matter," he said. "We can't let that happen again."

"What if we want it to?"

He turned away, raked his hand through his hair and expelled a breath that revealed just how much he'd been holding in. "Oh, God, Jess. I don't know what came over us."

"I wasn't drunk. Were you?"

"No," he said, "but..."

"I had my faculties about me. I knew what I was doing. Did you?"

"Well, yes, but I—"

"Then why are you acting like it was something that sneaked up on us and ambushed us? Why are you treating me like I've led you to hell?"

"Because it's wrong! That's all there is to it."

"You've never thought of me as a sister," Jessica shouted. "And as much as I've wanted to, I couldn't ever quite feel that you were my brother. You didn't act like it, and you didn't want it. Now, if you've lost interest in me after we made love, fine. Say it. But don't keep implying that we've committed some kind of incestuous crime. It doesn't fly, Cade."

"It does for me. And it will for anyone else who finds out."

"Since when have you cared what anybody else thinks?"

His face reddened as he started to answer, but the phone rang, and for a moment they stood staring at each other, faced-off and ready for the duel of their lives. But finally Cade broke his gaze and picked up the phone. "Hello? Yes, thank you."

He turned back to her. "The cab is here. We have to go."

She gritted her teeth and grabbed her carry-on bag. "This isn't over, Cade," she said as tears glistened in the corners of her eyes. "You'll have to come up with something better."

He went to the door and held it open for her. "Come on, Jess," he said in a quiet voice. "Let's go to Houston."

JESSICA WASN'T FOOLED when Cade pretended to be asleep before they were even off the ground. He was avoiding her, and as much as she wanted to shake him awake and insist on finishing their conversation, she didn't want the passengers around them to hear any of it.

She tried not to cry as it hit her that he might have been turned off by her passion. Maybe she'd been too aggressive. Maybe he'd noticed her lack of experience. Maybe he wished he'd just kept the fantasy in his head where it belonged.

Whatever it was, it hurt, and she spent the better part of the trip blotting the corners of her eyes with a handkerchief and trying not to sniff.

He didn't wake until the plane was back on the ground. By then, she was in her "to hell with him" mode, just daring him to bring it up, and swearing to herself that she'd said all on the subject she was going to say.

They didn't speak all the way to the hotel, and when they checked in, she waited in the lobby as he got the keys to their suite. When he came back, he handed her a key. "You're in 1420. I'm in 814."

"What?" she asked. "I thought you said we needed to stay together. To save money and all that."

He waited for the bellboy to take their luggage, then glanced back at her. "I thought maybe we needed to make an exception in this case."

"I see."

"It's just not a good idea, Jess. We probably shouldn't tempt fate any more than we have to, under the circumstances."

Heat scaled her cheeks. "What *circumstances* would you be referring to?" she asked, wanting desperately for him to say it.

"What happened between us was an accident, okay, Jess? That's all. Just a bad mistake. Even apart from the brother-sister thing, which in itself is a biggie, we're from two different worlds. Different leagues."

Tears sprang to her eyes unexpectedly. "What are you talking about? I've seen the women you date, Cade. They aren't exactly bikers."

"But I've never been serious about them. I couldn't be."

She stared at him with pain on her face, and a longing so great that she had to struggle with the urge to reach out for him. "Whatever you're trying to say, Cade, just do us both a favor and say it."

"All right, Jess," he said. "I just don't feel that way about you."

Her heart seemed to implode in her chest, threatening to suck her in. Blinking back her tears, she said, "I see. Then it was all just sex, right? Just a few minutes of madness?"

He couldn't take his lie that far, so he looked away.

"Well," she said, bending over to pick up her carry-on bag and slipping the strap over her shoulder. "That was all it was for me, too. You were a nice diversion after a hard day's work, and I was already wound up after my date."

She could see that the words struck home, and he didn't reply. "I'll see you later, Cade," she said.

He started to stop her and ask her about dinner, but something told him not to. Instead he let her go, and waited until she was on the elevator before making his way to his own room.

CHAPTER TWELVE

THE NEXT FOUR WEEKS were the most trying of Jessica's life. It took a Herculean effort to feign indifference to Cade, and to go out of her way to avoid him. They worked together when necessary, met each evening for a quick, cheap dinner and an update of what was going on, then went their separate ways. The days sped by, but the nights, lonely and packed with the stress of their standoff, crept along at a snail's pace.

Jessica had always thought of herself as strong, but now she realized she'd never been tested as she was being tested here. Her father's scheme was stressful enough—she had to spend every day with a beauty-pageant smile on her face, looking perky and upbeat and glamorous. But it was the trials Cade put her through that truly tried her strength and sapped her of the exuberance so vital to her job.

Yes, she was strong, she told herself as she sat in front of her mirror, applying her makeup for the third time that day, and trying not to think about the date who was on his way to pick her up. He was another news anchor in Phoenix, who had interviewed her that afternoon. Cade had been in on the interview, as well, and when Brick Sawyer—incredibly, that was not a stage name—had asked to take her to dinner, she'd seen the guarded look on Cade's face and had no choice but to accept. The last thing she wanted was for him to think she was pining for him.

Her hand froze as she brushed on her mascara, and she remembered that the night they made love had been after her date with Dave. Jealousy had made him rabid, and he had worked himself into a rage by the time she'd gotten home. That hadn't been brotherly protection, she told herself. And there had been nothing brotherly about the way he had made love to her.

Her eyes filled with frustrated tears, but she blinked them back and forced herself to finish applying her makeup. She had a date with a handsome, well-to-do man who *wasn't* her brother. There were women all over Phoenix who'd kill for a date with Brick Sawyer. He'd practically said so himself.

Wearily she dropped the mascara wand and looked through her bedroom door, across the plush sitting area, to the door that led to Cade's adjoining room—a concession he had found necessary, since they needed to be as close together as possible while still maintaining separate quarters. She wondered if he was home yet... what his plans were for the evening. And as she tore her eyes away and forced herself to finish getting ready, she wondered if life had gotten as lonely—and complicated—for him as it had for her.

Brick showed up just after seven, overflowing with compliments. Before they went out he popped a video of her interview in the VCR for them to watch together. As the interview played, Brick dwelt on the cuts to himself, the cleverness of his questions, the humor with which he reacted to Cade's comments.

Jessica was only interested in Cade's part in the interview—the easy, casual way he'd leaned back in his chair with an ankle over his knee, the tie that was perpetually loose at his throat, as though it was a reluctant concession to his white-collar image, and the shadow of stubble already darkening his jaw. He radiated virility and restrained passion, and for a moment, she wanted to find a graceful way out of her date and feign some reason for spending the evening with Cade instead. But it wasn't going to happen, she thought. She had to go on with her own agenda, and she supposed there were worse ways to spend the evening.

When they were at last ready to go to dinner, they stopped downstairs in the bar, where Brick was ogled by most of the locals there.

Jessica realized as she sipped her wine that Brick was the kind of man who fed on adulation, who encouraged it at every opportunity. She couldn't really say she blamed him, however. He was pretty. Too pretty. Just like Dave.

But not like Cade, who had a rugged, grudging handsomeness, and hardly seemed to notice when he turned women's heads.

"You know, Jessica," Brick said, glancing intimately from her to the mirror behind her head. "We make quite a couple. We're both blondes, we both have green eyes, and we both command a lot of attention when we enter a room."

She thought for a moment about how to respond to that. Thank-you didn't seem appropriate, so she only brought the wine back to her lips. Suddenly she felt very tired, and her temples were starting to ache.

"I think we're a *likely* pair," he went on. He found a hair out of place in his reflection and smoothed it back with his freshly manicured hand. "You own a company and are known around the world as *the* Jessica Hartman, and I'm climbing fast in my field. We complement each other, don't you think?"

She glanced around the room, wishing for a graceful way to escape spending the next few hours with this man, when she spotted Cade walking in with a redhead who looked remarkably like Julia Roberts. Except she was smaller. And thinner.

From deep within her, Jessica managed to find her world-weary smile, and touching Brick's arm, she let out a soft laugh, as if responding to his last line. He seemed pleased, though she didn't have a clue what he'd been talking about.

"No, really, I mean it," he chuckled. "I could take some vacation time, and meet you in Oregon..."

It was then that Cade spotted her, and she saw him hesitate, as if trying to decide whether to leave or stay. After a moment, he led his date to Jessica's table.

"Well, look who's here," Jessica said, her smile more radiant than ever.

Brick came to his feet and shook Cade's hand. His loud greeting drew every eye in the bar. Cade was low-key, as usual, wearing his James Dean aura like a leather coat over his three-piece suit. "Jessica, Brick, I'd like you to meet Kathryn. She's the cosmetics buyer for the Lacy's Department Stores. We're talking about putting a line of Jessica Cosmetics in her stores."

Jessica blanched. "It's nice to meet you, Kathryn. But we've always had our own stores for our products."

"How well I know that," Kathryn said. "But I'm trying to convince your brother that it would enhance profits quite a bit if you sold them in our stores as well. The overhead would be lower, and we get quite a bit more traffic through our stores..."

"Oh, I don't know about that," Jessica countered, her voice growing decisively colder. "Besides, your stores are usually located in malls where we already have stores. It would be counterproductive to have you compete with us that way."

She could have sworn Cade rolled his eyes, dismissing her misgivings. "Those are all things that need to be worked out, Jessica."

For a moment the tension in the air was palpable, and Jessica forced her smile again. "Well, we'd ask you to join us, but we have reservations. Don't we, Brick?"

Brick glanced in the mirror again. "Sure do. You're welcome to join us at Pointe of View, though. Probably wouldn't be too hard to change a table for two to a table for four."

"That's all right," Cade said, fixing his eyes on Jessica's. "We wouldn't want to barge in on you like that. Besides, we have our own reservations somewhere else."

"Fine." Her smile grew thinner the longer they faced off. "Are you ready, Brick?"

She took Brick's arm and they started away.

"Jess," Cade called after her. She turned back and confronted the brooding mechanic in him. "Go easy on the wine."

Her face reddened, and she didn't respond as they left the bar.

CADE DIDN'T REALIZE how long he'd stared after them as they left, but finally Kathryn shook his arm, pulling him out of his reverie. "Are you going to buy me a drink, Cade?"

"Of course." He smiled and offered her the chair that Brick had occupied before, and he slipped into Jessica's. It was still warm, and her scent lingered like a wounded spirit. But somehow he was the one who felt wounded.

He signaled the waitress, ordered their drinks, then glanced back to the door.

"Your sister's very beautiful, in a cold sort of way."

Cade turned to her, fixing her with his eyes. "Cold? How do you mean?"

"I mean, she has sort of a chilling presence. Do the two of you get along?"

He waited as the waitress brought their drinks, then took a sustaining sip of his before answering her question. "Of course we get along. Why wouldn't we?"

"Well, you know. Sibling rivalry, that kind of thing."

"We're adults, Kathryn. Not jealous kids."

"I don't know," she said. "I thought I detected a little note of tension."

"That wasn't about sibling rivalry," he said. "Or sibling anything. The truth is, we're not really sister and brother. I was adopted."

"Oh." She sat up straighter. "How interesting. I had no idea. I mean, I knew you were just half brother and sister, but... Well, that explains it."

"Explains what?" He was growing annoyed, and he regretted not following his instinct to rent a movie tonight and stay in his room. But he had known that he'd go nuts listening for Jessica to come home from her date with that moron.

"The tension. She's probably angry for having to share her inheritance with you."

He fought the urge to tell her that his inheritance was none of her business, but he didn't want to blow the deal they were discussing, just in case he decided it was a good move to make. "Jessica is the one who talked me into coming to work for Jessica Cosmetics, Kathryn. And despite the impression you have of her, she's a very warm, sweet person. Not at all like you seem to think."

"I'm sorry, Cade," she said, taken aback. "I didn't mean anything by it."

His jaw popped as he set his elbows on the table. "She's been through a grueling few weeks, just as I have. And all through that, she's been nothing but a trooper."

"All right," Kathryn said, glancing at the people at the table next to them who were beginning to stare. "I get the message."

"Good," he said. He gulped down the rest of his drink and sighed. "And as for what she said about competing with our own stores, I'm afraid she's right. The more common we make our product line, the less mystique it will have, and the less money we're likely to make. Truth is, Kathryn, I think we'll just keep doing things this way for a while."

Kathryn looked crestfallen. "Well, does this mean you're not taking me to dinner?"

His heart wasn't in it. All he wanted was to go back to his room, phone Ben, sleep for a while and be ready to greet Jessica when she got back. But he had asked Kathryn to dinner, and he wasn't one to renege.

"Of course I'm taking you to dinner. Where do you want to go?" He named five restaurants he'd picked out of the phone book, all of them relatively inexpensive. After a few moments of disappointed indecisiveness, she chose.

And as they left the bar and he thought where Brick and Jessica were dining that night—one of the most expensive restaurants in the Phoenix area—he realized, once again, how wrong they would be for each other. He was a beans and potatoes kind of man, and she was caviar.

So why couldn't he get her out of his mind, and why did he think he would go mad thinking about her with that ego-tripper tonight?

IT STILL WASN'T too late to call Ben when Cade got in that night, so he dialed the number, tossed his tie over a chair and began unbuttoning his shirt as he held the receiver with his shoulder.

It was Bridgit who answered. "Hello."

He ground his teeth at the sound of her voice. "May I speak to Ben?" His tone bordered on hostility.

He could almost see her smug smile. "He's in bed, Cade. Sorry."

"It's only eleven, and it's a weekend, Bridgit. Would you check and make sure?"

"Call him back tomorrow," she said. "I'm having a dinner party, and my guests are still here. I don't have time for this."

She hung up the phone before he could say anything else. Uttering a word he had associated with her many times over the past few years, he slammed the phone down. He lay back on his bed, hands behind his head, and stared at the ceiling, dreaming of being a father who was actually there for his son, a father who knew the intimate details of his child's life, the names of his friends, the things that made him laugh...

It wasn't going to happen with Ben, and he doubted he'd ever have the chance to do it right again. There wasn't a woman alive he could trust enough to put himself through that kind of abandonment or betrayal.

But then a voice inside his head said, *Jessica...you trust her.* He forced himself to ignore that voice.

He heard the sound of a door closing in her suite, and he sat up. For a moment he listened, every muscle in his body rigid, waiting for the sounds of voices. When he heard nothing, he got up and went to his front door, cracked it open and saw Brick in the hallway waiting for the elevator.

Jessica was alone.

Closing his front door as quietly as possible, he eyed the door that joined his room to her suite, and wondered why she'd come in so early. For a moment he thought of knocking, of asking her himself, but it was too obvious, too telling. She couldn't know that she had full possession of his mind these days, or that he'd cut his own date short to be here when she came in.

He touched the door, as if it could give him some indication of what she was feeling, but then backed away and slid his hands into his pockets.

This was crazy, he told himself. How had he gotten here, to the point where he was wearing three-piece suits for a cosmetics company and fantasizing about his sister? It had to stop.

But he knew it wasn't going to stop tonight.

He had to see her before he could rest, he thought. Just for a moment. Then he could sleep through the night. Then he'd feel better.

He opened his side of the door, then, raising his hand to lean on the casing, he knocked lightly on hers.

She opened it almost instantly, and for a moment took in the sight of his indolent stance as if she weren't sure if he wanted to pick a fight or apologize for his antagonism in the bar.

"I didn't expect you to be home," she said, stepping back and inviting him in.

He pushed off from the casing and went in, and felt her eyes sweeping to the hair on his chest at the vee of his T-shirt. She was still in the dress she'd worn on her date, but her feet were bare and she had let her hair down. It fell in full, sexy billows around her face, more exciting and sensual than he had been prepared for. God, she was so beautiful, he thought, turning away.

"You're kind of early, yourself."

"I was dead. It's been an excruciating week." While she spoke, she went to a small refrigerator in her wet bar and pulled out a bottle of Chablis. "I probably shouldn't mention this, after your crack in the bar about the wine, but one of the disc jockeys at the radio station where I went this morning gave me this as thanks for the interview. I plan to have a glass. Just one. Do you want some?"

He considered the grudging offer. "Maybe one glass." He took the bottle from her hands, rummaged through the drawer until he found a corkscrew. "I'm sorry about that remark. I was out of line. Tell me," he said in a grunt as he worked the cork out. "Is Brick as obnoxious as he seems?"

She shrugged. "He's a little narcissistic, but I wouldn't call him obnoxious."

"Right." The cork popped out, and he poured some wine into the glasses she'd gotten out. The fact that she hadn't defended him made him relax, and he went to the couch and sank down. "Listen, about my deal with Kathryn... you know, to market our product in Lacy's... I pretty much came to the same conclusion you did."

"Good. I was worried."

"I know you were."

She studied her glass for a moment, then ambled across the floor to sit down beside him. "At least it got you a few hours in a beautiful woman's company. That couldn't have been so bad."

He smiled. "Waste of time, really."

"Oh? She wouldn't sleep with you, huh?"

He grinned and shot her a look. "I didn't notice Brick hanging around when you answered the door."

She smiled. "I sent him on his way. I told you, I was tired."

"Brick," he scoffed. "Where'd he get a name like that, anyway?"

"Football," she said. "He played halfback, and he claims to have blocked like a brick wall." She grinned. "Hence the name."

"From football to journalism. Wonderful."

"Hey, don't make fun. He's a great interviewer. That is, if you get rid of all the mirrors in the room first. He does get a little distracted."

In spite of their efforts not to, they both laughed, and their laughter played itself out in soft sighs. The more relaxed he felt with her, the less he needed his facade. Finally he leaned his head back on the couch.

"I tried to call Ben tonight," he said. "Bridgit wouldn't let me talk to him. She was having some kind of party and didn't want to be bothered."

"Call back!" she said, as indignant as he had been when he'd hung up. "Demand to talk to him. Bug her to death, and she'll cave."

"No." He sat up and leaned his elbows on his knees. Rubbing his eyes, he said, "Truth is, he probably wouldn't have anything to say, anyway. Our phone conversations are pretty tough."

"It doesn't matter," she said, her voice softening. "You have to try, anyway. It's *not* trying that'll hurt him."

He stared at his empty glass for a moment. "Maybe. I'll try in the morning." For a moment, he sat beside her, totally comfortable, and he realized that he'd never met another woman who could make him feel so completely at peace at the same time that she drove him out of his mind. Her scent drew him with a magic summons such as he had never experienced before, teasing him, tempting him.

When their eyes met, he feared he might lose control and forget all the reasons that this couldn't work.

"You're easy to talk to, you know that?" he asked.

He wished she didn't look so sexy when she smiled.

"And not too bad to look at, either," he added.

Her smile faded, and her lips parted slightly.

He swallowed and willed his heart to pace itself. That look was there in her eyes, that look of longing, and he knew that it wasn't the wine. It was the woman. The one woman on the face of the earth whom he had to avoid.

Forcing himself to break the spell, he got up. "Thanks for the wine," he said. "I think I can sleep now."

She stood up, and he marveled at how small she seemed without her heels. Small enough to scoop up in his arms. "If you can't sleep, just knock," she whispered. "I'll be here."

Her words filled him with a warmth that he didn't want to embrace, and for a moment he looked at her, wondering if she meant she would be there to talk, or to repeat a mistake that he couldn't wipe from his memory. "Yeah," he said. "You, too."

But as he left, he knew that she wouldn't knock. His rejection had been too scathing, too humiliating. The ball was in his court, but he wasn't willing to play it.

JESSICA LAY AWAKE that night, alone in her huge suite where Brick had interviewed her that day and where others like him had showered her with attention and questions, and admitted she would give it all up for one more night with Cade.

I just don't feel that way about you.

Why didn't his words ring true to her, when he'd done nothing but prove them over the past few weeks?

Tears came to her eyes, and she told herself she was kidding herself. That look in his eye was pity, since he knew he'd hurt her. And the way he looked at her across rooms when he thought she wasn't looking...maybe it was brotherly pride. Then she reminded herself there was nothing brotherly about the way he'd made love to her.

She got up, went to the mini-bar and picked up the glass he'd drunk from earlier. Quietly she filled it with water, brought it to her lips and squeezed her eyes shut against the tears. Damn it, how could she have done such a stupid thing? How could she have fallen in love with Cade Hartman?

She went to their common door, laid her head against it and tried to determine if he was sleeping. No sound came through. She touched the knob, then let it go. She raised her hand to knock, but thought better of it.

He couldn't have been any plainer about his feelings, and yet...that night when they'd made love, he'd been consumed with jealousy over her date. He'd waited up, furious, anxious, and his anger had exploded into passion so fierce it could not have been misinterpreted. And tonight, when he'd come into her suite...hadn't he looked at her with that same longing she saw in her own eyes each time she confronted her reflection in the mirror?

Still, he didn't want her. Call it moral fortitude, or just plain indifference. It all came out the same.

She went to the couch and turned on the television in the dark, flipped to an old Humphrey Bogart movie and wiped away the tears that were beginning to fall.

She was lonely. And loneliness made her weak. It made her cower from life instead of facing it head-on. It took the joy out of the simplest things. Made difficult those things that should have been easy.

Like sleeping.

She turned off the television and decided to return to bed, when she heard an infinitesimal knocking on the door that joined their suites.

Not certain she'd heard it at all, she got up and went to the door. In a moment, the soft knock came again.

Her heart stumbled as she opened it.

Cade stood before her, leaning against the casing in nothing but a pair of shorts, his hair mussed and his eyes tired.

"Cade?" she whispered.

"I couldn't sleep," he said. "And I thought I heard your television."

"I'm sorry. Was it keeping you awake?"

"No, that wasn't it."

For a moment they stood staring at each other, and she became painfully aware of how exposed she was in the gown that laced over her breasts and clung all the way down her body until it reached the floor. As his eyes swept the length of her, she could see he was aware of the same thing.

When he spoke, it was in a broken whisper. "God, Jess, you're so beautiful."

Swallowing, she stepped back. "Don't, Cade."

"Don't what?" he asked. "Don't watch you when you're out with other men? Don't think all day about the way you smell? Don't have dreams and fantasies that would make you blush?"

She lifted her chin, realizing that, suddenly, the power was hers. "You don't feel that way about me."

He frowned, as if the reality tormented him. "Jess, you didn't buy that when I fed it to you the first time."

"You've spent a lot of time trying to convince me."

"I've spent a lot of time trying to convince myself," he said. "And look where I am."

He reached out, hooked a finger beneath her chin, and urged her closer until his lips touched hers. When she didn't resist, he pulled her against him, one hand sliding down her back while his other tangled in her hair.

The kiss was wild, euphoric, arousing to the point of madness, but after a moment, Jessica broke free and pressed her palms on his bare chest. "No more, Cade," she whispered. "Not tonight."

"Why?"

"Because I don't want to wake up tomorrow and find you gone and unable to look me in the eye. And

I don't want to think we used each other because we were lonely."

Cade slid his hand down her bare arm, then back up to the spaghetti strap over her shoulder. "If I'm lonely, Jess, it's because of you."

"It doesn't have to be all or nothing." Her voice trembled as her fingers tingled over the soft hair curling across his chest. "Either bitter enemies afraid to look at each other, or lovers who can't keep their hands to themselves. We could try being friends."

"I don't want to be your friend."

And I don't want to be yours, her mind cried. "We have to learn to be friends, Cade, before we could ever trust each other to be lovers."

She felt his heart racing against her hands, his nipple hardening into a pebble. His breathing came more heavily than it had since the first time they'd made love. And she knew that if he kissed her one more time, all her ramblings would go out the window and she would be his despite the consequences.

His mouth came down, but instead of touching her lips, it went to her neck. He nuzzled it, breathing in her scent, and she arched her neck back and sighed with tormented agony. Then, as if he'd found sustenance for a long, lonely journey, he let her go. "You're right."

She didn't want to be right, and she didn't want him to agree with her. She wanted an argument. But he was taking her at her word.

"I'm sorry, Jess. I shouldn't have come over."

"Yes, you should have," she said, tears crowding

her eyes. She hoped it was too dark for him to see them. "I'm glad you did. Really glad."

"Yeah?" he whispered.

"Yeah."

For a moment, neither of them moved, and she wasn't sure if the pounding in her ears was her own heart or his. His sigh was labored as he stepped backward into his room. "Well, I guess I'll see you in the morning," he murmured.

"Cade?"

He stopped before closing the door.

"Could we have breakfast together tomorrow? I'd really like that. However early you say."

He smiled. "How about seven?"

"Okay," she whispered. "I'll see you then. Good night."

"Good night."

She watched the door close and pressed her hand against it, as if she could capture his presence in the wood. And this time, when she went to bed, she felt more at peace. Cade wanted her, too. Maybe there was hope after all.

CHAPTER THIRTEEN

THERE WAS NOTHING Cade hated more than wasted time, but that was exactly what the next day became. His concentration level was at zero, and he kept forgetting what he was working on and losing his train of thought. He should never have had breakfast with Jessica.

It was all going to be innocent enough—just a quick bite and a moment to warm himself in her smile before they went their separate ways. But the moment he'd seen her—dressed in those spiked heels and that short skirt that revealed too much of her leg...the moment he'd looked into those bright green eyes...he knew the rest of the day was shot.

There was something important going on, and for the life of him, he didn't want to confront it.

Were they paving the way to be lovers, or just trying to forge a friendship? Whatever it was, he was certain this wasn't how it felt to be a brother.

When he finally gave up trying to accomplish anything, he drove back to the hotel, hoping Jessica would be home and not have plans for the evening, and hurried in from the parking garage in the basement. He cut quickly across the lobby to the front desk to check his messages.

"There's someone waiting for you, Mr. Hartman," the desk clerk told him. "We aren't authorized to give out room numbers, but I told him I'd let you know when you came in."

Cade frowned. "I didn't have any appointments scheduled."

"No, sir, I don't think it's an appointment. He said he was your son."

"Ben?" Cade swung around, scanning the people in the lobby, and the woman pointed to the divan next to a water fountain. His son sat motionless with his arms crossed, staring pensively into the fountain.

Cade launched across the lobby, and Ben looked up as he approached him. Joy mixed with confusion on Cade's face, and he pulled Ben up into a bear hug. "Ben, what are you doing here? Why didn't you tell me you were coming?"

"Just decided," Ben said awkwardly, stepping back. "I hope it's okay."

"Well, sure it's okay. I just wish you had let me know. I could have picked you up at the airport. Did your mother and Richard bring you?"

"Nope." He followed Cade toward the elevator, speaking in a matter-of-fact monotone. "Mom left for Greece this morning. I came alone."

"But...I talked to her just last night. She didn't tell me you were coming. All she said was to call you back today."

Ben turned around, adjusting the bag's strap on his shoulder. "Why didn't she call me to the phone?"

"She said you were asleep," he said. "She was busy, and it was late." He narrowed his eyes on his son. "Ben, she did know you were coming, didn't she?"

Ben shrugged and turned away, and started toward the elevator again. "I don't know. I might not have told her."

Cade tried to rein in his reaction, but it was impossible to hide his surprise. "Who *did* you tell?"

"You, okay?" the boy returned belligerently. "I'm telling you right now. I'm here, but if it's a problem, I can leave."

"No...no." He mussed his son's hair, then put his arm around him and squeezed him again. "No, let's not look a gift horse in the mouth. Let's go up, and you can tell me about your trip."

"Not much to tell," Ben said, hoisting the suitcase strap over his other shoulder.

"Here, let me get that."

"I've got it," Ben said as the elevator doors opened. Without waiting for his father, he stepped on. And as Cade followed, he told himself he shouldn't give the boy a hard time about coming all this way to find him. Ben was here, and that was all that mattered.

JESSICA HURRIED BACK to the hotel as soon as she finished her final interview of the day, anxious to see Cade and test the signals he'd given her last night and this morning. He'd invaded her thoughts all day long, making her stammer through things she'd said a thousand times, making her forget where the stories she told the reporters were headed. And then, when she'd autographed samples, she'd had to ask the customers' names repeatedly. She'd bungled so many tags that they'd had to open a new box.

What had it meant when he'd knocked on her door for the second time last night? And that kiss, which rivaled any other kiss she'd ever had in her life...what did it reveal about Cade's feelings?

She had been strong last night, and she was proud of that. But then she'd lain awake, anticipating the morning, knowing that if he kissed her today, if he made the slightest suggestion of intimacy with her, she would be nothing but mush in his hands.

Breakfast had been sweet but short, and then they had gone their separate ways, promising to meet for dinner that night. She had immediately canceled her date with Brick, who seemed flabbergasted that she would do such a thing. And now she couldn't wait to see Cade.

The door between her suite and his room was open when she went in, and she dropped her purse and key and went toward it. "Hello? Cade?"

"Come in, Jess."

Jessica's eyes instantly lighted up at the sound of his voice. Trying not to look so anxious, she stepped into his room. Cade and Ben sat across the table from each other, engaged in a game of cards.

"Ben!" she shouted. "What are you doing here?"

He smiled. "Just thought I'd drop by."

"In Phoenix? Don't tell me. You were in the neighborhood..."

Cade got up. "This kid just decided to hop on an airplane and fly over today. Can you beat that?" He walked toward her, and his eyes closed slowly as he caught her scent. When they opened again, they seemed to smile as they met hers. "How did it go today?"

"Great," she lied. "We set a sales record in the store. Don't know if we should credit your work there the other day, or mine today."

"Maybe a little of both," he said. He turned back to Ben. "I'll be real surprised if we don't reach our goal."

Ben shrugged and looked down at his cards again. "Can we go eat now?"

"Sure," Cade said. "We were waiting for you, Jess. You wanna make it a threesome, or is some local self-proclaimed celebrity waiting to take you out?"

She smiled. "No, I don't have any plans. Just let me change into something more civilized."

She went back into her suite, kicked off her shoes and, hooking them on two fingers, carried them to her bedroom. Sitting down on the bed, she sighed. Yes, she was happy to see Ben. She was happy that he had come to his father on his own. That was a giant step. But it dashed her hopes for the evening.

She should be glad, she thought, that Ben's arrival saved her from what might have been another mistake with Cade. It saved them both. But she wasn't glad, she thought dolefully. She was turning into a basket case.

She heard a knock on her door and looked up startled. Cade was leaning against her bedroom door, his biceps bulging as he crossed his arms over the solid gray T-shirt that stretched tightly over his chest. "What do you think?" he asked.

She felt as though he'd read her straying thoughts. "About what?"

"About Ben showing up like this. I can't get over it."

"Yeah, it is a little sudden, isn't it? But as long as his mother knows..."

"That's just it. She doesn't." He pushed off from the door and came closer. "Hey, would you do me a favor? Call his house and try to get a number where she can be reached? He says she left this morning for Greece."

"Sure, but do you think they'll give it to me?"

Cade hesitated. "You've got a point. They'd be more likely to give it to me. After you change, you can talk to him for a minute while I call. I don't want him to know about it. He might think I'm trying to get rid of him. I just think she ought to know he's here."

"They're probably worried sick," she whispered.

"I don't know," he said pensively. "Maybe, maybe not. All I know is he can stay with me as long as he wants."

He stood over her for a moment longer, gazing at her sitting on her bed, and finally whispered, "Hey, Jess, I know people have been telling you all day. But you really look great today."

The small intimacy sent a shiver scurrying up her spine. "Thanks, Cade."

"I'll see you in a minute."

She watched the door as he disappeared, then hurried to change.

A FEW MINUTES LATER, as Jessica was teaching Ben a card trick her father had taught her as a child, Cade slipped into her suite and called Ben's house. The maid answered on the third ring.

"Lowdon residence."

"This is Cade Hartman," he said. "Ben's father. I need to get in touch with Bridgit right away. Could you please tell me where I can reach her?"

"I'm sorry," the woman said in a snobbish twang. "I'm not authorized to give out that information."

Cade bristled. "Look, I'm not some stranger. It's about Ben. I have to talk to her."

"Perhaps you could leave a message, and I could relay it to her if she calls in."

He gritted his teeth. "All right. Tell her that our son showed up at my hotel in Phoenix tonight, and that he's going to stay here for a while."

There was no response, and he wondered sadly if she was writing the message down or simply letting it sink in.

"Hello? Are you there?" he asked.

"Yes," the woman said.

He frowned and stood up, clutching the phone tighter. "Let me ask you something. Who is in charge of my son when his mother is away?"

"The staff and I," she said.

"Well, doesn't it strike you as odd that he's not there and hasn't been seen all day?"

"He's in his room," the woman said smugly.

"Since when? Have you actually laid eyes on him today?"

"Well . . . just a moment, please."

She put him on hold, an act that sent him through the roof. What the hell was she doing?

After a few moments, she came back to the phone. "Uh...Mr. Hartman, it seems that you may be right. Ben's not in his room, and no one has seen him today."

He gave a sarcastic laugh. "It seems I may be right! Of course I'm right—Ben's right here with me! I can't tell you how reassuring it is to know that his mother leaves him with people as caring and attentive as you."

The woman didn't answer for a moment. "When may we expect him back?"

"When his mother decides to stop jet-setting and take care of him herself! Look, if she wants to speak to me, I'll be at the Phoenix Hilton for two more days."

"I'll give her the message."

"Thank you so much," he droned, then slammed down the phone.

He was near bursting point when he went back into his room and heard Jessica and Ben laughing aloud. His anger diminished a little at the sound of his son's uninhibited glee. But the boy quieted as soon as he saw his father, as though he couldn't make that small concession to his image of disgruntled son.

"Uh...let's go eat, guys," Cade said finally. "I'm starved."

BEN GOT ENGROSSED in a video game at the Pizza Hut before they had finished their pizza, and Cade and Jessica sat across from each other, able to talk alone for the first time that night.

"So what did Bridgit say?" she asked him in a low voice.

"I talked to the maid, who I might add is a bitch with a capital *B*. No wonder the kid ran away. Would you believe that no one even knew he was gone?"

"You're kidding."

"Nope."

"So...what happens next?"

Cade gazed across the room to his son. "I don't know. I guess I'll keep him here until she gets back." He smiled. "You know, as pissed off as I was about that woman, I have to say I'm kind of flattered that he would have come here to find me. I figured I'd be the last person he'd make an effort to see."

"Why? I thought you two got along great in Dallas."

"We did, until the last day. Then he acted like he couldn't care less if he ever saw me again or not. He barely said a word."

"Well, maybe that was because he knew you were leaving. Sort of a defense mechanism. Like he was bracing himself."

He gave her a stricken look—it was the first time that possibility had occurred to him. "You think?"

She nodded. "You also used to act like that. The few times you visited us, you'd get all grumpy and irritable the day you had to leave. Think back. How did you feel?"

He shook his head. "I don't remember. It was too long ago."

"Well, I do. And Dad would mope around for days afterward and he wouldn't call you for a while because he figured you didn't want to talk to him."

Cade felt that old bitterness rising inside him again. "Give me a break, Jess. I stopped coming to see him by the time I was Ben's age."

"Right. And he stopped inviting you because he didn't like hearing that you had better things to do."

Cade regarded his son, focused intently on the video game, and thought back to his own feelings when he was Ben's age. The feelings he still carried with him today. The feelings that, warranted or not, had colored his life ever since.

"Ben loves you, Cade, or he wouldn't be here. I think he's just starting to get used to the idea that you might love him, too."

"That's ridiculous. I'm his father. He must know I love him."

"It's not always a given, Cade. You know that."

Ben won the game and rushed back to the table, his face more animated than Cade had ever seen it. "Man, I beat it. I almost got zoned out there for a minute, but I tore it up."

Cade laughed. "Great. So...are you ready to leave, or do you plan to conquer that machine again?"

"We can go," Ben said. "There's a game on tonight."

Realizing his son was exactly where he wanted to be—with his father—Cade slid out of the booth, happier than he had been in weeks.

CADE WAS TAKING a shower to relax that night when the ball game ended, and Jessica finished reviewing her itinerary for the next few days, memorizing the names of various reporters and disc jockeys who would interview her. Covering her mouth, she yawned, and Ben glanced up at her. "Cardinals won."

She smiled. "Who were they playing?"

"The Reds," he said.

She laughed. "I'm sorry I wasn't watching it with you. It's probably no fun watching by yourself."

"No problem," Ben said sincerely. "I'm used to doing things by myself."

She picked up a small pillow from the sofa and pulled her feet beneath her. "Just like your father. He was a loner, too. Of course, he didn't have much choice. His mother was always working."

"Mine might as well be."

She detected the slightest hint of bitterness in his voice, and decided to seize the opportunity to dig further. "She stays busy a lot, huh?"

"Yeah. She thinks it's some kind of crime to stay in the same place for more than a couple of days."

She looked at him as he flipped the remote control from channel to channel to channel, but she sensed that he didn't see any of what was there. "How do you feel about that?" she asked tentatively.

"It's fine, I guess," he said with a shrug. "It's not like I'm some kid who has to be watched over."

She looked at the channels flashing by, thinking about how no one in that huge house of his had noticed his absence. He had hopped on a plane from

Texas to Arizona without anyone missing him. There was something terribly wrong with that.

"You know, your dad loves having you here. I've never seen him smile so much. It's against his nature, you know. Ruins his tough-guy image."

Ben grinned. "You sure he's not smiling because of you?"

Jessica's mouth fell open, and she gaped at Ben. "Why would you ask a thing like that?"

"Just the way he looks at you. Sometimes I forget you guys are sister and brother. You seem more like a couple to me."

Her face reddened, and she dropped her feet to the floor. "I'm sure he's told you that we aren't really related by blood. And as for us seeming like a couple, that's probably just because I'm always around. I hope you don't feel like I'm horning in."

"No," he said quickly. "You're okay."

The endorsement seeped into her heart, and she leaned her head back on the couch. "You know, there was a time when I thought your dad hated me. All the time I was growing up, I had the biggest crush on him. I just wanted him to notice me, to be my knight and my rescuer. But he couldn't have been less interested."

"Things change, huh?"

Again, she smiled. "You think so?"

He nodded. "I thought he hated you, too. Guess he just had to get to know you."

Jessica laughed at the little-boy bluntness coming from such a mature-looking face. "I guess we've learned to like each other," she said, sighing as she thought of last night, when Cade had pulled her into that kiss that had held such hope, such promise. She almost wished now she had allowed it to go further.

"So..." she said, trying to pull out of her reverie. "Are you coming to California with us in a couple of days?"

He shrugged. "Nah, I don't think I'll go with you. I kind of thought I'd stay here a couple of nights, and then it'll be time to move on."

An alarm went off inside her, and she dropped her feet again. "Move on? You mean, go home?"

He shook his head. "I'm not going home. But you and dad have a lot of stuff to do without having to worry about me. And I'm old enough to be on my own. I made it here alone, didn't I?"

"Ben, your father is never too busy for you."

He didn't seem to buy it. "Well, I just mean it's not like he's prepared to have a kid with him all the time. He has his own life. If he'd ever wanted me, he coulda had me. I don't even think Mom would care. He's real busy, you know..." He hesitated and looked up at her. "Hey, when he gets rich and everything, do you think he'll buy back his bike shop?"

"I don't know," she said.

"That'd be cool." He thought about it for a moment. "Maybe I could come to work for him sometime."

"If he doesn't, he could get you a job at JC, after we get our shares."

Ben tossed her a deprecating grin. "No offense, but I don't see myself selling makeup."

She laughed. "Neither did he. But he's doing a great job."

She heard Cade coming back into her suite, and turned around. He was dressed in a pair of cutoff jeans and no shirt, and the shower steam glistened on the thick curls of hair across his chest, reminding her of the way his chest had felt beneath her fingers last night.

"Who won the game?"

Jessica tore her eyes away from him. "The Reds," she said.

Ben scoffed. "No, the Cardinals." He looked at his father and rolled his eyes. "She was zoned out, Dad. She doesn't know."

Cade grinned and grasped his son by the shoulders. "We'll teach her, buddy. There's still hope."

Jessica laughed at the growing harmony between the two men in her life.

BEN FELL ASLEEP before his father, and quietly Cade tested the door between his room and Jessica's suite. She hadn't locked her side, so he slipped it open and went in.

She was in her bedroom, so he knocked quietly and heard her whisper, "Come in."

She was wearing that same white gown that trailed to the ground, and Cade caught his breath on a heartbeat and told himself that he needed to remember the vision she created tonight. If he put her in a commercial looking like this, they'd sell out of cosmetics within twenty-four hours. But it wasn't the makeup, the perfume or the lingerie that made this woman a vision, he thought. It was Jessica. Just the idea of Jessica, the essence of Jessica, the presence of Jessica.

She came to her feet when she saw him, and his eyes dropped from her soft, unadorned face, to the lace barely concealing her breasts. "Is Ben asleep?"

"Yeah," he whispered. He swallowed and fought the urge to step nearer. If he did, he wouldn't be able to stop himself. And he couldn't bear to hear the word "no" again from her lips. "That look you gave me when we were going back to my room tonight... did I misunderstand or were you hinting you needed to talk to me?"

"I did," she said. "About Ben."

Disappointment shot through him, and he rubbed the back of his neck and nodded. "Oh. What's wrong?"

"I just thought you should know that he told me tonight that he's going to be 'moving on' in a couple of days. Not going home, 'moving on.' He seems to think he's a burden to you here, and that he's old enough to take care of himself. He even said that if you wanted him, you could have had him. The fact that Bridgit has custody seems to be proof that you didn't want him."

Cade groaned and looked at the ceiling. "And the fact that I rarely visited him didn't help that attitude any." He sighed. "I didn't know he thought that."

"He feels the same way you felt as a kid, Cade. The similarities amaze me."

"There are no similarities," Cade said. "I love my son. I'd do anything for him, and if he wants to live with me, it would make me the happiest man in the world."

"Same way Dad felt."

He gave a mirthless laugh and shook his head. "No. Our father had another family. He replaced my mother and me, real neatly."

As she always did when they got into these conversations, Jessica felt her defenses rising. "That's just your interpretation," she said. "And it could have been just as wrong as Ben's."

Cade thought of his son traveling across the country with a backpack and a credit card, looking for a place to ease the pain of neglect. "Poor kid has been taking care of himself for so long already, he's probably right about being able to do it. But he's not going anywhere."

"You're going to have to do a lot of convincing to make him believe you want him here. He really thinks he's in the way."

Cade brought his eyes back to her. "Why does he tell you stuff like this, and not me?"

"Because," she said with a smile. "I'm a member of the female species. Guys talk about football and motorcycles and movies. Women talk about feelings."

He frowned. "I wonder if he talks that openly to Bridgit."

"There was nothing so open about it, Cade. He still holds a lot in. But no, I doubt he talks to his mother. She doesn't sound like she has much time for him."

He thought for a moment, then lifted his chin. "Jess, I'm going to tell him in the morning that I want him to stay with me all summer. That'll mean he'll be with us all the time. I know it'll be hard for you to have both of us to deal with, but—"

"Cade, don't be ridiculous," she cut in. "I love Ben. I would love having him around all summer, and even though he thinks he doesn't need taking care of, I'll help do it. You don't know how I've always wanted a big family, with brothers and sisters and nieces and nephews. This is almost heaven to me."

Almost. His eyes softened as he looked at her, wondering what it would take to make that heaven complete. "But what about us?"

She was surprised that he'd be so open with his question. "What *about* us?"

He glanced at those barely covered breasts again. "Do you honestly think I can keep seeing you dressed like that and keep my distance?"

A slow heat rose to color her face. "Oh," she said softly, "I would say you're doing a pretty good job so far."

Stepping closer, he whispered, "There you go again, making assumptions about me."

When he touched her, every nerve in her body urged her toward him, and this time she didn't fight it. His fingertips on her bare arm made her shiver, and as he moved closer, she looked up at him, wetting her lips unconsciously.

Slowly he dropped his lips to her neck, breathed in her scent, then, taking a handful of her hair, guided her face to his. Just before he kissed her, he whispered, "Tell me why that perfume doesn't smell the same on anyone else..."

Their lips met tentatively, softly, and his touch was gentle, sweet, savoring. His hand slid down the sleek, filmy fabric and pressed on the small of her back, until he moaned with the pressure of her against his arousal.

His lips journeyed down her face, across her throat, and with one hand he slid the tiny strap off her shoulder and peeled back the lace that stretched over her breast. The sight of it bare almost made him groan, and he touched it the way an artist might touch a valuable piece of sculpture, feeling the silky texture of her breast, the turgidity of her nipple, the heat that seemed to radiate from her skin.

That touch made her heartbeat race, and she ran her tongue through the soft curling hair of his chest, finding the flat male nipple that was right at her mouth's level. She flicked, then bit it lightly, and felt his body buckle. He trembled, and she trembled, and in its agony, the moment was the most wonderful—and the most terrifying—she could remember in her life.

He bent low and his mouth closed over her breast, making her legs go weak. With one hand he wadded the fabric of her gown until he could reach beneath it with the other. She had worn nothing there, and the thought that she could have wanted him, could have hoped for this, accelerated his desire.

Almost roughly now, he pulled her other strap down, peeled the lace off her breast, and watched the gown fall to the floor to puddle at her feet. He went back to close the door, then beheld her for an excruciating moment.

She stood before him, unashamed, her breasts heaving with desire, and their eyes locked as he released the button of his shorts, pulled down the fly and stepped out of them.

When he took her into his arms again, it was with a ravenous intention, a mighty hunger, and their desire was so great that they each feared they would hurt the other even as they sought to give pleasure. He gave unselfishly to her, until she arched back and reached for the pillow to muffle her moans.

And she gave unselfishly to him, bringing him right up to the moment of completion, then torturing him to wait, until finally he grabbed her wrists, turned her over, held them above her head and completed the act in the most violent, most excruciating and most fulfilling release he had ever achieved. Her excitement at his climax brought on one more of her own, until they smothered each other's cries in a kiss of ultimate torment.

Their hearts still raced like athletes' as they clung to each other afterward, still tangled and enraptured in the love that had erased all barriers and taboos, and made it not just a need for them to be together, but destiny itself.

NEITHER OF THEM meant to fall asleep, but when they heard a sound in the living room of Jessica's suite, they both woke with a start. Cade looked at the clock and saw that it was six a.m. "Oh, no," he whispered. "I didn't mean to sleep here."

He got out of bed and pulled on his shorts, then cracked the door enough to peer out. Ben was at the mini-bar pouring Coke into a glass. "Damn," he whispered, turning back to her.

Jessica grabbed her gown and slipped it over her head. "Cade, don't go out there. Wait a minute. Maybe he'll go to the bathroom or something, and you can come out."

Cade's face reddened. "It's not like he hasn't already noticed I'm gone. What'll I tell him?"

She thought for a moment. "Run out my door and get a paper, then bop back in like you'd gone out for that. He'll buy it."

They waited with breath held, and finally Cade peeked out again. "He's back in our room, but I can't tell if he's in the bathroom or not. I guess I'll have to take a chance."

"No!" she whispered. "Please, Cade. We can't let him know you were in here. Just wait a minute until you're sure."

Cade sat down on the bed and raked a hand through his hair. "Damn. I could be in here all morning. Come on, Jess, he's bound to have figured this out."

"I don't care," she shot back. "He'll unfigure it." She caught her breath and went for her robe. "I know. I'll go out as if I was in here alone, and get some orange juice, and I'll ask him where you are. When he goes into the bathroom, I'll signal you to make your getaway. And come back in with a newspaper or it won't look real."

"This is asinine," Cade bit out. "Just crazy."

"It can't happen again," she said. "Not while Ben's with us."

He took her hand and stopped her before she made it to the door. When she paused to look at him, he whispered, "I have no regrets. Do you?"

"I'm not sure," she whispered. "Let's see what happens."

Cade sat back on the bed as she left the bedroom, closing the door behind her.

A few minutes later, she came back. "He's taking a shower. We're both real baffled as to where you went." She handed him some change. "Here. Bring back some more sodas from the machine and a newspaper."

Dropping the change into his pocket, and then slipping into his room long enough to get a T-shirt to pull on, Cade left through her suite. When he came back a few minutes later, Ben was just coming out of the bathroom.

"Hey, kiddo," he said, tossing him a canned drink. "Didn't think you'd wake up this early."

Ben popped the top and watched his father drop the newspaper on the bed.

Cade shot Jessica a grin that told her that this time, they'd gotten out of the mess without a catastrophe. Jessica's returned glare, however, told him it was the last time they would take the chance.

FOR THE NEXT FEW WEEKS, Jessica stopped referring to Cade in interviews as her brother. Instead she made it clear at every opportunity that he was her *adopted* half brother. Each time someone introduced them as sister and brother, Cade would politely correct them and say that they weren't related biologically.

Nights grew longer and longer as they tried to stay away from each other around Ben, who was always there, watching, listening, with an insight too keen for a twelve-year-old.

And as Jessica fell more and more deeply in love with Cade, she found herself feeling more and more guilty.

One night, as they were riding home in the back of a limousine the mayor of the small California town had loaned them as transportation to the campaign dinner in his honor, they found themselves alone.

A strange melancholy had fallen over Jessica, and she couldn't shake it. "They introduced us as brother and sister tonight."

"Yeah, I know."

"That's what everybody thinks we are. Can't blame them, I guess," she said on a sigh as she set her elbow on the door of the car. Peering out, she said, "Same last name, same father. I guess it's what we are."

Cade thought for a moment. "I spent my whole life hating the adopted-child label. Now I can't wait to tell them I'm not your biological brother." He reached for her hand, but it was slightly limp as he held it. "This is really bothering you, isn't it?"

She nodded. "I've been thinking about the other night. When Ben almost caught us together. And I wondered if it was just the fact that we were almost caught sleeping together that bothered me, or the fact that we're two siblings who were almost caught sleeping together."

He stroked each finger individually, studying the shape and the contours. "Probably a little of both."

"What would he think?"

"About us as a couple? I don't know, Jess."

She sighed and looked over at him. "And what about in a few weeks, Cade? After our jobs are done, and we've gotten our shares of JC? What's going to happen to us then?"

Cade hadn't really thought past the next few days. He'd been too busy, too preoccupied. "You mean, are we going to come out of the closet about our feelings for each other, or pretend it never happened and go our separate ways?"

The way he phrased the question didn't bode well, she thought. "Something like that."

Cade thought for a moment and set her hand back in her lap. "Would it bother you if people knew we were an item?"

She drew in a deep breath. "It might be a little weird at first."

"Yeah, it might," he said. "We could keep things secret for a while."

She looked out the window, at the waters of the Pacific pounding against the rocks on the shore. "I've never been involved with anybody before who wanted to keep me a secret."

"You've never been involved with your brother."

Her head snapped around. "That's it, isn't it? You're still thinking of me as your sister?"

"No, I'm not," he argued. "You're the one who brought this up."

"Well, it would just be pretty strange, since you never treated me like I was related to you before Daddy died."

"I told you, I don't think of you that way." Setting his arm across the seat behind her, he slid his fingers through her hair, and pulled her close to him. "You're the first thought I have each morning," he whispered in a deep rumble, "and the last one I have before I fall asleep. You're the one who's making my life more difficult than it's ever been. You're the only one who's ever made me wish for one night without Ben."

Her eyes sparkled, and she tried to hold back the tears. "Then what's going to become of us?"

"I don't know," he whispered. "I don't want to embarrass you, and I don't want to blow Ben's mind. And I don't want you to put your reputation on the line."

"The Board might not want me as spokesperson anymore if they found out. They're champing at the bit for a reason to replace me."

"That's because they're fools." He kissed her forehead, then glanced up at the driver who, through the window separating them, appeared to be unconcerned with them. "We don't have to decide anything right now, do we?" he asked.

Jessica shook her head, but feared that her heart was going to be deeply wounded when their jobs were finished. Cade would cut her loose and go back to his old, safe, risk-free life.

And no one would have to be embarrassed.

CHAPTER FOURTEEN

BEN WAS ON THE telephone when Cade got back to his room, and Cade knew instantly that something was wrong.

He set down his room key and listened to Ben's monosyllabic replies. "I don't know. No. Why? No."

Cade glanced at his son as he shrugged out of his jacket, tossed it over a chair and slid off his tie.

"Guess so. Yeah. When?"

Cade didn't try to pretend he wasn't listening, and finally he sat down and watched his son struggling with the emotions battling on his face. "All right. I said I would. Yeah. Bye."

He dropped the phone a little too loudly, then pulled his feet up in his chair, rested his elbow on his knee, and covered his mouth.

"Who was that?" Cade asked.

"Mom." Ben set his eyes on the television, as if there were nothing more to say.

"She's back from Greece?" he asked.

"Yep."

Cade's stomach tightened. "So what did she say?"

He shrugged. "Wants me to come home."

"Oh, she does, does she?" Cade got up and looked down at his son. "Well, I hope you told her you were staying for a while longer."

Ben didn't answer. "School starts next week."

Cade raked his suddenly shaky hand through his hair, leaving it ruffled. "Oh, yeah. School. Well, this tour will be over in another month. I could get you a tutor until I get back to Atlanta..."

Ben shook his head. "No. You still have a long way to go. I'll just go back."

"Go back?" Cade's voice came too loudly, and he tried to quieten it. Sitting down, he looked at Ben. "Is that what you told her?"

Ben couldn't meet his eyes. "She wants me to leave tomorrow."

"Tomorrow?" Cade felt as if he'd been knocked in the stomach. He tried to breathe out a dry laugh. "Nothing like a little notice, is there?"

Ben's eyes were wide and fragile as he looked at his father. "I'll pack myself. You won't have to do anything."

The injustice and absurdity of his son's concerns almost made him angry. "Do anything? Do you think I'm upset about getting you packed?"

Ben turned back to the television again, and for a moment Cade was torn between screaming for him to answer him and begging him not to go. Frustrated, he turned the set off, making the boy flinch in surprise. Standing in Ben's line of vision, he forced his son to look at him. "Ben, I'm upset because I wasn't ready to let you go. I like having you here. Do you understand that?"

Ben still couldn't meet his eyes, and his mouth trembled as he admitted, "We've had some laughs."

"We've had a lot of laughs," Cade said. "And I don't like sending you back to your mother. I used to always think she was what was best for you, but this summer, I've had an awakening. Maybe she's not the best thing for you. Maybe I am."

Ben's eyes collided with his, and Cade could see the carefully hidden pain there. It was like looking into a mirror, only he was confronting a younger version of himself—the version whose father never said the things he needed to hear. Cade wasn't sure he could say them, either. "I'm just saying that, if things aren't good at home, you have a choice, you know. You always have a choice." The words weren't very eloquent, but Cade felt Ben understood.

"If you get the inheritance and get rich," Ben asked seriously, as if it had some connection to where he would live, "would you still ride Harleys?"

Cade hesitated, again uncertain if his life-style embarrassed his son. "Well . . . I don't know."

Ben let it go, but his face looked lifeless as he propped his head on his hand. "She said I had to be on tomorrow's flight home."

Cade caught his breath again, then with great effort, swallowed the lump in his throat. "Fine," he said finally, knowing he couldn't stop him if Ben really wanted to go. "Then go home. But know that you can come back anytime."

Ben didn't answer for a moment, and Cade wasn't sure if he was struggling with his own emotions or seeking a way to break the news to his father that he'd rather be neglected in style by his mother than to live within his old man's means.

"Why don't you just think about it, buddy?" Cade's voice was hoarse, and he cleared his throat. "Whatever you decide, I can live with it."

Ben nodded. "I'd better get packed," he said.

And Cade couldn't fight the feeling that he'd lost his son again.

JESSICA WENT to the airport with Cade and Ben the next morning, and found herself getting teary-eyed as the boy was called to board. Without giving him the chance to object, she pulled him into a hug and whispered, "I'm gonna miss you, kiddo."

He didn't smile, but stepped back and gave his father an awkward glance. "Thanks for letting me stay with you so long."

Jessica ached at the pain in Cade's eyes. "Anytime, Ben," he said. "You know that."

Ben slung his duffel bag over his shoulder and started toward the line where the passengers were boarding. Cade grabbed his arm to stop him. His eyes misted as he bent to Ben's eye level. "How about a hug for your old man?"

Ben dropped his bag and gave his father a stiff, quick hug. "See you, Dad," he said, then quickly turned and started away.

Jessica waited for Cade to shout after him that he loved him, but the words didn't come. And she wondered if he thought Ben knew. Just as her father had believed Cade knew.

Frozen, Cade watched through the window until the plane taxied out of sight. Finally he said, "Well, that's the end of that."

Jessica looked at him. "What do you mean? He's still your son."

Cade sighed and started walking. "I'm just wondering how long it'll be before I see him again. I told him he could come live with me, but you know how that goes."

"No, Cade. How?"

"Oh, he'll go home to that Taj Mahal he lives in, have a couple of people waiting on him every time he breathes, start his private school with the sons of the richest people in Dallas, and forget about the boring summer he spent in hotels with his father."

"He might think *you'll* forget *him.*"

Cade didn't answer.

"Cade, don't give up. He needs you. Keep calling him, keep letting him know that you love him, that you're there for him. He needs to know that."

Cade didn't say a word as they made their way to their rental van.

THAT NIGHT, after they'd both returned from their busy workdays and come together for a glass of wine to unwind, Jessica saw that Cade's mood had not lifted.

"Why don't you call and make sure Ben got home all right?" she asked.

Cade shrugged. "I did. Bridgit said he'd gone somewhere with a friend."

"Oh." She sipped her wine. "Well, you can call later."

"Yeah, if she'll ever let me get through." He shook his head. "I'll tell you, Jess, it's hard not to hate sometimes."

"I know," she whispered.

He looked at her, at the silk pajamas she was wearing and the shiny hair piled up on her head, which gave her the look of a cool socialite, much like all the others he had dated. What was it that had made him marry Bridgit and keep going out with women with that kind of aura about them? Was it Jessica? Was it that he'd always felt so inferior to her in his father's eyes that he had spent his entire adulthood trying to be her equal?

No, he thought. That was why he'd started repairing bikes. He had refused to compete. It was fine that she was better than he was. It was no contest.

He turned his eyes away and drained his wineglass.

She got up and refilled his glass, then began to pull the pins from her hair, allowing it to fall full and billowy around her face.

He glanced up, almost grudgingly, and let his eyes linger on her a moment too long. Then he tore them away. "It's late," he said. "I should go back to my room."

Her heart crashed, but she didn't show it. Absently she shook her hair around with her hand and stared into her glass.

"Unless..."

She looked up. "Unless what?"

"Aw, hell, Jess," he said in an almost agonized whisper. "I don't want to go."

Her eyes were steady, certain, when she said, "Then stay."

He closed his eyes. When he opened them, she was slipping off her shoes, and he wondered why the sight of her bare feet did so much to his libido.

"I told myself we wouldn't do this," he whispered.

"Do what?" she asked innocently.

Groaning, he got up and went to her, knelt in front of her and touched her face. Slowly his fingertips feathered down her neck, to her chest, and across the silk over her nipple.

"I don't want to hurt you, Jess."

Her eyes were serious, pained, as they locked with his. "Why would you hurt me, Cade?"

"Because things are uncertain. And scary. And I don't know who I am or why I do anything anymore."

Her eyes filled with tears. "I'm scared, too, Cade. Scared that you'll walk out of here tonight."

With a gentle touch to her chin, he pulled her face to his, and just before his lips grazed hers, he whispered, "There's nothing to fear tonight."

His kiss was sweet, torturous, and as he pulled her into his arms, she knew that everything would be all right.

At least for tonight.

THEY DIDN'T TALK about the future, or their relationship, or what they would tell people, for the next few weeks. They worked with a vengeance, knowing their time was coming to an end, and at night when they collapsed into bed they collapsed together.

Their lovemaking became a natural thing, an act that grew more wonderful and intimate as the days progressed, but it held no certainties, no promises, no commitments.

And Jessica wouldn't let herself think of what might happen when reality intruded again and they went back home to their real, separate worlds. There would be time enough later to figure out where they stood. But they would never have insulated, private time like this again.

All too soon, their whirlwind came to an end. And as they flew home to Atlanta for the final time, Jessica couldn't escape the foreboding sense that her tour wasn't the only thing coming to an end.

THE LONELINESS of Cade's house assaulted him like a jealous lover when he arrived back home. It was too big, he thought as he ambled through the rooms, trying to remember why he'd ever bought it. A single man had no need for three bedrooms—especially when two were empty.

He'd always planned to make one into a guest room. But with no family and no close friends, he hadn't seen the point when it came right down to it. The other room was reserved for Ben.

He walked into the empty room that mocked the boy's absence, and wondered what Ben's room at the mansion looked like. It could be anything he wanted, he thought, from a Gremlins theme one year to Jurassic Park the next. Bridgit would have spared no expense to make his room spectacular.

But when he'd bought the house, the most he had expected to furnish the room with was a set of bunk beds, a dresser and a chest of drawers. He'd never even made himself go that far. Ben had never visited him here, and somehow the thought of a fully furnished room for his son had made Cade uneasy—it would be a daily reminder of all the days that Ben was not a part of his life.

But that could change now, he thought with a fragile hope. Maybe Ben had gotten home and found that he missed his dad. Maybe he'd had enough of his mother's neglect. Maybe he would make the choice that no child should ever have to make, and decide to live with Cade.

Suddenly anxious to speak to his son, Cade picked up the phone and called him. To his surprise, Ben answered the phone.

Bridgit was getting sloppy, he thought. Before she knew it, Cade would be able to reach his son anytime he tried.

Ben was as cool as usual as they exchanged a round of pleasantries. Finally Cade decided to get right to the point.

"So how's everything at home?"

"Fine."

"Do you like school?"

"It's okay."

"The schools here are great. The junior-high football team hasn't had a losing season in ten years."

"Really?"

"Yeah. You could probably still get on the team. They need big guys like you."

Ben was silent, and Cade wondered if he should have even brought it up. Now, backtracking, he tried to lift the burden of choice he'd put on his son. "So...when do you think you can come see your old man?"

Ben hesitated. "I don't know."

Cade sighed and wondered why it was so hard to be straight with his son. Was he afraid of rejection? Getting angry at himself, he tried to remember Jessica's warning not to leave their relationship to chance. There were things that had to be said straight out.

"You know, Ben, things don't have to be terrible for you to come here. I hope you realize that there's nothing that would make me happier than to have you come here anytime you want."

He paused for a moment, and when Ben didn't respond, he wondered if his wording had been wrong. He didn't want Ben to feel responsible for his father's happiness. If Ben was happy, nothing else mattered.

"Look," he said finally. "I just mean the door's open all the time, okay?"

"Sure," Ben said quietly.

When he hung up the phone, Cade collapsed on his bed and asked himself why Ben's lack of response had been so disappointing. Hadn't he known that his son wouldn't jump up and down, anxious to pack? What, after all, did Cade have to offer him?

He thought of the money he would inherit if they'd reached their goal. Tomorrow he'd learn just how much he was worth. But none of it meant anything if it was just for him, he thought. What was he going to do with part of a cosmetics company? He had no more business being involved in that than he had being involved with Jessica.

He closed his eyes and thought of how beautiful she was, how her tour had enhanced her image and made her not only a household name but a household face. She had been approached by celebrities and politicians, tycoons and star athletes while they were on tour. Why had she opted to spend every free moment with him?

He wondered what she was doing now, and realized it was the first time in almost six months that he'd come to the end of a day and not had her to look forward to. Damn it, he missed her.

But it was time to make a decision. They were from two different worlds, two different leagues. She was class and beauty and sophistication. He was rough edges, laid back, and a loner. Even if he had money, he still wouldn't ever quite live up to her.

She deserved better. She deserved someone who wouldn't taint her name and make her the subject of scandal. She deserved someone who knew how to act at a black-tie fund-raiser and could contribute to conversations at elegant dinner parties.

Not a man who, until six months ago, had spent most of his day with grease under his fingernails.

Feeling despondent and unable to quell the unease in his heart, Cade called Jessica at home and asked her to have dinner with him. "We need to talk before the board meeting tomorrow," he said.

"All right," she whispered. "Do you want to pick me up?"

He thought of his truck, and the fact that she deserved to ride in a limo. For the first time, he hated being known as a cheapskate. "Yeah," he said. "How about seven-thirty?"

"Fine." They were quiet for a moment, and finally she whispered, "Cade?"

"Yeah."

"I miss you," she said.

He would have smiled, but instead his eyes grew misty. "Yeah," he said. "Same here."

JESSICA SAW from the brooding way Cade avoided her eyes that night that something was wrong. They were both quiet all the way to the restaurant, and even though he ordered a bottle of champagne—a rare and extravagant treat for him—she had the sense that he was preparing to break her heart.

"So...do you think we did it?" she asked quietly.

"We'll find out tomorrow," he said. "But if my calculations are right, we should have not only achieved but surpassed what we set out to do."

She leaned back in her chair and sighed. "Gosh, it'll be good not to have to kill ourselves. Imagine just working regular hours, coming home every night, having a life."

His smile was strained. "Yeah, it'll be nice."

Her smile faded and her eyes widened as a sudden overwhelming wistfulness took over her. She leaned on the table, getting closer to him, and gazed up into his eyes. "Thing is, it wasn't really that bad. It was really nice coming back to the hotel and knowing you'd be there at night."

He looked down at his plate. "Yeah."

Growing more sullen at his silence, she reached out to take his hand. "What is it, Cade? There's something you want to say, isn't there?"

He sighed and withdrew his hand from hers, and crossed both of his in front of his face. "I've been thinking."

"Yeah, I thought you had."

He met her eyes, knowing she anticipated what he was going to say, but somehow having to say it anyway. "Jess, the past six months have been an experience..."

"An experience," she repeated, unbidden tears coming to her eyes.

"Yes. I mean the work. It was good for me. Taught me that I had it in me. I wasn't sure before."

"Oh, you have it in you, Cade. It wouldn't have worked without you."

"There were other things," he whispered, meeting her eyes, "things that I didn't know I had in me. But you showed me a part of myself I had denied for a long time. You brought out whatever good there is in me."

She held her breath. "But?"

"But...I think it's time to look at reality. And the future. And I don't think we can go on with this."

Her heart plummeted even farther than it had when she'd gotten the phone call about her father's death. She glanced around, wondering if anyone would see the tears moistening her lashes. "How did I know you were going to say this?"

"Jess, it's your reputation. If word gets out that we've been sleeping together, it's not going to help business. It may hurt it a lot. People won't understand."

"Sleeping together," she said. "Funny. I thought we had more than that."

"It doesn't matter," he said. "People will see—"

"I don't care what people see," she said too loudly. "And I don't care what they think. And frankly, I'm surprised you do."

"I'm thinking of you," he whispered.

Her eyes stung as she shot him a look. "Don't do me any favors."

They were quiet for a moment, and finally he went on. "Jess, we're from two different worlds. You're classy and sweet and open with your feelings, and I don't even know what I feel half the time, much less how to express it. I'm a motorcycle mechanic, for God's sake."

"For the past six months, you were the pivotal employee in a company that was dying. You brought it back, Cade."

"But it was a one-shot deal. I'm not going to keep working for JC."

Her face twisted, and she felt the heat scaling her cheeks. "But you have to. You'll own part of it after tomorrow."

"No," he said. "I've decided that if we win our inheritance, I want to sell my shares. And I'd really like to sell them to you. If you can't swing it at first, I understand. I don't need the money now. I could just sign them over to you, and—"

"No!" she said too loudly, then caught herself and lowered her voice. "I won't take them!"

"Then I'll sell them to someone else, Jess," he said. "I don't want them."

"Why?"

"Because," he said. "I don't belong in this company, and I don't belong with you. We have to end this thing between us, Jess, and we can't as long as we're tied together."

A tear rolled down her cheek, and she blotted it away. Her lips were stiff as she spoke. "So let me get this straight. You don't want to see me anymore, so you're cutting any ties you might have to me. And we not only won't be lovers, we won't be anything. Not co-workers. Not friends. Not brother and sister. Nothing."

Cade felt helpless at her tears, and he fought the urge to reach for her. "You don't want to be friends, Jess, and neither do I. And I sure as hell don't want to be your brother."

She covered her mouth as it began to tremble. "I'd rather have you that way than not see you again."

He wiped away a tear she missed, and leaned toward her. "It's better this way, Jess. Besides, you're the Jessica in Jessica Cosmetics. It's your birthright, not mine."

"This is not about birthrights, Cade!" she whispered through her teeth. "Or...maybe it is. Maybe you still can't get past that resentment you have toward me. You feel like JC is my turf, and you don't feel comfortable there. Or maybe deep down you still hate me..."

"I never hated you."

"Then what *do* you feel, Cade?" she demanded. "Indifference?"

"No, Jess. I'll never feel indifferent toward you."

But he couldn't say how he did feel, and she suspected he never would. Not even to himself.

She covered her face, tried to recover, but finally gave up, no longer caring what anyone around them might think. "Daddy wanted us both in the company, Cade. He wanted us to learn something before we took over the company. We learned it, and I think we would have made him proud. He was trying to do what was best for both of his children, because he loved us both."

"I don't know why he did it, Jess, but I don't think that was the reason. And I know for sure he wouldn't have done it if he'd known we'd wind up sleeping together."

"There you go again," she whispered. "Sleeping together. It was so crude, so simple. Just a satisfaction thing." She wiped her eyes with a trembling hand. "Let me tell you something, Cade. I've never just slept with anyone in my life. I *feel* more than that."

"I know you do," he whispered.

His agreement only made her more livid. "I told myself all these months that you were changing. That you had grown, and stopped being bitter and resentful. But you're still just as ungrateful as you were six months ago. And I think you're afraid to be successful because you don't want to be like Dad. In fact, I have to wonder if what you said about him was true. He was probably giving you money all your life, and Cade the martyr probably sent it back. I can see it, Cade."

"That's not true, Jess."

"What? That you're a martyr, or that you're too proud? You know, you're reaping what you sow, Cade. Your son is just like you, and he's never going to be happy until someone shows him a way to let go of his pride and his resentments. But it won't be you, will it, Cade? You'll insulate yourself behind all those motorcycles, pitying your life away and beating yourself with that short end of the stick you keep getting. And no one but I will know that you threw it all away."

Before he could answer, she had slid her chair back, grabbed her purse and was storming out of the restaurant.

CHAPTER FIFTEEN

WHEN HE SHOWED UP at the board meeting the next morning, Cade wore jeans and an MMU T-shirt, which on the back spelled out Motorcycle Mechanics' University and showed a professor in leather scholars' robes putting together an engine.

He hadn't slept a wink last night, hadn't even bothered going to bed—he knew he couldn't escape the memory of how he had hurt Jessica. Worse, his own pain cut much deeper than he would have guessed. Was he going to face a lifetime of sleepless nights, helpless memories, agonizing wishes? he wondered.

He'd finally concluded that he would endure it so that Jessica could move on to the better things waiting for her. His decision to buck the executive garb he'd worn for the past six months had come this morning as he realized he didn't need these bigwigs' approval. He'd saved their butts, and now he would show them that he could walk away without looking back.

Jessica was already waiting in the Jessica Cosmetics boardroom when Cade walked in, and at the sight of him she averted her eyes and took her place at the table. He heard murmurs of disapproval at what he was wearing, and took some satisfaction in stirring up the board members. Jessica would understand his need to thumb his nose at them, he thought, if she could ever get past her bitterness toward him.

He took a place at the table and allowed himself to look at her, though she refused to meet his eyes. She looked almost regal, he thought. Her makeup was flawless, just like in the PR pictures they'd given to so many newspapers along the tour, and she held herself with an aura of dignity that no one he'd ever met could match. But there was no joy in her expression, no excitement at the fact that she was about to be made rich.

Damn, he'd blown it with her, he told himself, forcing himself to look down at his hands. And in a way, he supposed that was exactly what he'd intended to do. It had been his idea that they make a clean break and never see each other again. But now, as he was getting his wish, he realized it wasn't what he wanted at all.

The mood in the room was somber as the board members came in one by one, and when Thurgood finally arrived, carrying a stack of papers that held the verdict for him and Jessica, Cade felt the tension mounting.

After a prelude that seemed to take forever, including thanks to the two of them for all their efforts, the CEO took his glasses out of his pocket and perched them on his nose. Slowly, meticulously, he began to pass out the quarterly reports. "I believe you'll see by the figures indicated here that the Hartmans have managed to honor their father's request. In fact, they've surpassed the half a million in profits that

Andrew called for in his will, and it looks as if Jessica Cosmetics is on an upward swing. It appears, ladies and gentlemen, that we are no longer in the red."

A round of applause broke out around the table, and Cade let out a sigh of relief. His eyes met Jessica's, and he saw the relief on her face, as well. A hint of a smile crept across her face, but just as her eyes met his, it fell.

When the applause had died, Cade leaned forward. "So what's the next step for Jessica and me?"

The CEO cleared his throat, adjusted his glasses and gave Cade a look still full of as much disgust as it had been before he'd reaped the profits of Cade's work. "I suggest you meet with your lawyer this afternoon for an accounting of the number of shares Andrew held, and have them signed over to you."

Cade waited for something to be said about a change of the guard, about his and Jessica's votes upsetting the structure of the board of directors, or something indicating that Thurgood felt some respect, and not just gratitude, to the two people who had saved his own skin.

But nothing more was said. Cade sat back as the meeting rolled on, wondering if perhaps he had missed something.

When the meeting broke up, he waited at the door until Jessica reached it. "We did it," he whispered.

Jessica tried to smile. "Yes, we did."

He caught her arm as she started away, and she turned grudgingly to him. "Don't you think it's odd that nothing was said about our owning the majority of the shares, or the changes we plan to make in the future, or the restructuring of the board?"

She frowned slightly. "Well, I did keep waiting for something like that, but I just thought they wanted to wait until it was all legal." She stopped and looked at him fully. "Or that you'd already told them you planned to sell out, so it really didn't matter."

"No," he said. "I hadn't told them. Had you?"

"No," she said. "I haven't spoken to anyone." She glanced at his T-shirt. "Maybe they figured it out from the way you were dressed. It certainly succeeded in making your I-don't-give-a-damn statement."

"Good," he said, surprised that her comment had stung him. "Because I don't." He slid his hands into his pockets and looked broodingly around the room as the board members left one by one. In the far corner, Thurgood was embroiled in a very low-voiced debate with one of the members.

Something wasn't right.

Cade turned back to Jessica, trying to ignore the indictment in her eyes. "Come on," he said. "Let's go right over to see Morgan and get this all settled."

She pulled back. "I'll take my car and meet you there."

"Come on, Jess," he said. "Don't be like this."

Her face reddened. "Be like what? You're the one who wants out of my life, and you'll go to such amazing lengths to do it. I'm just making it easy for you."

Sighing, he let her go.

SAM MORGAN'S EXPRESSION was grave when he greeted the two of them and ushered them back to his office. When they were settled, he took his place behind his desk.

"Sounds like the two of you pulled off quite a coup. Frankly I don't think anyone expected you to do it."

"Obviously not," Cade said.

Sam leaned forward on his desk, frowned deeply and regarded Jessica. "You must be exhausted. You've worked really hard."

Jessica nodded. "It's been a long six months. In a lot of ways."

Cade stiffened and rubbed his chin with a callused finger.

Sam sat back, took off his glasses, cleaned them on his tie, then put them back on. "Well, I suppose you want to get down to business. There are...uh...just a few things we need to talk about first."

"What things?"

Sam sighed, and gave them another reluctant look. "You see, your father drew up this will about two years before he died. At the time, he had fifty-one percent of the shares of stock at Jessica Cosmetics. But I wasn't aware until yesterday that things had changed between the signing of the will and his death."

Cade leaned forward slowly, fixing his eyes on Sam. "What things?"

"His financial situation, for one thing." Sam opened a file and pulled out a few papers. "Cade, I knew your father for years. And I know that outward appearances suggested he was wealthy."

"He was loaded," Cade said. "Not that it did me any good."

Jessica shot him a here-we-go-again look.

"That's just it, Cade," Sam went on. "Most of the time I knew your father, he was knee-deep in debt. There were several times over the years that he seriously considered bankruptcy."

Jessica frowned. "How could that be, Sam? I had everything, growing up."

Sam shrugged. "Jessica, the truth is that your father was able to get Jessica Cosmetics under way only after he invested your mother's inheritance. Even then, it was a constant struggle to keep it afloat. And, with all due respect to your mother, she does like to spend money. Sometimes it got out of his control."

Jessica gaped at him. "But I never heard a word about money problems."

"He was embarrassed by them," Sam said, "and he tried to shelter you from it. That's why he never insisted that you be more active in the business." Sam leaned his elbows on his desk and focused on Cade. "And I wouldn't be a friend to him, Cade, if I didn't tell you how guilty he felt over his relationship with you."

Cade rolled his eyes, as if he'd heard it all before.

"Your mother despised him after the divorce, Cade, and he never had a civil conversation with her again."

"Maybe she had good reason," he said.

"Maybe. He knew the child support he gave her was inadequate, but at the time, he was literally living off of his wife's inheritance. The profits from JC had to be reinvested in the company to keep it going."

"Give me a break," Cade said. "They lived in a godforsaken mansion. He drove a Rolls-Royce. A few hundred dollars a month wouldn't have made any difference."

"Barbara bought all those things with money she got from her family. She gave him the Rolls for his birthday, and the house was in his name because he didn't want anyone knowing he'd used her money. Unfortunately her inheritance ran out a few years ago."

"Wait a minute," Jessica blurted. "Are you telling me that my mother squandered away her inheritance buying things that we couldn't afford?"

"I'm afraid so," Sam said. "That's why the will called for her selling so much of it."

Jessica shook her head. "I can't believe this."

"It's true, Jessica."

She looked at Cade, who hadn't said a word, and realized that he couldn't have been less interested. None of that wealth—whether real or imagined—had anything to do with him. "Wait. I still don't understand," she said. "Whether it was my mother's money or my father's, it still doesn't explain why Cade wasn't given adequate child support."

Sam obviously didn't want to respond to that. He shifted in his chair, then cleared his throat. "Your mother isn't here to defend herself, Jessica. I don't really feel free to go into it—"

Cade leaned forward, setting his elbows on his knees. "Let me help you, Sam." He rubbed his chin, his face bland. "Barbara didn't want any of her money going toward my support, and my father didn't have the balls to cross her. It was a control thing. Am I right?"

Sam hesitated, then finally whispered, "Something like that."

Jessica's eyes filled as she stared at Cade. "Oh, my God."

Cade's expression only seemed to grow harder. "So what's this got to do with our inheritance?"

Perspiration dotted Sam's upper lip, and he shifted in his chair again. "Well, it has a lot to do with it, actually. You see, since the writing of this will about two years ago, your father incurred some major debts trying to keep the company afloat. And to avoid bankruptcy, he got a personal loan using his shares as collateral. He put the money into the company. Unfortunately the loans hadn't been paid off by the time he died."

Jessica glanced at Cade. "Well...we could pay them off now, couldn't we? Mr. Thurgood said we were in the black."

Sam rubbed his temples and looked down at his file, as if he couldn't bear to meet their eyes. "I'm afraid it's not that simple. You see, the loan was paid off shortly after your father's death... but apparently it wasn't done with company funds."

Jessica stared at him for a moment, trying to follow. "Who paid it off?"

"John Thurgood," he said. "Apparently, there was a stipulation that the stock would be turned over to whomever paid it off in the event of Andrew's death. Thurgood was the one to do it. He used personal funds to pay it off, and obviously, that gave him controlling interest in the company."

"What are you saying?" Cade asked slowly. "Are you telling me that we get nothing? That we've been had?"

"No," Jessica blurted, her voice trembling. "That's not what he's saying, is it, Sam? We just don't get as much as we'd hoped."

Sam took off his glasses and looked at them both from behind steepled fingers. "The fact is... your father died owning only about a hundred shares of Jessica Cosmetics. That amounts to about two percent of the company...or roughly two thousand dollars' worth of shares at the current market rate. That's all he left for the two of you to divide."

Cade's heart took a nosedive, and as he tried to regain his equilibrium, he looked at Jessica. From the way she was gaping at Sam—the color had gone from her face and her expression was incredulous—he realized that she was even more stunned than he was.

Slowly she came to her feet, but, too shaky to stand on her own, she bent over Sam's desk. Her voice was quiet with restraint. "You're telling me that my father started this company from scratch, built it into a huge corporation, and died owning only two percent of it?"

Sam shook his head wearily. "I've spent all night trying to find a way around this," he said. "I hated to be the one to tell you, but it's rock solid."

Something within Cade snapped. He shot up, his teeth clamping together. "Why the hell didn't someone tell us all this before we busted our butts trying to reach some goal that didn't exist?"

"First of all, this transaction didn't occur until you and Jessica were already on the tour. That's probably why Thurgood didn't encourage you to work for JC. He didn't want you snooping around while he did this."

"That sounds like grounds for a lawsuit," Cade said. "Conspiracy, fraud, extortion, mental anguish..."

"Wait." Sam held up a hand to stem Cade's rambling. "You were definitely had. But the truth is, none of what's happened is illegal. Your father signed his shares over to the bank of his own free will, and he outlined the terms of his will. You abided by those terms, and you're now being awarded his hundred shares. Thurgood, meanwhile, paid off the loan and legally wound up with the stock. And he could argue that you were paid while you worked for JC and that the company took care of all your expenses."

"But we rescued the company, damn it! We wouldn't have lived out of hotels for six months and worked like demons if we'd known they were going to stab us in the backs."

"He's right," Jessica said, her nose reddening as her eyes began to sting. "Cade gave up his business for this. I wouldn't have encouraged him to do that if I'd known." She caught her breath, went to the window and stared out through the mini-blinds. "Damn it, Sam," she whispered as tears rolled down her face. "Why did Daddy do this? He knew better than to leave a gaping loophole like that. If he'd left me nothing, I could have adjusted. But to dangle something in our faces so we'd scurry after it like little mice in a maze..."

"I'll tell you why he did it." Cade raked his hand through his hair. "Andrew Hartman had a penchant for cruel jokes. This time he just included you. You were lucky. At least he waited until he was dead!"

Jessica turned on him. "You bastard!" she said under her breath. "What do you care, anyway? You were going to walk!"

"I care for you, damn it! It was bad enough for me to be set up like some godforsaken prince, then have it all jerked out from under me. But now he's doing it to you, his little princess, and by God, you don't deserve it!"

"Well, we don't always get what we deserve in this life, do we, Cade?" she cried through her teeth. "The past six months have at least taught me that."

Cade glared at her. "Are you still defending him?"

Gritting her teeth, she spun around and looked helplessly at the ceiling. "I don't know what to think, Cade. This is nothing to you. You wanted out, anyway. You wanted your motorcycles and your privacy and your distance. My whole life was Jessica Cosmetics. I grew up with it. And now I find out that the past six months were a farce? What will I do? Do I sign on to keep working for them, knowing how they tricked me?"

Suddenly Cade's anger was gone. He stood quietly, looking at her, wishing with every fiber of his being that he could pull her into his arms and make the pain go away. But he knew she wouldn't let him touch her.

He was the last person who could give her comfort now.

Turning back to Sam, he said, "Look, just give my shares to her. I don't want them."

"I can't do that," Sam said. "I have to assign them to you first. After that, you can do whatever you want—"

Cade jerked the pen out of his hand. "Give me the papers."

Sam shuffled through the stack on his desk and pulled them out. Turning the pages around, he indicated where they should sign. Cade scratched his name, then handed the pen to Jessica. With great effort, she signed.

"I can draw up the papers to sell your shares to Jessica now, if you want," Sam said.

"I don't want to sell them," Cade returned. "I just want to give them to her."

"You still have to sell them, even if for a dollar apiece, just to keep things neat legally."

"No thanks, Cade," Jessica said, her voice hollow and weary as she went for her purse and dug out her keys. "I appreciate your offer, but I can't afford any more favors."

She was out the door before he could stop her. "Jessica!" he shouted, but she didn't turn back. Turning back to Sam, Cade said, "Just draw up the papers. I have to go after her."

He bolted out the door and through the offices, where they'd spoken to each other for the first time in years so many months ago. But last time it was she who had followed him. A lot of emotions had been spent since then. A lot of mistakes made.

She was almost to her car when he caught up to her. "Jessica!"

"Just leave me alone, Cade," she cried, surrendering fully to her sobs. "I just want to be alone."

He grabbed her arm as she started to get in, and turned her around. When he pulled her into his arms, he felt how weak she was, how exhausted, how drained. Her body shook with the strength of her sobs, and he held her against him, wishing he could ease her pain for her.

Instead he just kept contributing to it.

"Come on," he said finally. "I'm taking you home. We'll come back for your car later."

As if she had too little energy to fight—or just didn't care anymore—she allowed him to guide her to his truck. When she got into the passenger seat, she told herself to pull herself together. She couldn't let Cade see her like this. But there were too many shattered pieces already, too many broken illusions.

Jessica cried silently as Cade drove her home, and when she got her keys from her purse, he took them from her and opened her door. As they walked inside, she stepped on an envelope that had been slipped beneath her door.

For a moment she only looked at it, wondering what new horror awaited her. Finally Cade picked it up.

He looked at the envelope and saw the Jessica Cosmetics return address. Someone from the board had rushed over here to leave it before she got home, and he was damn sure going to find out what it was.

"Open it, Jess. Let's see what those wimps have to say."

"No...I can't." She collapsed on the sofa, clutching the envelope in her hand. Her voice was openly miserable when she whispered, "I don't know how much more I can take." Cade sank down next to her on the couch, feeling more helpless than he'd ever felt, and overcome with the irrational feeling that he was somehow to blame, directly or indirectly, for all the injustices in her world.

Suddenly he knew that he had the power to soothe that pain, and that by doing so, he would end his own pain as well.

"Here," he whispered, taking the envelope. "Let me."

She surrendered it, and didn't watch as he opened it and pulled out a letter.

His jaw ticked as he read, and finally, he wadded the letter and threw it across the room.

"They're firing me as their spokesperson, aren't they?" she whispered.

Cade stood up, arms akimbo and shoulders heaving. "They didn't even have the balls to tell you to your face." He turned back around. "Jess, they can't do this."

"Oh, but they can. They've planned it all along. Right from the beginning. And why not? It's not like my father left any provisions for keeping me in the company!" She threw up her hands and clutched her head. "I feel so stupid! I spent the past six months working toward nothing but mirages." A sob broke her voice, and she drew in a deep breath. "Am I supposed to *learn* something from this?"

The phone rang before he could say anything, and furiously, Jessica snatched it up. "Hello?" Her voice was weak, hollow.

Cade thought of leaving now, but somehow he couldn't make himself do it, not with her still crying, and those dappled red patches beside her eyes, and her nose glowing with the intensity of her pain. And there was something else, too.

He didn't want to take the chance of not seeing her again. After last night, he had no reason to. It was over. They had their separate lives now, their separate agendas, their separate futures. There was no reason for the twain to meet if they didn't want to.

But who was he kidding?

The thought of not seeing Jessica tomorrow, and the day after that, was more than he could stand right now. Later, he told himself. There was time to end it all later. Right now, she needed him.

And he needed her.

"No," she said, her face twisting and turning a deep red as she clutched the phone to her ear. "No comment." She hung the phone up, and instantly it started ringing again.

This time she didn't pick it up. "Word's gotten out, Cade," she said, standing up. "We were duped. All this publicity we did for the past few months...we had everybody rooting for us. Now they'll all know how stupid we were!"

He went to her, tried to pull her against him, but the phone kept ringing.

Finally she flung herself away from him and knocked the phone off the table. The receiver fell off, and she hung it up and jerked the cord from the wall. "You can go on home now, Cade!" she shouted. "Your phone's probably ringing, too. You can tell them how you were right, and how it's all behind you now."

He didn't move. "I'm not going anywhere, Jess."

"Why not!" she shouted. "What are you hanging around here for? Your work's over, and you've ended whatever we had between us. You're a free man! Take off, Cade!"

He shook his head. "I told you, Jess. I'm not going anywhere. At least not without you."

She laughed too loudly, the harsh sound revealing just how close she was to breaking. "You've got to be kidding!" she said bitterly.

He started for her bedroom. "I'm going to pack you a bag."

Her face twisted. "What?"

"You'll need a change of clothes. I'm taking you home with me."

Furious, she followed him and watched him pull a small bag from her closet. "Cade, I'm not going anywhere with you. I have to decide what I'm going to do with my life!"

"You can decide later. Right now, you just need to get out of here." She dropped down on the bed, her own emptiness making her numb as she heard him opening drawers, rattling hangers, clanging things in the bathroom.

All that kept going through her mind was that her father was dead, her mother was a thousand miles away with no plans to come home soon, she had no job, no hope, and the only man she loved had made it clear that he wanted to be rid of her. Today, she had no patience with his mercy or his pity.

In a few minutes, he came back into her room and began taking clothes from her drawers. "You might want to get out of those heels and put on something more comfortable." He found a pair of white leggings and a big T-shirt to match. "Here. Wear this."

She skewered him with a look. "I told you, Cade. I'm not going anywhere with you."

"Yes, you are." He finished with her bag and zipped it shut. "I'm going out to load these into my truck now. If you haven't changed when I come back in, then you'll go in what you're wearing."

Still gaping at him, she muttered, "You're out of your mind."

"Fine," he said.

She watched him take her bag out and sat still, refusing to make any effort to do as he'd told her. After a moment, he came back in. "Wearing that, huh?" he said. "Okay. You ready?"

She sighed and clutched her head where it was beginning to ache. "Cade, this is getting ridiculous."

"Tell me about it." Grabbing her arm, he yanked her up, but she struggled to free herself.

"Stop it, Cade. I'm not going with you."

"Either go get in that truck of your own accord, or I'll take you myself."

"No!"

Smiling, he said, "Okay, baby. Your choice." Bending over, he grabbed her legs. Before she knew it, he was standing up with her hanging over his shoulder.

She screamed and beat impotently at his back. "Let me down!"

Laughing, he set the lock on the door, grabbed her purse and headed out to his truck. When he dropped her into the passenger seat, she glared up at him.

"Where are we going?"

"My house, where I can pamper and protect you. Where we can chill out...and think."

"I can do that here!" she shouted.

"No, you can't," he said. "Not in the state you're in."

He went to his side and slammed the door. "Besides, what else have you got to do? You have some big company you have to run?"

She sighed. "No, Cade. I have nothing better to do. But I'd still rather do it without you."

His voice softened as he pulled out of her driveway. "Well, you're not going to," he said. "From here on out, we're in this together."

Jessica closed her eyes, not wanting to dwell on what that did—or didn't—mean. It didn't pay to hope, she thought, and it didn't pay to dream. The best she could do was brace herself for any more arrows life chose to fling at her.

WHEN THEY REACHED his house, Jessica was quiet as she went inside and watched him unplug the phones. He poured her a glass of wine, put his Pachelbel CD on the stereo, and came to where she sat on the couch. Leaning over her, he whispered, "I'm glad you're here, Jess. This house was real lonely last night."

"So was mine," she whispered.

He gazed into her eyes for a moment, his own dark with meaning, though she didn't have a clue what they were saying. She wanted to believe that he'd changed his mind, that the "in this together" he'd referred to had meant that they weren't going their separate ways. That it wasn't over.

But she knew better.

"I'm gonna take a shower," he whispered, his lips too close to her face. "And then I'm going to cook you the best dinner you've ever eaten." His voice was soothing as he went on. "So just sit here and zone out, as Ben would say. Don't think. Just be."

She didn't say a word, and finally he stood up and disappeared into his bedroom. Her eyes followed him until he was out of sight, and something stirred in her heart. He was the picture of virility, a rugged, handsome icon in her life against whom no other man would ever measure up. Did that mean that once he was out of her life she was destined to be alone, to remember the brief few months of bliss when her hope was grounded in reality?

Dolefully she realized that he had lost, too. He had lost Ben, and he was losing her—and whether it was his idea or not, he would be alone, as well. He didn't have a job or a company, either, and the pain she was feeling was just as much his.

The same hoax that her father had played on her had been played on him. The only difference was that he wasn't surprised by it. He'd had these disappointments before.

She drew in a deep breath and laid her head back on the seat, and thought of the pictures her father had of Cade as a little boy, when his family was still intact. The joy and love of life that shone in his eyes spoke of a child who was well loved and encouraged to be and do whatever he wanted. But that joy had died when their father had found another woman. And had another child with that woman.

Yes, Cade knew disappointment, for he'd had to rebuild his life around it at an age when his greatest worries should have been passing his math test or being the first one to find a treasure in the neighborhood creek. By the time she had known him, Cade's light had died, and instead he was an angry, disillusioned young man who didn't dare make any further investment of love in the man who had betrayed him.

And now her beloved father, the man who had doted on her and spoiled her, had betrayed her as well.

Fresh anger stirred inside her, and she wished she had never been the daughter of a rich man, had never known the attentions and whims and indulgences that he had afforded her. She wished she had grown up like Cade, expecting nothing, so that now she wouldn't have so far to fall.

Where would she start, now that her whole purpose was gone? She got up and went to the back door, opened it and stepped onto the deck overlooking Cade's backyard. He had been working in it since they'd come back, she saw. The hedges were freshly trimmed and the lawn had been recently mowed. He took a lot of pride in this place, she told herself. He took a lot of pride in a lot of things.

Tears came to her eyes again, and she blinked them back as she heard Cade return from the shower.

Vaguely she wondered if she and Cade were going to act like brother and sister or lovers while she was here. Were they going to spirit around like ghosts in the same house, avoiding each other, or go back to the way they had been on the tour, pretending he'd never told her it was over?

Before she could come to any conclusion, he stepped out on the deck behind her, slid his arms around her and held her as tightly as he would have held a china doll that might break with the wrong pressure. "I told you not to think," he whispered against her hair. "But you're doing it anyway, aren't you?"

She sighed, trying not to lose herself in the feel of his arms. "It's gonna be all right, Jess," he whispered. "I promise."

She didn't want to think about it now, didn't want to confront the awful loneliness waiting for her back home, or the aimlessness of her life, or her search for a direction. And she didn't want to think about how cold she would be when Cade let her go.

All that mattered was that his arms were around her now. He was here with her, and no matter what that meant or didn't mean, she was going to cling to it while she could.

"Let's go get you another glass of wine," he whispered.

Taking his hand, she followed him inside. He poured her another glass, and she brought it to her lips. "It just occurred to me that I've never seen the rest of your house," she said. "That was the first time I saw the backyard. I don't even know how many bedrooms there are."

His eyes grew serious as he looked at her, and finally he took her hand and pulled her against him again. "If you're trying subtly to ask me where you're sleeping, I was hoping it would be with me."

Her heart jolted, but she told herself not to be stupid. Sleeping in the same bed with her was not tantamount to a commitment. Still, his arms felt so good, and when he bent down and kissed her neck, she let out a breath of sweet relief. His mouth came down gently on hers, and as their tongues mated softly, her tension seeped out, and the pain and grief and sadness were all replaced with a fragile seed of hope... right next to the longing that had overgrown in her heart.

Trembling, she pulled back. "If we're through, Cade, let's be through," she whispered against his lips. "You want out of this. You said so last night."

"Shut up," he whispered.

She shook her head. "I can't. You said it was over. Am I supposed to forget that?"

Framing her face with both hands, he fixed his eyes on hers. "I also said I'd never work for JC, but I did. And I said nothing could happen between us, but a lot happened. When are you going to stop listening to me?"

She took in a sharp breath. "Are you saying that you didn't mean what you said last night?"

"I'm saying that what I know I should do and what I find myself doing are two different things." He pressed his forehead against hers and took a long, agonizing breath, as if breathing in a life-giving scent. "I just want to be with you, Jess. I want to hold you and cherish you and feel warm and whole again. You're the only one who can make me feel this way."

Tears flowed down her cheeks as he kissed her again, and this time she didn't pull away.

DAWN'S RAYS warmed the room through the huge window at the back of Cade's bedroom, stirring Jessica from her sleep. Opening her eyes, she beheld the sight of the sunlight painting the room in bright colors.

Cade stirred behind her and, rising up, pressed a kiss on her neck. "Good morning, Sleeping Beauty," he said.

She smiled and leaned back into him. "Is the sun this beautiful every morning?"

"No," he said. "And it'll never be more beautiful than it is today." He rolled her onto her back. Bracing himself on an elbow, he smiled down at her. "I was watching you while you slept. You're gorgeous drenched in sunlight, did you know that?"

She smiled. "How long have you been awake?"

"Long enough." He kissed her shoulder, then pushed her hair back to bare her neck. "You know how early morning sometimes brings bursts of clarity? Like all the answers to life's problems are suddenly, painfully obvious?"

"Did you have one of those bursts?"

He grinned, and then his grin faded and a serious sweetness colored his eyes. "I sure did, Jess. I sure did."

He kissed her then, and as he pulled her against him, her body was newly aroused by the feel of his skin against hers. And this time when they made love, she allowed herself to feel that elusive hope. Cade was right. There was something about early morning that brought clarity to a blurred world. And whether she was kidding herself or not, she was going to believe in it for now.

THEY WERE STILL IN BED two hours later, when Cade, sleepy and relaxed, propped himself on an elbow and traced her cheekbone with his finger. "This morning, I was watching you sleep and thinking how beautiful and serene you look, and what a perfect image you gave the company," he said. "And I was thinking what a stupid move they've made in cutting you loose."

Her smile faded, and that sadness crept back into her eyes. "So what else is new?"

"Our company," he whispered. "That's what's new. We're going to start our own company."

"What?"

"You and I," he said. "We're going to start a competing company, and name it something romantic and mysterious, and your face is going to be all over it. Jess, if we did that, we could blow JC out of the water."

Jessica sat up, pulling the sheets around her in sudden modesty. "I don't know, Cade. Where would we get the capital?"

"Borrow it," he said. "We're Hartmans. We pulled JC out of the dumps ourselves, and everybody knows it. We could convince investors to set us up. I know we could. All the work we've done for the past six months would then be in our favor. It's your face that's in everybody's minds. Who do you think customers will follow? The name of a company, or the real woman they're trying to emulate?"

"But I thought you wanted out of the cosmetics business."

He thought for a moment. "That was before."

"Why now?" she asked. "Is it because you feel sorry for me?"

Smiling, he stroked her shoulder. "No," he said. "It's because I'm so angry at them."

"So angry that you'd get into a line of work that you hate?"

"I don't hate it, Jess. The past six months were a real rush to me. I didn't want to admit it, but I enjoyed it. Besides, I don't think it would come down to actually starting our own company. I think it would just be ammunition."

Jessica finger-brushed her hair back from her face and tried to follow him. "I don't understand what you're saying."

He grinned. "I'm saying that the threat of our starting our own company is enough to shake them up. Enough, even, to keep you as spokesperson. We might even be able to get them to give you the stock you should have gotten, just to get you to stay."

Slowly she saw the genius in his plan, and stared at him for a long moment. "What about you?"

"I was going to leave, anyway," he said. "Right now we need to get you back where you belong, and show those idiots where their success has come from. They don't want us competing with them, Jess."

"And if they don't bite?"

"Then we'll go ahead with the plan. And within a year, we'll blow JC right out of the water."

Her smile came from the center of her heart, where the lights had all been burned out the day before. With fragile joy, she believed it would never be dark there again. "All right, Cade. Let's do it."

CHAPTER SIXTEEN

THE BOARD MEMBERS of Jessica Cosmetics had not been easy to gather at an hour's notice, but when Cade had outlined his plans to Thurgood in his office that morning, he'd gotten the man's attention.

Now, he and Jessica found themselves at the table feeling quite a bit more powerful than they had before. They knew they had something to say that the board did not want to hear. And the best part of it was that they weren't bluffing.

In the past few days, they had talked to two investors and three banks who were willing to put up the money for Cade's and Jessica's new company. Now it wasn't just ammunition. It was a real possibility, and the board members knew it.

Cade and Jessica sat side by side, listening to the CEO's condescending tone and his diatribe about how they'd consider taking Jessica back on their own terms.

Cade laughed. "You don't seem to understand something," he said, rubbing a spot off the table with his finger. "Jessica doesn't need you. You need her."

"We've already started our search for our new Jessica," the man said, as if the whole conversation bored him.

Again, Cade laughed. "You people are pathetic. It's Jessica's face that's been all over the media for the past six months, and before that, she was the main identifier for this company ever since she started wearing makeup herself. You're not going to be able to replace her, but if you're stupid enough to try, and we take her face and her image to our company, it's a safe bet you won't be in business to lord it around this table for much longer."

Silence filled the room as all eyes turned to the woman for whom this fight was being waged.

Jessica sat regally in her seat, calm and unruffled, meeting the eyes of the people her father had trusted to build his company. "The fact is, I don't like the way I've been duped," Jessica said, speaking for the first time since the meeting had been called to order. "I don't have much respect for people who cheat and lie."

"Wait a minute," Thurgood said. "No one lied to you."

"It was a lie to send us on a mission for you with some nonexistent prize at the end. You knew my father didn't have much stock when he died. But none of you bothered to tell us. And no one dared mention that Mr. Thurgood, here, was buying my father's stock for himself while we spent six months killing ourselves so that stock would be worth something."

Leaning forward at the table, she crossed her hands in front of her. "The truth, ladies and gentlemen, is that Cade and I look forward to the prospect of starting our own company. And frankly, we think we can do a heck of a lot better job than you have."

Thurgood's jaws reddened. "That's a mistake, Jessica. This is not the kind of economy conducive to starting a new company. The market shares won't be—"

"*Don't* tell me about market shares," Jessica cut in. "We know the reality of this business. We're the ones who've been out there in the trenches for the past six months. The fact is that we'll be going into this with a lot of name recognition, and we'll be taking it away from you. That's a lot more than my father had when he started this company."

"And you would compete against the company that your father started from scratch and built with his bare hands?" someone asked.

It was Jessica's turn to laugh, and she looked at Cade, offering him the chance to respond. Smiling, Cade shifted in his chair. "Frankly, people, we have no qualms about it at all. In fact, if he were here to see the position we've been put in, he'd probably jump ship with us."

The board members were silent for a moment, and finally one of the members looked at the CEO. "I think we need to talk about this, John. Why don't we ask the Hartmans to give us a little time to work this out?"

The CEO mumbled something incomprehensible, then asked Cade and Jessica to leave so the board members could discuss the matter. They would call them when they came to a decision about how to proceed.

The moment they stepped out of the room and the door closed behind them, Cade and Jessica grinned at each other.

"Gosh, Cade," Jessica said. "I think they're finally taking us seriously."

Cade laughed and took her hand. "Come on, let's go have lunch."

AS IF THEY WERE A JURY that had just reached a verdict, the board of Jessica Cosmetics contacted Jessica and Cade that afternoon and asked them to return for another meeting.

They knew when they walked into the room that the attitude of the board had changed. Suddenly people were smiling, offering them coffee, making small talk that had never been bothered with before.

Thurgood, however, did not look so happy as he took his place at the head of the table. Clearing his throat, he waited until everybody was seated, then got right to the point. "The members of the board have decided that it would be in our best interest to keep Jessica on as our spokesperson. We're prepared to offer her a much larger portion of stock than her father left her, and give her a seat on the board." He handed her a paper with their terms outlined, and Jessica took it.

"What about Cade?" she asked.

"Cade could continue working at JC in the same capacity as he has for the past six months. We could pay him ten percent more than we've been paying him . . . all of this under one condition."

He shifted in his seat and clasped his hands. "It has come to our attention that the relationship between the two of you has the potential to create a scandal. We can't offer either of you anything unless we have your assurance that you will end whatever is going on between you."

Jessica caught her breath and looked at Cade, who stared at Thurgood, stunned. "Mr. Thurgood," she said through compressed lips, "our personal relationships—whether they're with each other or anyone else—aren't now, and have never been, any of your business."

"Oh, but it is. We don't want our customers thinking of incest whenever they see your face."

"She's not my sister!" Cade bit out. "You know that as well as I do!"

"But much of the world will find it scandalous anyway," Thurgood said.

Jessica leaned forward, livid. "Then much of the world needs an education. And we're just the ones to give it to them. I think the place to do that is from the forum of our own new company."

She stood to leave, but Cade stopped her. "Wait a minute, Jess." His eyes were dull as he turned back to them. "It's not worth the fight. As for me, you have my assurances that there won't be a scandal. But I don't want anything you have to offer me. And Jessica shouldn't either, unless you offer her more stock."

Jessica looked at him as if he'd just shot her in the heart. The rest of the board gaped at him as if he'd just rolled in on a hay truck knowing more than he ought to know. "I'm afraid that would be impossible. We've all had to cut into our own shares to give those to her."

"You should have cut into the shares that Thurgood rooked us out of," Cade said.

"I beg your pardon," the man bit out. "Your father made his own choice to use those shares as collateral, and I found it in JC's best interest to buy them back rather than letting the bank have them."

"But all that will be a waste, won't it, if we start a competing company and draw your business away?"

Thurgood's hand came down on the table. "What would you have to gain by doing that?"

"Control, for one thing," Cade said. "We wouldn't be cut out of the profits. Nobody could tell us with whom we're allowed to have relationships. And we'd know we weren't being manipulated to put money in the wrong people's pockets."

"We weren't manipulating you," one of the members said.

"Conning us into saving JC by making us think we would get something out of it is not manipulation?"

"If you recall, we didn't care whether you came to work for us or not," Thurgood said. "As a matter of fact, we had plans to proceed without either of you."

"Yes, I do recall," Cade said. "I recall the plans to cut Jessica out and find a new Jessica, just as you've threatened to do lately. And that, I suppose, could happen anytime down the road. Unless she has enough stock that her input carries some weight."

The CEO leaned back as if he were extraordinarily weary of it all, and gave a disgusted look around the room. "Then if you'll excuse us, Mr. Hartman, it looks like we have a little more to discuss."

Cade slid his chair back from the table and stood up as Jessica put their offer into her briefcase, fighting back the tears threatening her. "Tell you what. The next offer you make should go through her lawyer. Sam Morgan can speak for us."

The man gave him a go-to-hell look, and muttered, "Very well."

The moment the door closed behind them, Jessica turned on him. "How could you?"

"How could I what?"

"How could you just ignore what they said about our relationship?"

"Because your future is at stake, Jessica. I want them to give you what you deserve."

"And what about us? Am I supposed to forget how I feel about you to satisfy them? Do you think a seat on the board will replace what we've had?"

Cade's eyes grew fiery, and he struggled to make her listen. "You're *the* Jessica. The only one. The whole company revolves around you. It's absolutely ludicrous for them to consider cutting you out . . . for any reason. And I'll do whatever is necessary to keep them from doing it!"

"Even if it means saying goodbye?"

Cade looked at his feet, unable to answer.

"What about our business together, Cade? What about our plans? What about our being 'in this together' from now on?"

"I meant all that, Jess. But I don't want you to lose everything because of me." His voice broke, and she saw the tears forming in his eyes.

Jessica's mouth trembled as she uttered the most nakedly honest truth she'd ever uttered in her life. "None of it means anything to me without you, Cade. When are you going to believe that?"

DRIVING HOME was difficult, as Jessica's tears blurred her vision. She had left Cade behind, hurt by his own hand. And as angry as she was at him for negotiating away their relationship so easily, she couldn't help thinking it had cost him more than he wanted her to know.

She reached her apartment and realized that something had to be done. She couldn't let them dictate her emotions or rob Cade of what was rightfully his, even if he was willing to abdicate it. He had fought to help her. Now she could fight to help him. And if he still wanted to say goodbye after that, at least it would be an emotional decision and not a business one.

Turning her car around, she headed for Sam Morgan's office. When his secretary showed her in, she took a deep breath. "Sam, we have to talk. I have some new demands for staying with JC. And I won't settle for anything less."

THE OFFER that Sam Morgan brought Cade and Jessica that afternoon was one that had never crossed Cade's mind, but the moment he heard it, he knew something was fishy.

"Let me get this straight," he said as he sat with Jessica and Sam at his kitchen table, studying the terms of the offer. "Not only did they come up on Jessica's number of shares, but they've offered me an equal number of shares, *and* a seat on the board? I don't get it. I didn't ask for that, and I know damn well they didn't just throw it in for good measure. In fact, with her shares and my shares combined we'd have a substantial vote in the company. Why would they do that if it wasn't one of our demands?"

"Well, it was one of your demands," Sam said, glancing at Jessica.

Jessica wished Sam hadn't exposed her, and she gave Cade a guilty look. "I'm not taking any offer without your getting your fair share, Cade. I had Sam call them after our meeting today."

Cade looked down at the offer again. "Jessica, I appreciate your effort here, but I don't need anybody going to bat for me. I don't even want to be a part of this company. I told you—"

"And I told you. Either you do this with me, Cade, or I'm out."

Bristling, he got to his feet. "Look, I know you mean well. And this is a good deal. But take the shares they're giving me and put them together with yours, Jess. Then you'll be set for life. They won't ever be able to cut you out again."

"They can't cut me out anyway," she said, "even if you take your shares." She stood up and faced him head-on, and made him look at her. "Look, Cade, I know that our father let us down. I know the executives of the company duped us. It was a sleazy trick to pull, but something good is coming out of it. Because of what Dad put in his will, we learned an awful lot. We both got a crash course in what makes JC tick, and we learned that together we can do anything. Dad did give us that."

Cade looked down at Sam, still sitting at the table. "Sam, I need to think this over. Could we meet with you in the morning?"

"Sure," Sam said. "I'll block some time out for you."

They waited until he left, and finally Cade turned back to Jessica. The air was charged with expectation, and she waited, hoping, praying, that they could accept this latest victory. But something in Cade's eyes told her they could not.

"I don't want you fighting my battles, Jess," Cade said. "And I don't want handouts. And I don't want something just because you blackmailed them into giving it to me."

"It's not blackmail," she said. "It's negotiation."

"It's blackmail," he said. "They were desperate to keep you from competing, and you used that to get something for me."

"Let me get this straight. If you do that, it's negotiation, but not if I do it?"

His face reddened, and he turned away from her, walked to the counter and whirled back around. "I don't need anything from you, Jess! I don't need your help or your handouts. I've done just fine all my life!"

She leaned back against the table, unable to believe what was happening. "You're going to throw this opportunity away, aren't you?" she asked, astounded.

"You're going to give up the chance of a lifetime, something you've earned, something that was your birthright, just because of your stupid pride?"

"What do you care?" he shouted. "If they'd give me this much, then they'd give you more if I pass. And they'd know we'd be less likely to create a scandal. Why do you want me there so badly?"

"Because I love you, Cade!" she shouted. "Sue me! I realize that's a stupid, foolhardy thing to do, and that it'll probably cost me the biggest heartbreak of my life, but I love you anyway. And I don't know if I'm going to have you in my life after all this is over. But I made it clear to them that my love life was none of their business, and I dug out all of the interviews I'd done in which I explained that we aren't really related. I found almost fifty, Cade! So many people realize it already. And they had to admit that our relationship is more a love story than a piece of scandalous gossip!"

Cade raked his hair, his face betraying his confusion.

"If you want to end this, Cade, I'll have to accept it. But at least I'll still see you sometimes, and together, we can make this company grow into something huge and wonderful. I'll at least have you as a business partner, and maybe even as a friend."

"Not as a brother?" he asked sarcastically.

She shook her head and wiped the tears just beginning to spill from her eyes. "No, Cade. Never as a brother again."

Cade looked up at the ceiling, frustration rampant in his eyes. "Damn you, Jess."

"Damn you, Cade."

He looked at her again, taking in the stark refreshment of her beauty. She loved him. Why didn't that make him happy?

He closed his eyes and waved a hand in the air. "I have to think, Jess."

She drew in a deep, labored breath, then let it out in a rush. "Okay. I'll leave you alone, then. You know where you can find me."

CADE DROPPED onto the couch when she left and, lying down, stared up at the ceiling. This wasn't how he'd expected things to turn out, and for the life of him, he couldn't figure out why he hated it so much.

Was it really his pride?

Or was it fear? Fear of not measuring up to the class and dignity that Jessica carried with her like a passport to any place she wanted? Or was it fear of failing with JC?

Funny thing, he thought. He'd always thought of himself as fearless. But since he'd gotten to know Jessica, he'd never been more afraid in his life. A mechanic's work was easy, risk-free. But working for JC had been the hardest work he'd ever done. There was such a high chance of failing. Such a high chance of proving what he'd always believed about himself. What he thought his father had believed.

The doorbell rang, and he sat up, wondering if Jessica had come back to try one last appeal. He hoped not, since he was no closer to an answer now than he'd been earlier.

Slowly he went to the door and opened it, but it wasn't Jessica who was waiting.

It was Ben.

Catching his breath, Cade pulled his son into a quick embrace. "Ben! What are you doing here?"

As usual, Ben pulled stiffly back and came inside. "Hope it's okay that I dropped in."

"Of course it's okay! How did you get here?"

"Amtrak," he said. "I figured they wouldn't look for me there."

"Oh, no." Something in Cade's heart fell, and he took Ben's shoulders and made him look him in the eye. "You didn't run away again, did you?"

"Dad, I'm practically grown," Ben said. "I wouldn't call it running away."

"Then what would you call it?"

"Going out on my own," the child said. "I've got a plan."

"A plan." Cade tried not to sound deprecating as he took Ben's duffel bag and set it down. "And what kind of plan would that be?"

"I'm going down to Florida," he said. "I have some friends living there. I can stay with them."

Cade tried to put aside the hurt that his son would deliberately not consider the obvious choice of staying with him. "Look, why don't you tell me what happened?"

Ben looked toward the kitchen. "Okay, but you got anything to drink?"

Cade kicked himself mentally and told himself that he should have offered his son food and drink immediately. His failure to do so only showed how deficient his fathering skills were. He got up and poured his son a Coke, then pulled some things for a sandwich out of the refrigerator and set them down in front of his son.

Ben started making a sandwich, his face still somber.

"So... are you gonna tell me?"

"It's really no big deal," he said. "I just don't like it there."

"So you thought you'd just move on."

"Well, yeah. Pretty much. I figure it'll be three or four days before Mom even notices I'm gone."

He watched his son quietly as he bit into his sandwich. The boy was vacuum-packed with pride, just like Jessica had said he was, and just like Cade himself. He'd rather go off to Florida than to ask his own father if he could live with him.

Maybe Ben just needed it spelled out, he thought. Maybe, for once, Cade needed to ask him, straight out, to come live with him.

"You know, there is an alternative to Florida, even though it may not be quite as adventurous," Cade said, his voice soft and tentative.

Ben washed his bite down with a gulp of soda. "Yeah?"

"Yeah. You could live here with me."

Ben didn't answer for a moment, and Cade felt he had to make the sales pitch a little stronger. But somehow he didn't feel he had much to offer.

"I realize it's not exactly like your mansion in Arlington. And I sure as heck don't make as much as

Richard does. Matter of fact, I don't even have a job right now."

Ben frowned. "I thought you owned part of JC."

Cade rubbed his eyes, wishing his son had never known him as anything other than a motorcycle mechanic. It would save him a lot of disappointment. "That didn't exactly work out like we hoped. I mean, we raised profits like we hoped...but my father didn't hold as many shares of JC as we thought, and..."

"You're broke, then?" Ben asked him, trying to follow.

"Well, yes and no. I mean, they've offered me a big hunk of stock and a position in the company and on the board, but—"

Ben waited for what followed the "but," but Cade knew that there was no way he'd ever understand why he didn't want to accept their offer. "I'm thinking about turning their offer down...for a number of reasons. I might be opening another bike shop...or something like that."

"Cool."

Cade frowned. Had Ben said what he thought he'd said? Didn't he understand the difference in income between a bike mechanic and a top executive in a public company?

"The thing is, I'll never get rich with my bike shop. And I won't be some big shot with clean fingernails. I'll never have a lot of money to throw around."

"That's good," Ben said, taking another bite. "All money does is take people away."

The impact of his words surprised Cade, and for a moment he looked at his son, wondering how the boy had learned the same lesson that had been such a smothering force in his own life as a child. Money did take people away. It had taken his father away when he was a child. It had taken Bridgit away. It had taken Ben. And, if he wasn't careful, he was going to make it take Jessica away, as well.

"That's a tough lesson for a kid your age to learn," Cade said quietly.

Ben shrugged.

"When I was your age, I thought the same thing," Cade went on. "And I told myself that people always did a lot better after they left me. Look at my father. He made millions of dollars after he walked out on Mom and me. And now Jess. She's going to be a rich lady, too."

"What do you think now?" Ben asked, setting the leftover crusts down.

Cade thought for a moment. Had his ideas really changed all that much since he was a child? Did he want Ben to know that he was still that cynical? "I don't know," he finally admitted.

Ben reached for two more slices of bread and started making another sandwich. "Well, you could be rich, too, couldn't you? I mean, you said they offered you some things."

Cade bristled again. "I don't need handouts."

"You just don't think you deserve it."

His son's insight hit him right in the gut. "What do you mean?"

"I mean that might be why you want to fix motorcycles. It's not very hard for you. You never have to live up to anything."

Cade's forehead pleated as he stared at the boy. "I thought you liked me having a bike shop."

"I do," Ben said. "It's cool. But I just keep wondering why you do it when you could do just about anything."

"Maybe I'm bucking the system," Cade said. "Maybe I'm making sure nobody else chooses my path for me. I'm in control."

"I know the feeling," Ben said. "That's why it feels good to leave home. I'm in control. I can go anywhere I want, and do anything I want. No expectations, no disappointments."

Cade leaned forward, his gaze intent on his son. "You're twelve years old, Ben. Like it or not, you're still a kid. You're not going anywhere. You're staying here with me, or going back to your mother. That's your choice."

Ben's eyes were belligerent when he met his father's gaze. "Well, I'm not going back there."

"Good," Cade said. "Then you'll live here with me."

"You can't afford me," Ben said. "It costs money to raise a kid. I eat a lot."

Cade didn't know how to answer that. "I didn't say I was broke, Ben. Just that I'm not rich."

"Well, you won't like spending money on me. It'll make you mad after a while."

Cade's face twisted as he tried to figure out where his son got such logic. "That's not true. I'd rather spend money on you than anyone else. I wouldn't sweat over one cent. I just meant that it wouldn't be like it is at your mom's, with millions coming in. I wouldn't let you carry a credit card in your pocket, not even if I had the money."

"Fine," Ben said. "I only use that for traveling."

"You wouldn't be doing any more traveling, Ben. If you choose to live with me, you have to follow the rules. And one of them is . . . no running away."

Ben looked at him seriously, but after a moment, he broke into a grin. "Yeah, it seems like Mom had that rule, too. She still doesn't know I broke it."

Cade got the point. "Well, maybe you won't want to run away."

"You think?"

The question set a new worry forming in his mind, the worry that he wasn't good enough to be a father, wasn't worthy of having his son, didn't deserve to know that kind of loving responsibility. Was it just another example of his feeling that he only deserved the worst of life's offerings? The leftovers?

And why did he feel that way?

Maybe it was time he did something about that, he thought. Maybe it was time for life to make a few things up to him. And maybe it was time to put aside that pride and embrace the moment.

He watched Ben finish his sandwich, then leaned across the table. "Listen to me, buddy."

Ben wiped his mouth and gave his father a serious look.

"Your coming here might be the best thing that could have happened to me tonight. And I can't think of a better time to turn my life around."

"How?"

"By growing up," he said. "By being a father, for the first time in my life. By admitting that I love you more than any father ever loved a son."

Ben glanced away, as if searching for a change of subject, but suddenly his eyes filled with tears, and quietly he reached across the table and took his father's hand. "Yeah, me too, man."

It was a catharsis, a moment of awakening, a liberation of a lifetime of baggage that they were both vowing to throw off, each in his own way.

"You're the legal age to decide which parent you live with," Cade said. "And I would like nothing better than to have you live here."

Ben refused to wipe his eyes, even though a tear dropped onto his cheek and rolled down his face. "Are you sure?"

"I don't have a doubt in my mind," Cade said. "And...as for the bike shop...maybe that's not really what I want to do, after all."

"Doesn't matter to me what you do," Ben said. "But if you work for JC, will you still have to travel a lot?"

Cade's heart sank. "Maybe."

Ben shrugged. "Then maybe I could stay with Jessica when you're gone."

A slow grin, just like the sunshine the morning Jessica had awoken in his bed, dawned on his face. "Maybe."

"Or maybe she could just stay here."

Cade's frown tainted his grin.

"You two are an item, aren't you?"

When Cade didn't answer, Ben said, "She'd be a terrific stepmom. Where's my room?"

Cade laughed, and following his son as he bounced up the stairs, he realized that maybe life wasn't a series of misguided flukes, after all. Maybe there was a path for him. And maybe he just had to grow up enough to take it.

JESSICA DIDN'T SLEEP at all that night. She lay awake for hours, then paced her apartment, stared out the window, gazed at the phone, and wondered if Cade was going to let her down. The next morning, she showered early and dressed, just in case, then paced the living room of her apartment, back and forth, back and forth, waiting for word from either Cade or Sam. But somehow, she knew that she was waiting in vain. Cade was going to disappoint her. It was the beginning of the end for him. Turning his back on JC's offer would be turning his back on her. It would be the perfect time to cut her loose again. The perfect time to carry out his plan to forget her.

The doorbell rang, and she rushed to open it. Cade stood there, his face soft and vulnerable and unshaved, and her heart leaped at the mere sight of him.

"Come in." She turned away from the door as he closed it behind him.

"I've come to a decision, Jess," he said.

She put up a hand to stem his words—she didn't think she could bear the disappointment. "I know, Cade. You're going to turn it down. You're going to go back to repairing motorcycles, and pretend we never meant anything to each other, and pretend you never pulled an ailing company out of the dumper by your will and determination." Tears assaulted her, and she dropped onto her couch. "I've been expecting it all night. I just didn't want to hear it."

Sitting down next to her, he pulled her hair back from her neck and nuzzled a kiss there. "No, Jess," he whispered. "That's not it."

Her nose was red from the emotion wrenching her when she finally brought her face up to his. "What then?"

"I'm going to take their offer, Jess. As long as you'll take mine."

"What?" she asked on an incredulous whisper.

"Will you marry me?"

She caught her breath and more tears rushed forward. "Oh, Cade!"

He pulled her into his arms, and felt her body shaking with her sobs, as if all the pain she had endured last night, certain that it was their end, were now draining out in a flood of relief. "Just one thing," he went on softly. "Ben's coming to live with me. In fact, he's already here. So if you take me, you have to take him, too."

She laughed through her tears, and pulled back to look at him. "Yes, Cade, I'll marry you."

It was his turn to get teary-eyed, his turn to feel stark relief. "I love you, Jess."

"Oh, Cade," she cried. "I love you, too."

EPILOGUE

THE AFTERNOON after they'd closed the deal with Jessica Cosmetics, Cade, Jessica and Ben breezed into the justice of the peace's office and exchanged vows. From there, they went to the airport, where Cade had reserved first-class seats on the Concorde to Paris.

"You sure you want to take me on your honeymoon?" Ben asked as they settled into their seats. "I mean, it is kind of weird. I didn't go with Mom and Richard. Matter of fact, I hardly ever went with them on their vacations."

"We're going to be a different kind of family," Jessica said. "Besides, you've been to Paris more than either of us. We need you to show us around."

"You probably won't have time," Ben said. "You'll be working the whole time."

Cade laughed. "Not the whole time. Once I get the new shop underway, we'll have time to do whatever we want."

Jessica shot Ben a look, and they both laughed.

"What?" Cade asked.

"We're amazed at the way you can work business into your honeymoon so that your extravagance isn't really an extravagance, Dad. You have to justify spending money, don't you?"

"I guess I do," Cade said with no apologies. "That's why I'm going to make JC the biggest cosmetics company in the world within the next five years. You just wait and see."

Jessica snuggled up to him. "I'm so proud of you, Cade. I know you can do it."

"We'll do it together," he said, and not caring who witnessed it, pulled her into a kiss that made Ben roll his eyes and turn his head away.

THAT NIGHT, after they'd gotten into Paris and fought their way through customs and cabs, they got to the suite where they would be starting their lives together.

Cade swept her into their bedroom, a huge luxurious room that overlooked the Champs-Elysée, and pulled her into his arms. "How did I ever deserve the most beautiful woman in the world?"

"How did I deserve the most wonderful man?" she whispered.

His lips met hers, and vaguely she remembered that they hadn't closed the bedroom door when they'd come in.

A knock sounded, and they jumped apart. Ben stood on the threshold with a pair of headphones on. "Hey, Dad. Can I talk to you for a second?"

Jessica's heart sank, and she hated herself for wishing, even for a moment, that Ben wasn't with them.

Cade went to his son, and the boy put his arm conspiratorially around his shoulders. "Hey, listen, Dad. I know it's kind of tough for you to express yourself and everything, but this is your honeymoon. You need to try to be a little romantic."

"I do, do I?"

"Well, yeah," Ben said. "So I just wanted you to know that I'm gonna be in my room tonight with my headphones on, turned up real loud. It'll be like I'm not even here. And I won't hear a thing."

Surprise colored Cade's face, and his eyes twinkled as he regarded his wife. "Thanks, buddy," he said. "That sounds like a good idea."

Ben patted his back, as if offering a vote of confidence that his father would do what was expected of him. When Ben was gone, Cade fell against the wall, laughing.

Jessica had heard enough to burst into giggles, too. "He's some kid, Cade."

"Tell me about it."

He closed the door and locked it, just in case, then turned back to his wife. "Now... where were we?"

"You were making yourself at home with me," she whispered.

He smiled. "For the first time in my life, I know what home feels like."

And as he brought her back into his arms, he realized how true that was. For the first time in his life, he knew what it was to belong.

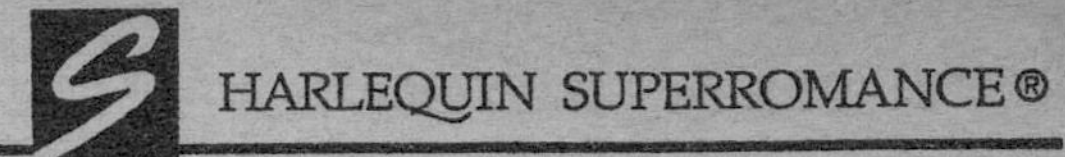

COMING NEXT MONTH

#598 WEDDING INVITATION • Marisa Carroll

Brent Powell was marrying Jacqui Bertrand, and Weddings, Inc. of Eternity, Massachusetts, was planning to showcase the wedding. No expense was spared and no detail overlooked.... Except perhaps for a few trivialities: the bride was no longer speaking to the groom, his mother was less than thrilled with her future daughter-in-law, and Jacqui's kids were in no mood to accept a new dad.
Wedding Invitation is the first book in **Weddings, Inc.**.
In July watch for *Expectations* by Shannon Waverly, Harlequin Romance #3319.

#599 PIRATE MOON • Peg Sutherland

Daron Rourke had a secret life in Bali, a dangerous life, a life that made up for all the years she'd lived in the concrete jungle of North American commerce. Then Grant Hilliard appeared on the scene. But who *was* Grant? He seemed to have two faces, two personalities. Both of which posed even greater danger to Daron.

#600 DARE TO LOVE • Tara Taylor Quinn

Policewoman Andrea Parker had always been able to handle tough men—until she met Doug Avery, one of the officers she had to train for the DARE program. He was rude, crude and arrogant—not the sort of man who'd be good at helping street kids. So why couldn't she throw him out of the program...and out of her life?

#601 TILL SEPTEMBER • Ginger Chambers

When Robin Farrell was a child, a man drowned while saving her life. Twenty years later, she was still confused and consumed with guilt...especially when she found herself falling in love with Eric Marshall, her savior's orphaned son! How on earth could she tell him that *she* was the woman he blamed for his father's death?

AVAILABLE NOW:

#594 THE PRINCESS AND THE PAUPER
Tracy Hughes

#595 NOT QUITE AN ANGEL
Bobby Hutchinson

#596 DANCING IN THE DARK
Lynn Erickson

#597 THE YANQUI PRINCE
Janice Kaiser

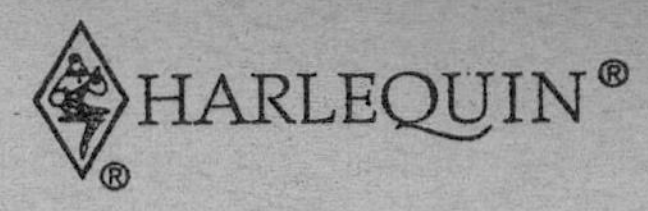

Harlequin Books requests the pleasure of your company this June in Eternity, Massachusetts, for WEDDINGS, INC.

For generations, couples have been coming to Eternity, Massachusetts, to exchange wedding vows. Legend has it that those married in Eternity's chapel are destined for a lifetime of happiness. And the residents are more than willing to give the legend a hand.

Beginning in June, you can experience the legend of Eternity. Watch for one title per month, across all of the Harlequin series.

HARLEQUIN BOOKS... NOT THE SAME OLD STORY!

WEDGEN

INDULGE A LITTLE 6947 SWEEPSTAKES
NO PURCHASE NECESSARY

HERE'S HOW THE SWEEPSTAKES WORKS:
The Harlequin Reader Service shipments for January, February and March 1994 will contain, respectively, coupons for entry into three prize drawings: a trip for two to San Francisco, an Alaskan cruise for two and a trip for two to Hawaii. To be eligible for any drawing using an Entry Coupon, simply complete and mail according to directions.

There is no obligation to continue as a Reader Service subscriber to enter and be eligible for any prize drawing. You may also enter any drawing by hand printing your name and address on a 3" x 5" card and the destination of the prize you wish that entry to be considered for (i.e., San Francisco trip, Alaskan cruise or Hawaiian trip). Send your 3" x 5" entries to: Indulge a Little 6947 Sweepstakes, c/o Prize Destination you wish that entry to be considered for, P.O. Box 1315, Buffalo, NY 14269-1315, U.S.A. or Indulge a Little 6947 Sweepstakes, P.O. Box 610, Fort Erie, Ontario L2A 5X3, Canada.

To be eligible for the San Francisco trip, entries must be received by 4/30/94; for the Alaskan cruise, 5/31/94; and the Hawaiian trip, 6/30/94. No responsibility is assumed for lost, late or misdirected mail. Sweepstakes open to residents of the U.S. (except Puerto Rico) and Canada, 18 years of age or older. All applicable laws and regulations apply. Sweepstakes void wherever prohibited.

For a copy of the Official Rules, send a self-addressed, stamped envelope (WA residents need not affix return postage) to: Indulge a Little 6947 Rules, P.O. Box 4631, Blair, NE 68009, U.S.A.

INDR93

INDULGE A LITTLE 6947 SWEEPSTAKES
NO PURCHASE NECESSARY

HERE'S HOW THE SWEEPSTAKES WORKS:
The Harlequin Reader Service shipments for January, February and March 1994 will contain, respectively, coupons for entry into three prize drawings: a trip for two to San Francisco, an Alaskan cruise for two and a trip for two to Hawaii. To be eligible for any drawing using an Entry Coupon, simply complete and mail according to directions.

There is no obligation to continue as a Reader Service subscriber to enter and be eligible for any prize drawing. You may also enter any drawing by hand printing your name and address on a 3" x 5" card and the destination of the prize you wish that entry to be considered for (i.e., San Francisco trip, Alaskan cruise or Hawaiian trip). Send your 3" x 5" entries to: Indulge a Little 6947 Sweepstakes, c/o Prize Destination you wish that entry to be considered for, P.O. Box 1315, Buffalo, NY 14269-1315, U.S.A. or Indulge a Little 6947 Sweepstakes, P.O. Box 610, Fort Erie, Ontario L2A 5X3, Canada.

To be eligible for the San Francisco trip, entries must be received by 4/30/94; for the Alaskan cruise, 5/31/94; and the Hawaiian trip, 6/30/94. No responsibility is assumed for lost, late or misdirected mail. Sweepstakes open to residents of the U.S. (except Puerto Rico) and Canada, 18 years of age or older. All applicable laws and regulations apply. Sweepstakes void wherever prohibited.

For a copy of the Official Rules, send a self-addressed, stamped envelope (WA residents need not affix return postage) to: Indulge a Little 6947 Rules, P.O. Box 4631, Blair, NE 68009, U.S.A.

INDR93

INDULGE A LITTLE
SWEEPSTAKES

OFFICIAL ENTRY COUPON

This entry must be received by: JUNE 30, 1994
This month's winner will be notified by: JULY 15, 1994
Trip must be taken between: AUGUST 31, 1994-AUGUST 31, 1995

YES, I want to win the 3-Island Hawaiian vacation for two. I understand that the prize includes round-trip airfare, first-class hotels and pocket money as revealed on the "wallet" scratch-off card.

Name______________________________

Address ____________________ Apt. __________

City______________________________

State/Prov.________________ Zip/Postal Code__________

Daytime phone number________________________
(Area Code)

Account #______________________________

Return entries with invoice in envelope provided. Each book in this shipment has two entry coupons—and the more coupons you enter, the better your chances of winning!

 MONTH3

INDULGE A LITTLE
SWEEPSTAKES

OFFICIAL ENTRY COUPON

This entry must be received by: JUNE 30, 1994
This month's winner will be notified by: JULY 15, 1994
Trip must be taken between: AUGUST 31, 1994-AUGUST 31, 1995

YES, I want to win the 3-Island Hawaiian vacation for two. I understand that the prize includes round-trip airfare, first-class hotels and pocket money as revealed on the "wallet" scratch-off card.

Name______________________________

Address ____________________ Apt. __________

City______________________________

State/Prov.________________ Zip/Postal Code__________

Daytime phone number________________________
(Area Code)

Account #______________________________

Return entries with invoice in envelope provided. Each book in this shipment has two entry coupons—and the more coupons you enter, the better your chances of winning!

© 1993 HARLEQUIN ENTERPRISES LTD. MONTH3